ROMA
RUMA
ROMA
ROME

Seed of Fury:
Zolia's Revenge

by: Joe Antony Sebastin

Let Us Unite all Genders

A friend was driving me to the Miami Airport when talk on AM radio turned to abortion and abused women. The commentator cited a list of Bible passages "proving" God chose everyone from the womb: Galatians 1:15, Isaiah 44:24, Jeremiah 1:5, Psalm 139:13-16, and Job 31:15.

My friend, hearing this, switched the channel. "Sorry about that," she said. "I do wonder, though, how we could possibly address an issue as nuanced as aborting the fetuses of abused women."

"It seems to me," I said, "that God forfeits His decision by allowing rape in the first place. Most of the talk, like the radio there, is thoughtless bluster. It is a mother's choice. It is her body that was so cruelly abused; she should have full say over how she recovers. No other soul in the universe has any authority over the abused woman and the child she carries. There must be rules and consistency, even for God."

The argument occupied my thoughts during the flight. I realized it was a much bigger problem than I'd originally thought. How can we stop abuse in the first place, for all genders and regardless of age?

Eventually I came to a conclusion. Perhaps a mason or a nurse would find a different solution, but as a writer, I know we can change minds through our stories. I was determined to stop abuse through a story.

I decided to create a friend, someone the reader would grow with and love. In this way, we make abuse immediate. We make it something that must be stopped whether it happens to woman or man, young or old.

Suffering anywhere ultimately hurts us all. We can only end abuse and its fallout through the realizations that we are all humans on Earth and the things that separate us are nothing more than invisible walls.

Gender, sex, age, and ability; none of those things divides us as much as life connects us. When we lift up those who are abused, those who suffer, those who are judged to be less, we lift ourselves up as well.

Seed of Fury is four separate novels, set in different times and studying different situations. Each one shows the lessons we've learned from abuse and its fallout.

We start with a famous atrocity of the classical world: The Rape of the Sabine Women. The Romans were at the height of their power when this happened, and their wanton and hideous treatment of the women they abducted has drawn focus to the abuse of women ever since.

This story, though set in the midst of an actual historical event, is fiction. But it is my hope that, through the lens of fiction, we can lift our spirits and create a better world for our fellow humans. Even if you feel it's good story and nothing else, I pray that the light of the sisters in this novel, Ronica and Zolia, will live on within you.

— Joe Antony Sebastin

CONTENTS

PART III :

Ronica

Zolia

Introduction:

Ronica's Oath to Destroy the Roman Empire

Do you hear the cries of the Sabines? Do you hear our desperation? The forest is cold from the night and filled with driving rain that washes away the filth of the Romans, but does not cleanse us of our agony.

Are they ahead or behind us? Our tormentors are everywhere but nowhere. Every sound is theirs. Our tears and the falling rain make the path away from Cures more treacherous with every step.

I hold hands with my younger sister, Zolia, until she trips, gashes her head, and falls to the wet ground. Her motionless form is but a few feet away when lightning flashes across the sky and my painful memories sweep over me.

***

When the Romans came, we were dragged to the square where a gathering swelled. I was tied to a stake, my tunic ripped from my back. Each lash cut to the bone. The scorching pain set my skin afire. When I fainted, the next strike snapped me back. Sheer agony followed every snap of the whip.

After the ten, they cut the ropes. I crashed to the ground. My back was all I could feel. A pregnant woman covered me and helped me to the side.

Like a warrior, Zolia stood to the post. As the soldiers tied her, the Crusader did not resist. Her body squirmed with each snap of the whip, but her mind seemed elsewhere. The Crusader never looked away from Romulus or his stooge rapist. Her eyes welled but she would not cry. The rapist and his king saw Sister would not surrender.

After thirty lashes, her legs caved and the ropes could not support her. Her peeled flesh lay on the ground around her. The warrior raised herself. "Roman whips are as weak as the penis of pirate Proculus. Finish it!"

The executioner stared at her filleted back and handed the whip to another slave driver. No person wanted to administer the last ten lashes. Roman men and women turned away from the sight.

One Roman slave driver administered the final blows and cut Zolia free. Sister lay on the ground, scarred and drenched in blood. A woman passed her a covering. The Crusader lifted her head to Romulus. "I spit on Rhea Silvia's womb. Her son shames all men!"

***

In the here and now, I pulled Zolia into my arms and held her to keep her warm. The Romans' rain, Jupiter's thunder, and Quirinus's lightning stole her breath. I force air and hope into her mouth but she remains unconscious.

Cruelty

I looked up into the skies and made a promise to the goddess Minerva. "Neither my sister nor I will die today," I swore. "Vengeance will be ours!"

The thunder argued back, confronting us with disfigured hallucinations of the faces of our Roman tormentors. With rage seething through my body, I swear: "Lord Quirinus, hear your daughters' cries! We will live to vanquish Roma. Strengthen us to fight and destroy their king!"

The skies hear my voice. The thunder and lightning stop. The vanishing rain marks our first victory. We have quieted the fury from the Roman skies. We are away.

Where does our story begin? It matters not. Our tale will end in misery, for the Romans have already abused and tortured and maimed us.

My tale is told in my own words. There were some things I did not learn of until later, though I relate them to you as they happened. Listen, now, to the story of the Sabine Women from one who was there.

Tragedy

Part I:

Chapter 1: The Enemies on the Other Side

For more than three hundred years, the Sabini managed peaceful and productive cohabitation with neighboring Latin and Etruscan tribes. The despicable Romans were another matter. Driven by an unquenchable thirst for wealth, fame, women, and ego, Romans constantly initiated wars, conflicts, and subterfuge.

In Cures, we came to understand that Roman culture, politics, and governance were encapsulated in the monumental events surrounding the most beautiful woman in the world: Helen of Troy. We learned Helen was actually Helen of Sparta, the daughter born to Leda… Leda whom Zeus raped while he was in the guise of a swan. The two Athenians who abducted Helen – Theseus and Pirithous – triggered a chain of events that would scar the world for hundreds of years.

I believed that Helen was similar to all women, a victim of male ego and lustful desires and empowered by an overriding need for revenge. But my sister Zolia saw Helen differently: as a conniving seductress who used her body and her sexuality to control men and determine her fate. Also, my intelligent sister viewed the entire Trojan War as a myth and hoax. She believed it was the gods who sent the Sea Peoples to destroy the Trojans.

By the end of the ten-year war between the Spartans and the Trojans, the wondrous city of Troy was burned to the ground, her last king was dead, and his army was destroyed. A single Trojan leader, Prince Aeneas, the son of mortal Anchises and goddess Aphrodite, survived.

Aeneas hoisted his father Anchises on his back and escaped the kingdom with his young son, Iulius, and a flock of followers. After years of scavenging the world, the survivors discovered Laurentum, home to several Latin tribes. Aeneas named his new land New Troy after his native land.

The Trojans took to plundering crops from their neighbors, a breach that so infuriated native farmers that their king, Latinus, was forced to respond. Latinus quickly discovered that his forces were overmatched by Aeneas and his army of battle-tested Trojans. After a short fight, Latinus was assassinated, his army was slaughtered, and the citadel was seized.

Aeneas immediately assumed sovereignty over all Latin tribes. To solidify his reign, the Trojan leader married Lavinia, daughter of Latinus, who was attracted by the conqueror's legacy as a fallen prince and avowed son to goddess Aphrodite.

We were taught that Aeneas was driven by the prophecy of a sow that had farrowed a litter of thirty pigs. According to the prophecy, known as The Three, The Thirty, and The Three Hundred, Aeneas's New Troy would collapse in three years. This prophecy was fulfilled when the Trojans united with Latin natives to form Lavinium.

After thirty years, Iulius founded Alba Longa, a new kingdom surrounded by lakes and a mountain ridge and resting on the plains close to the Tiber River. Iulius colonized thirty towns of the old Latin confederacy that would be ruled by Trojan descendants for three hundred years. During this time, Alba Longa prospered and continued to expand its territory.

After nearly three hundred years, King Procas sired two sons: Numitor and his younger brother, Amulius. Kind and generous, Numitor fathered two children: Prince Atys Numitor and Princess Rhea Silvia. By that time, Alba Longa had become home to rough, independent hunters, shepherds, and warriors, whom Numitor found to be lawless and distasteful barbarians.

Rather than rule a mob, the king preferred life on his ancestral farm with its lush gardens and flocks of plump sheep where he was surrounded by servants he could trust.

Unlike Numitor, the self-serving Amulius was vicious, greedy, and ambitious. He used inflated credentials to degrade his brother and gain favor with the people of Alba Longa. And though aware that Amulius conspired against his rule, Numitor remained aloof, uninterested in conflict, and unwilling to shoulder the task of civilizing his kingdom's barbarian culture.

Seizing the opportunity, Amulius rallied his followers, marched to the citadel, overthrew the guards, and proclaimed himself King of Alba Longa. Numitor's uninspired troops surrendered rather than fight. Amulius quickly assumed control, stationing soldiers at strategic positions throughout the kingdom. Disenchanted inhabitants rushed to Numitor's farm to inform their former king who, to their surprise, seemed relieved.

Amulius so terrorized the land, and so antagonized his subjects, that he feared retribution from Numitor's offspring. To quash this threat, he imprisoned them. When Numitor demanded the return of Atys Numitor and Rhea Silvia, Amulius responded by killing the son and confining the princess to the temple as a virgin priestess to goddess Vesta. With the prince dead and the princess destined for a virgin life, Amulius continued his savage rule unencumbered by worries of rebellion.

Mourning his son and suffering the sequestration of his daughter, Numitor prayed to the gods that his son be resurrected. With his dream of ascension fulfilled, Amulius embraced a life of debauchery and philandering while the people of Alba Longa came to loathe their king.

Seven years after the rebellion, Rhea Silvia escaped in the dark of night. This prompted Amulius to launch a massive inquiry revealing that the princess had been assisted by her lover, a respected warrior and protector of cattle named Silvanus. Once again, Amulius feared for his throne.

Silvanus, whose protective nature led friends to call him "God of Mars," had first met Rhea Silvia at the temple. The couple enjoyed such a powerful physical attraction that the "God of Mars" helped Rhea administer rituals by day and bedded her at night. Their five-year relationship peaked when they escaped for their imminent marriage.

One year later the rivers and lakes of Alba Longa overflowed, flooding the land. As fearful farmers and shepherds rushed to save their cattle, two herders came upon a forlorn woman perched high on a cliff above the Tiber. The shepherds called to the woman to come down; but she ignored their pleas, prompting the men to climb to her.

"Woman, are you Rhea Silvia, daughter of good King Numitor?" called the nearest shepherd.

"For the sake of my father, King Numitor, save his grandchildren in this basket!" cried Rhea Silva, before casting her robe aside and plunging to her death. Discovering twin boys in her basket, the shepherds quickly covered the infants with the mother's discarded cloak and headed home, all the while fearing Amulius would kill them and their families for harboring his nephews.

After tending the babies for two days, the herders carried the boys to the king. He was stationed at the citadel to better monitor the floods, and there the humble shepherds knelt before him and pleaded for leniency. "Lord, please accept these two newborn boys."

"Why do you bring these twins to your king? Did the flood wash away their families?" Amulius asked.

"No, master. These twins are your nephews, left by Rhea Silvia before she drowned herself."

"If you are troublemakers, I will end your lives here and now!" Amulius drew his sword, but when one shepherd tossed Rhea's cloak at Amulius's feet the dumbfounded king sheathed his sword. "That is Rhea Silvia's cloak. How do you have this?"

The shepherds recounted the mother's suicide and their rescue of the children, whereupon the king shouted, "Remove these evil boys from my sight!"

Amulius ordered his treasurer to reward each shepherd with a bursa of gold. "Loyal shepherds of Alba Longa," he began, "take this gold in exchange for rendering an important service. So that their bodies can rest with their mother, drown the boys in the river. This is a necessary service but one you must never discuss with anyone. If you value the lives of your families, heed my words."

The shepherds packed their gold, placed the cloak and children in the basket, and departed. After they reached the river, they were unable to reconcile ending the lives of two healthy infants. Because their allegiance lay with Numitor and Rhea Silvia, the herders struggled to find a solution until a wooden vessel used to feed lambs drifted through the mist and settled before them. The shepherds cleaned the float, lined it with Rhea Silvia's cloak, enclosed the boys along with several gold coins, and set the makeshift barge adrift.

When the boat disappeared, the shepherds returned to King Amulius with clear consciences. "All of Numitor's seed has drowned in the river. King Amulius and his offspring shall rule Alba Longa for eternity," they announced.

❀❀❀❀❀❀

Chapter 2: Corradeo and Bionca

Our lives began with a melody and a smile in Cures, a town in the Sabini hill country where ancient traditions still prevailed. Neither home nor country, Cures was a paradise filled with integrity, spirituality, hard work, patriotism, and warriors from the gods. Here, we were born to Corradeo, a farmer, shepherd, and hunter, and his beloved wife, Bionca, mother of two daughters: Zolia the Crusader and me, Ronica the Revolter.

From the first, we pressed our parents about how they had met and fallen in love. One night after a day in the fields, Father faced the firelight, huddled us on the rug floor, and began his recitation. We basked in his every expression, celebrated his every word. "One day in the market, there was a funny girl trying to sell two puny fish," he chuckled.

"Was that Mother? How old were you? What did you talk about?" we pressed.

"Ah, my curious daughters interrupt? This story is long enough. Hold your questions until the end." Father shrugged, and sighed an exaggerated sigh before restarting his saga:

> "A lifetime ago, when I was twelve and your mother ten, I worked with my two older brothers and my father managing the cattle and doing the lowliest farm

chores. That was when we started raising sheep, cattle, goats, and pigs, and growing cabbage, lettuce, fennel, and olives. There was always much to do.

"While bringing two sheep home to Mother, I passed through the crowded market where this spunky girl was selling fish. Her disheveled hair hung over a white tunic but, when she turned, I recognized her as Bionca, the victim of my many pranks. She and her father were well known to our family."

Before continuing, Father looked to see that Mother Bionca approved his recital.

"The girl insisted one bronze coin apiece was right for her two puny fish. 'Why does the young girl of Cures rob her neighbors? Your fish are the size of tadpoles,' I quipped. Bionca tilted her head pensively. 'Hmm, prankster shepherd boy. Tell me how much you charge for your scrawny mutton?'

"When I answered 'two silver pieces,' she feigned fainting. 'Tell me, shepherd boy, why do you overcharge for sheep the size of mice?' I wrapped my arms around one heavy sheep and asked, "Do my plump sheep look like mice to you?'

"'If my fish are tadpoles, your sheep are mice. My fish have added value because I scoured the river and wrested them from the toothy jaws of a vicious alligator to bring them to market for you to buy. Even a lazy shepherd boy can see my price is right.'

"'Ha! Ridiculous! Gather round, good people of Cures, to see this witch who parades two tadpoles as fish in our marketplace!' I called to the square.

"The alligator conqueror tightened her fists; but before she could pick a fight, Fabricius, her father, returned from the river. Noticing his daughter's ferocity, the fisherman inquired, 'Why does my child squint her eyes and scrunch her nose at our neighbor?'

"Bionca described our disagreement with great animation. When she concluded, Fabricius winked at me. 'Enough squabbling, my children. We have made our share today. Tomorrow waits. Take these fish, young Corradeo. Share them with your family so that Bionca's bravery does not go wasted,' he laughed.

"The ferocious alligator conqueror kept grumbling until Fabricius suggested we take our mid-day meal together. I quickly seized the opening and invited them home."

At this point in his story, Father paused so that we could absorb the scene. We begged him to continue.

"My daughters should know that it was either because Bionca's mother had died young, or because Fabricius had raised her as a son, but either way she was a rough cut: pretty and cute, but with jagged edges. On the way home, Bionca's incessant flirting blinded her to my adoration.

"At home, Mother welcomed our guests but gave Bionca a quizzical look when she was presented with the tadpoles. Thankfully, Fabricius added a few real fish so that Mother could set about preparing our midday meal.

"While my daughterless mother cooked, she questioned Bionca. 'My girl, why is your hair unruly?

This is no way for a young woman. Come here. Let me dress your hair.'

"Fabricius sighed. 'My girl grows so fast. She has no teacher for womanly things. She can fish and pull her weight, but…'

"'Worry not, Fabricius. Your Bionca can come to me anytime. I shall teach her and care for her. She is pleasant but she must soon become a woman so that when the time is right, Bionca will marry my young shepherd, Corradeo, and become my daughter.'

"Fabricius gasped. 'Wonderful! This would be a dream come true! And, when Bionca bears a child for the Avitus family, I shall build an eternal temple to honor the goddess Minerva.'

"My heart leapt with anticipation, but I posed the obligatory protest. 'Me and this seller of pricey tadpoles? Surely my mother is not serious!'

"Thankfully, Mother could not be swayed. 'My son, Bionca is a special girl. In the name of Quirinus, you must promise Fabricius and me that you will always honor and care for her.'

"That day I pledged to the world to be kind, gentle, and protective of Bionca, my beautiful wife, your mother. When my father and brothers returned from the fields, we ate well on fine fish, lamb stew, and cabbage – a fitting celebration filled with harmless teasing."

❀❀❀❀❀❀

Chapter 3: Romulus and Remus

The shepherd's barge did not sink; instead, it stalled downstream against a clogged pile of logs. When the children awoke, they wailed so loudly that they were discovered by a she-wolf who was searching for her missing whelps. Drawn to the newborns, the wolf used her paws to pull the vessel ashore where she welcomed her new litter by licking their faces.

After a time, the she-wolf placed the boys on the cloak and dragged them to her cave, positioning them favorably for the sun but keeping them invisible to invaders. For nourishment, the twins suckled her, enjoying wolf milk for the first time.

The mother wolf cared for Rhea Silvia's cubs like they were her own. Birds sang to the twins during the day and owls watched over them by night. By their first birthday, the twins had bloomed healthy and strong.

The she-wolf decided it was time for the boys to receive parenting from humans. Stealing a lamb from a nearby farm, she lured farmer Faustulus to her cave. When the farmer discovered two children, he assumed the she-wolf had not only stolen his lamb but had also abducted the children. Faustulus swung his ax and decapitated the kidnapper.

The farmer wrapped the infants in the cloak and hurried them to his farm, where his wife, Acca Larentia, warmed and fed the boys. Believing she recognized the cloak, Acca asked, "Is this not the cloak of priestess Rhea Silvia?"

While the couple argued about how to manage their discovery, their own twelve children interceded and convinced the parents to reverse their inclination to return the children to Amulius. The parents agreed, but stipulated that the origin of the new arrivals must remain a family secret; the true identity of the twins must never be divulged.

So it was that Acca Larentia claimed the boys and named them Romulus and Remus.

Chapter 4: Ronica and Zolia

Mother Bionca joined us on the floor and Father Corradeo continued his narrative.

"After our engagement dinner, I showed your mother our farm and our plump livestock. 'Corradeo, my future husband, why was your price two silvers for those sheep?'

"'Bionca, for those sheep, I fought a lion and pried them from his belly. My price was fair.'

"My future wife grinned. 'Ah, Corradeo, you are a storyteller like me! We will indeed be happy together.'

"Mother Bionca has loved our farm ever since that day when she playfully chased my favorite white-and-black goat until we lay on the grass, watching a brilliant sunset. Pointing to an early star, Bionca whispered, 'My father says that star is my mother. When I look at her, I see how beautifully the other stars are aligned, but Mother is the only one who always smiles upon me.'

"Feeling Bionca's sadness, I tried to change the conversation. 'You know, future wife, I can dress your hair.'

"'You do not like my hair? Worry not, shepherd boy. Soon enough, my hair will brighten your every day. Now that I have met my future husband, I shall be well spruced from this day forward. But–'

"She shook her finger at me. 'Do not misunderstand me, Corradeo. You may not touch me before our marriage. If you try, I shall complain to Father,' she teased, fitting into my chest. 'Perhaps, this one time, we could be cozy.' We cuddled innocently and Bionca whispered, 'We shall marry, Corradeo, and I will make you always proud.'

"Every day thereafter, Bionca came to work and learn maternal things with Mother. Our family treated her as our own, and my love for the pricey tadpole seller grew… and still grows."

Father looked to see that we had absorbed his story and his commitment to Bionca, our mother, before he continued.

"Occasionally, Father Avitus would take us hunting. My daughters should understand that Mother Bionca was a fearless hunter. It was right that we arrived at love together. When it was time to marry, the sun, star, and moon gods were content.

"When your mother was pregnant with Ronica, Fabricius fulfilled his promise. He built a temple for Minerva in the same spot where Bionca and I had embraced to enjoy the stars. The temple was forty paces square and housed a statue of Minerva. Four oil lamps rested in the corners. The open roof allowed the gods from the skies to consult Minerva.

"For the temple's consecration we invited the town's young Sabini priest, Cnaeus Augur, who wore a lengthy white cloak under a black vest. The cloak's hood covered his head. The head of his gold-coated staff was engraved with a spear, a bow with a mounted arrow, a bolt of lightning, and a strand of wheat. The augur blessed the temple with water from the Tiber Valley. After Father sacrificed a heifer, the priest dispersed the animal's blood around the temple.

Goddesses

"Cnaeus Augur then closed his eyes to ask Semo Sancus, the tribe's principal god, for a revelation. When the priest opened his eyes, he solemnly addressed the assembly.

"'Semo Sancus declares that Minerva will be divided into two halves that will be born to Corradeo and Bionca. The daughters will arise, fight, and shine as bright as the stars. Until the death of both daughters, the goddess Minerva will remain in the land of the Sabine. Upon the passing of the sisters, Minerva will be carried away from these lands to other empires and will be a forgotten memory here in her homeland.'

"The audience became agitated. One elder inquired, 'What misdeeds have we done to cause Minerva's abandonment?'

"The augur answered, 'You have done no wrong, but the cries of Minerva's unborn daughters disturb her. To preserve our spirituality, she will divide in two to allow us more time.'

"I knelt before the augur. 'Do you say we will have two daughters from Minerva?' He touched my head. 'Yes, Corradeo, you will sire the two mighty female warriors of this earth. Minerva's soul will be bestowed upon them. Your two mothers of bravery will be marveled at by all generations of an empire that is yet to be born.'

"With the augur's prophecy deemed true and divine, the town began to offer daily prayers to Minerva. And so, my curious daughters, this is the true story of how your mother and I met and how we came to know that you, Ronica and Zolia, would be here to share our story."

●●●●●❖●

Chapter 5: Roma

Romulus and Remus reached adulthood as a farmer's sons, meaning they were vigorous, hard-working, and respectful young men who honored the gods. Faustulus taught the boys to hunt, work, pray, and live together. The twins became known for bravery while protecting the cattle and chasing down thieves who stole their livestock.

The farmer was mindful of the pair's obvious leadership qualities. Romulus developed loyal followers known as Quintilii, while followers of Remus were called Fabii. On Palatine Hill, the two shepherds and their followers tended flocks owned by Amulius while other herders tended flocks owned by Numitor on neighboring Aventine Hill.

As time went on, the brothers recognized the advantages of Aventine Hill due to its favorable exposure and abundant full grasses. This motivated the twins to try grazing their flocks on the richer hill, but Numitor's vigilant shepherds quickly chased the gatecrashers away. The incident caused King Numitor to plot the capture of the trespassers.

Not long after the first incident, Romulus was summoned to Caenia for a sacrificial tribute to the gods. During his absence, one of King Amulius's finest lambs mysteriously disappeared. Remus suspected a kidnapper.

When he spotted the lamb tethered to a rock on Aventine Hill, Remus became incensed and set out to rescue the animal. He crawled to the hostage, cut the rope, and prepared for his return. But Numitor's shepherds sprang from behind tall rocks, overcame the trespasser, and promptly led their captive to Numitor, who had instructed that no mercy should be afforded any burglars.

Aware of the irony, Faustulus appeared at the court saying, "My only lord, King Numitor, I beg you to spare this boy."

"What say you, shepherd?" asked Numitor. "Why would I set such a dangerous precedent and spare the life of your trespassing son?"

"My king, this boy is not my son. He is Remus, one of two true sons of your departed daughter Rhea Silvia."

The king studied the trespasser with new interest. Recognizing the possibility, Numitor ordered that Faustulus explain what had transpired. After hearing the shepherd's fantastical description of the wolf, the cave, and the discovery of the twins, the king demanded proof.

Faustulus quickly produced the torn but unmistakable cloak of Rhea Silvia. The king clutched his daughter's cloak and came to see her face in his captive. "The boy has the eyes of my princess!" proclaimed Numitor. "My grandson, come close to your true king… your only grandfather."

Guards unshackled Remus, who knelt before his king to receive his grandfather's attention. Shortly afterward, Numitor asked the whereabouts of Remus's brother. At that moment, Romulus and a squad of fighters charged into the chambers. The king quieted Romulus by asking, "Where have you been, my son?"

Puzzled, Romulus looked to Faustulus for an explanation. When satisfied, he responded to his grandfather. "I have just returned from Caenia to free my brother. Forgive my ignorance in this treacherous game, but I am now here for you, my king and grandfather." Romulus laid down his weapons and knelt beside his brother.

Numitor stroked the faces of his newfound grandsons. "My sons, you resemble your mother, who was only briefly known to you. It is not right, but at long last Rhea Silvia has returned to her home." The king rose from his throne. "My faith in the gods never waned. I asked for my only son to be resurrected, and my prayers brought the sons of Rhea Silvia, my grandchildren, home. Now I leave it to my ancestor's gods to steer my course."

Romulus and Remus lifted Rhea Silvia's cloak to their grandfather and assumed seats next to the king. All members of the court scorned Amulius and sensed the need for vengeance. The twins only needed direction. "We await your command," said Romulus.

Members of the court rose, calling out, "Down with Amulius! Let Romulus and Remus lead us to freedom. Defeat the demon king!"

"So be it!" declared Numitor. "My sons Romulus and Remus will lead the assault and assert their rightful claim to the throne. My grandsons will take whatever force and weaponry are needed to slay Amulius, the murderer of their mother and uncle."

Engrossed in his sinister existence, Amulius was unaware of the vengeful plot. When Romulus and Remus approached the citadel with Numitor's brigade, the surprised forces of Amulius offered little resistance. The victory was swift.

Staring at defeat, Amulius bribed a captain of Numitor's militaris and escaped. But as he fled, his requests for shelter were ignored by his abused subjects. Exhausted, defeated, and with no hope of reclaiming his throne, the king fell to the ground, where Palatine shepherds clubbed him to death.

Alba Longa rejoiced that the patient, peaceful king had regained his throne, his kingdom, and his grandsons on the same day.

❊❊❊❊❊❊

Chapter 6: The Sisters

Zolia and I now understood that our parents had started their lives peacefully together, with cattle in the field, fish in the river, and soothing wind music blowing through the trees.

When I was born, the augur's prophecy inspired Father to host a grand feast to celebrate my birth. According to tradition, all people of Cures enjoyed their measure. Cnaeus Augur blessed and anointed me. "With Ronica the Revolter, one half of Minerva has fallen from the skies."

My parents wrapped me in fine clothes and carried me around the temple first to the right, then to the left, and then to the right again before carrying me to the Sabini hilltop where the sacred stone of Semo Sancus rested.

After many rituals to our tribal god, Father hosted an unforgettable festival. Town musicians played lyres, salpinxes, and psalteries. Young and old villagers danced and rejoiced. Small flower girls presented peace offerings of hyacinth and larkspur to Bionca. Town elders proclaimed this the first birth festival ever celebrated with such ceremony. When Titus Tatius, king of Sabinium, sent presents and gifts, there was due cause for my birth festival to be recounted for decades.

Word of the augur's prophecy had spread to other Sabini towns. Visitors from Reate, Trebula, Mutuesca, Nursia,

Amiternum, and Eretum came to Cures to see Minerva's first daughter. It was a happy time for the town and for my parents.

When sister Zolia the Crusader was born two years later on during the earliest days of spring, I loved her from birth. Cnaeus announced, "The remaining piece of Minerva is born in Cures. The future of Minerva and of our town is balanced on the shoulders of the two mothers of bravery." Zolia's birth celebration was even more historic than mine.

While we grew up, our parents stayed righteous and caring. Mother groomed us and combed our hair, always putting our best front forward. Zolia shared Mother's thick, long, black mane and soon gained her favor. From the outset, I was Father's daughter. His first gift to me was a pole for catching fish.

With hair that reached her hips and perfectly accented her ash-colored eyes, Zolia grew to be strikingly beautiful. Always high-spirited, outspoken, and insatiably curious, my sister's disposition bordered on provocative. We tried not to notice, but her personality was hard-charging from birth.

I was the opposite. Curly yellow locks flowed to my shoulders but my face was thinner, my nose more delicate. I was a gentler spirit but, as different as we were, every eye turned our way when we walked the town. Father proudly took us to market, where old women pinched our cheeks and said, "May Tiber Valley overflow with your beauty." Ever contentious, Zolia would mumble, "If the Tiber overflows, the flood will drown the town. Do my grandmothers forget it is in their best interests that Minerva's daughters live long lives?"

We suffered our first disagreement after Zolia turned five. At dawn, we rushed to see a newborn cosset. The pink lamb was small, hardly able to open its eyes, barely able to suckle her mother's milk. Zolia and I cleaned the newborn and covered her in a small blanket, but we argued over who would name the cosset.

I resented that Zolia always named our newborns and stubbornly rejected her choice, "Blandina," in favor of my more thoughtful selection, "Vita." When Mother overheard the argument, she favored my choice for the first time in memory.

Zolia stormed away, crying her way home. After she left, I realized the cosset's mother should name her daughter. As the day in the fields unfolded, a heavy sadness overcame me. When Father and I returned home, Zolia stormed into our bedroom, unwilling to face me.

Seeing my distress, Mother looked to Father, who reported my day of sulking. At dinner, I faced east and Zolia west. We endured a silent soup and vegetable dinner until Mother asked. "Will you talk to your sister, Zolia?"

"Ronica has a new sister named Vita. I am without a sister."

Father raised his voice. "Hush, my daughters. You waste each other. Behave like good sisters."

Zolia sipped several spoons of soup, pushed her bowl aside, and announced, "Everyone tells me what to do because I am the youngest, but you will all watch me fly!" she declared, defiantly stomping off to our room.

Mother cast me a look. "Are you happy now, Ronica? Why are you not nicer to your sister?"

"But Mother, Zolia always names our animals. This is my time. Why are you angry with me?"

Father lifted me in his arms. "My Ronica is right. Why does Mother's little tadpole misbehave and pout?"

Mother feigned anger. "My Zolia is of the alligator. Do you forget? Never call her a tadpole again, or Ronica will be known as the mouse."

Our laughter quickly lured Zolia to Mother's side. Sister's brilliant smile warmed Bionca, but her narrowed eyes burned into Father and me.

That night, Father slept at the farm and I bedded with Mother, who patiently explained that the older sister bore eternal responsibility to care for the younger one. She suggested I apologize to my sister.

Gathering myself, I went to Zolia, who was turned to the wall and had burrowed under piles of sheepskins. I slipped next to her and started massaging her neck, untangling her hair with my fingers.

"What are you doing, Ronica?" she whispered, in her most melodic voice.

"Taking care of my little sister," I told her sincerely.

"I thought your sister was that cosset."

"Zolia, you will always be my only sister. There is no one better than you. When I fry the cosset for your breakfast, you will know how dear you are to me."

Wide-eyed, Sister swiveled to face me. "No, Ronica, you must spare the newborn! I could not bear her death."

"So be it. But understand that I will destroy anything that dares come between us," I answered, squeezing her for emphasis.

Zolia's intensity bore into me. "Tell me, Ronica. Are you still my true sister?"

"Always, Zolia. Your true sister."

Reflection

"What will you name the cosset?" she lamented.

"The cosset was not born to us, so her mother will decide her name."

Zolia lit up. "How smart my sister is! She makes the best decisions. The babe is not our daughter," she said, and then hesitated before going on. "Tell me, Sister Ronica. When the time comes, what will you name your daughter?"

"Zolia."

"My name? But why?"

"Because there is no sweeter or stronger person on this earth than my sister, Minerva's other half."

She giggled. "Will my sister be my mother, too, Ronica?"

Bringing her face to my chest, I answered, "I am your mother, your father, and your sister, who will protect you as long as I breathe."

Mother, who listened at the door, leaned in to ask, "Then, who will be my mother, my daughter?"

"Me!" we gleefully shouted in unison.

Mother snuggled into bed, hugging and kissing us so many times our cheeks nearly went numb. With the passing of our first sisterly argument, our bond tightened, as it would after every disagreement for the rest of our lives.

❋❋❋❋❋❋

Chapter 7: The Hills

For several years, Romulus and Remus followed their grandfather's lead until they wished to build their own towns. "And where will my grandsons construct their towns?" asked Numitor.

"On Palatine Hill," answered Romulus.

"Aventine Hill for my site," added Remus.

"And why do my grandsons choose these two hills?"

"These hills are where we grew up. We understand the soil, the pastures, the grasses, and the forests."

Numitor approved the reasoning and granted permission for the construction of the twin towns, thus fulfilling the three-hundred-year prophecy.

For the daunting projects, Romulus and Remus began with their most rugged followers: mostly pioneers, shepherds, and hunters. As development of the hills progressed, pirates, robbers, and warriors added more muscle to the workforce. It was natural that competition ensued and eventually spilled over to the brothers themselves. The dispute intensified as a debate over which hill, Aventine or Palatine, would house the capital city.

Desiring a peaceful resolution, Faustulus offered his stepsons an ancient solution. "When we want to settle debates like this, augurs cast birds for answers." The proposition was confirmed by Numitor, who added that the practice was derived from the Etruscans. So, the brothers agreed to resolve the debate in a traditional way.

Romulus took his followers to Palatine Hill, where he used his crooked staff to delineate sacred space on the hilltop. This would be where he would receive the vision of his birds. Remus led his group to Aventine Hill, where he prepared the hill's sacred space.

On the eve of the competition, heavy clouds covered the sky and blocked the moonlight. To mask their anxiety, Romulus and Remus covered their faces with cloaks. At dawn, clouds still hid the sun; but as the skies crept open, Remus spotted his birds and shouted, "I see six vultures in the sky. The augury favors me!"

"Remus has found six vultures. The augury favors Aventine!" shouted his followers on Aventine Hill.

But when the sun broke through, Romulus bellowed from atop Palatine Hill. "Twelve vultures fly to me and Palatine Hill! Victory is mine!"

Romulus's followers roared approval. "We will build the capital on Palatine Hill, and it will be known as Roma in honor of Captain Romulus!"

Faustulus confirmed that the auguries favored Romulus and the new capital city would be built on Palatine Hill. Remus bitterly suffered defeat and began a sustained strategy of defaming his twin.

It was amidst this tense brotherly conflict and resentment that Romulus and his loyalists founded Roma. The new town was not far from Cures and the Sabini region, and it was vowed that no unclean entity would pass through Roma's gates.

At the city's festival of Pales, country people took to purifying themselves with fire and smoke, cleansing themselves with spring water, and drinking milk mixed with the juice of grapes. When the smoke settled in the stalls, the burning sulfur, incense, rosemary, and firewood purified the livestock. The loyalists of Romulus lit a giant bonfire of hay and straw and danced wildly to music of cymbals, flutes, and lyres.

To plan the construction of Roma, Romulus and Faustulus sought advice from learned Etruscan priests. The builders forged a large circular pit from the earth's hard clay. Into the pit Romans threw in their "first fruits" and other earthy objects. An altar was erected and the pit burned as an offering to the gods, thus consecrating the new center of the city.

Romulus instructed his men to draw boundaries around Palatine Hill and to use a bull and a heifer to till a deep moat. When Romulus's plow reached the city gates, it was discovered that the furrow had been dug inwards, toward the city. Despite structural flaws and the random path of the plow, the moat was considered holy ground by Romulus, whose prayers had been answered by Jupiter.

It was a new day. The ominous prophecy of the sow was fulfilled. After three hundred years, Alba Longa gave way to the new Roman kingdom and its new king. Those two changes caused alarm among the enemy on the other side… among my people, the Sabini.

Chapter 8: Young Warriors of Sabinium

Our young grew to be respected warriors. The fearless prowess of Cures warriors was rooted in a long tradition of discipline and training. At seven years of age, boys attended the school of martial arts. Children who preferred reading, writing, or the arts pursued these skills but were still required to practice sword handling, spear throwing, archery, or martial arts for at least a part of every day.

Girls in Cures could choose gardening, flower arranging, cooking, or dancing classes. Some girls, like Zolia, preferred more masculine pursuits. Sister's training was as rigorous as that allotted to our young men. An understandable desire for boys and girls to compete interchangeably arrived at early ages.

Mother Bionca, the best cook in Cures, proudly taught me her secrets. I learned to season meat, flavor vegetables, make soft breads and cakes, and measure delicious spices, salt, and olive oil. Zolia and Father loved my cooking.

Sister avoided domestic chores, instead pursuing dance and soldiering with equally determined fervor. After her first day at dance school she set her sights on winning Coelus le Terpsichore, the most prestigious dance contest in Sabinium. The contest was celebrated on every year some twenty days before the summer solstice. A stage would be erected in Cures center, and townswomen and children would spend many days adding colorful trimmings.

The competition was open to any Cures girl age eighteen or older with the stipulation that competitors were only permitted one attempt in a lifetime. The stakes were high; only the winner would be allowed to continue dance classes. As with all Cures competitions, victors continued training and losers took up another skill. Defeated dancers tended to shoulder more domestic responsibilities, a most unappealing consequence for Zolia.

For Coelus le Terpsichore, dancers drew one of five cards, each of which bore the name of a Sabini god. The dancers would perform their most interpretive dance as testimony to their chosen god. Spectators came from near and far to behold the contest. The grand prize was awarded by King Titus Tatius himself.

Just as important, the winner was deemed a worthy bride for an eligible prince from a royal family. It was an outcome that most young girls in Cures fancied, but an option that repulsed the Crusader. For Sister, the idea was simpler: to win.

Given her usual determination, victory seemed inevitable. When the Crusader set her eyes on the prize, only a matter of time remained before she achieved her triumph. That was one reason why the girls and boys in Cures shied away from Sister.

Though it was never spoken of, other children were wary of Zolia's physical strength and mental toughness. Sister had an uncanny confidence that encouraged her to say what she felt, regardless of time or place.

Zolia and I shared only one skill, and that was archery. Father started us early, insisting we practice on the farm in a large hut where bows and arrows were stored. Our targets were made of finely tanned goatskin that presented concentric circles with a dot in the middle. Zolia was a sharpshooter and much more skilled than her domesticated sister. I was not equal to either her skill or her tenacious will.

Even as a child, the Crusader pursued archery, swordsmanship, and dance with Spartan drive. Her competency became known in the far corners of Sabinium, and Sister competed on an equal footing with the young men of Cures. As her confidence flourished, her courage soared. Whatever she undertook, Zolia only saw herself as the best. Her days were filled with dance and martial arts.

Meanwhile, I helped Father with the farm and helped Mother with the home, learning what I could about life's subtleties.

❂❂❂❂❂❂

Chapter 9: Great Orgy of Roma

With triumph in his heart, King Romulus started building a wall around Palatine Hill. Tents for laborers and a palatial stone residence for Romulus and Remus sprang from the ground, and Roma's busy workforce started their labor with a strong sense of purpose.

But Romulus's design was poorly executed and the wall was uneven and weak. Remus, who bitterly ridiculed his brother's crooked wall, and his followers were disenchanted. As resentment between the twins mounted, Romulus came to realize that his brother was undermining both his authority and vision.

One afternoon, Remus taunted his brother by leaping over the flawed wall. Romulus lost his temper, quickly grabbed a spade, and repeatedly struck his brother's skull. Remus fell to the ground, forever subdued.

"What have you done, captain?" asked Commander Fabius. "Your brother's blood is on your hands!"

"Yes, his blood is on my hands. Roma is my vision and will be a powerful, eternal empire. From this day forward, any person who leaps her walls or undermines my vision will perish."

Fratricide

Fabius was assigned to administer funeral services and bestow false honors on Remus. Romulus and Fabius conspired to blame the murder on Celer, a migrant worker who hastily escaped to Etruscan lands. Romulus convinced his subjects that his brother's death validated his own divine powers and the wisdom of his own vision.

As construction progressed, a massive fort, several citadels, and altars for the gods rose from the landscape. Foreigners, many of whom had loathsome pasts, arrived to join the effort. To house the misfit workforce, Romulus built a new and larger asylum.

Rife with endless opportunities for trade, Roma was soon flooded with gold and silver. The city's imposing infrastructure spread across the five hills of Capitoline, Aventine, Caelian, Quirinal, and Palatine.

To accommodate a workforce of murderers, thieves, and sexual predators, the king allowed a more permissive society than did his neighboring communities. To strengthen his militaris, Romulus divided his soldiers into legions of three thousand infantry supported by three hundred trained cavalry. For governance, the king recruited one hundred noblemen and landowners and declared them patricians or senators.

The face of Roma slowly took shape.

But rumors that the spirit of Remus haunted Palatine Hill persisted. Reports of Remus sightings caused many citizens to stay boarded up in their homes at night. Roma's malaise further intensified when a pestilence swept the city. To lift the cloud from his people, Romulus planned sacrifices and festivals and placed an empty throne for Remus next to his own.

While Roma's labor force expanded, Romulus obsessed over the city's dearth of women. Compensation and residence

Debauchery

were offered to women willing to service the workforce. Any women willing to participate in the "Magna Surrexerunt Ludere de Roma" or "Great Orgy of Roma" were assured profit and abundant opportunity. Soon, prostitutes willing to accommodate the lustful workforce arrived by sea, carriage, and on foot from Greece, Africa, Babylonia, Egypt, and Persia.

When the female population swelled, Palatine Hill became known for notorious public orgies. City streets, public baths, gardens, parapets, and landmarks steamed with so many bodily fluids that outsiders joked the mountain fog and snow had disappeared.

To stimulate libido, men and women used herbal powders and added bull and goat testicles to their soup. Sexual predators were so active during the Great Orgy that no Roman claimed innocence. Even King Numitor succumbed to repeated fellatio administered by trollops from Egypt, Africa, and Mesopotamia, as well as from Urnfield in the distant west. The orgy lasted seven days and seven nights. Romans lost track of their partners until Romulus addressed his exhausted subjects on the last day of faceless sex.

"We have proven there are no differences between Roman men," said King Romulus. "We have shared our women as brothers. Our kingdom signifies unity, strength, courage, and power. Hail Holy Roma! Long live Roma!"

Almost immediately, prostitutes bearing caches of gold and silver began to depart the city. Only handfuls of women chose to remain. Bewitched by the powerful penises of Roma, the remaining harlots either procured wealthy husbands or stocked Roma's infamous whorehouses.

❋❋❋❋❋❋

Chapter 10: Corradeo's Family

Father's oldest brother had three sons and two daughters. The sons were Neiro, Iulius, and Julius, and the daughters were Ableasia and Memmia. Father's younger brother had two daughters – Domitia and Sulpicia – and one son, Naevius.

Of our eight cousins, Memmia, Sulpicia, and Naevius were our age. Our strongest cousin was the eldest, Neiro, a fearless hunter and warrior known throughout Sabinium.

Father often took our cousins with us to hunt boar, wild cattle, and birds. Father stressed that good hunters were not only good marksmen but were patient, ever aware of their habitat and prey.

As an average archer, I relied on my senses more than my skill. My kills were more a measure of my discipline than my marksmanship. On the other hand, Zolia relied on her archery prowess to overcome her impatient hunting style. She and Naevius shared charging styles.

One afternoon, Sister's unfettered brashness put our hunting party in jeopardy. Father had cautioned that we should never shoot at one of the wild cattle while it was in the herd. So, when our party came upon a grazing herd, we busily prepared traps.

But when Zolia spotted a young bull, she grew impatient and let fly an arrow – which missed its intended target. Instead, the arrow pierced the neck of a wandering calf, which immediately dropped at the feet of a large cow.

The protective mother spotted the attackers and without hesitation charged ahead of the herd. With the beasts thundering at us, Father and Lunius rallied their children and took flight; but the herd would surely stomp us and rip away our flesh before we could hope to get back to the village.

While hunting in the woods, Uncle Neiro heard the commotion and came running with his spear and sword poised for battle. "Cover the children," he commanded. "The herd is mine!"

Zolia could not resist. She lurched from Father's arms, grabbed Neiro's hand, and screamed, "I fight with you, Uncle!"

"Zolia Minerva, warrior princess of Cures, so be it." Father, Lunius, and I formed a wall, firing arrows over Zolia and Neiro at the charging beasts. Neiro's spear felled the lead cow at his feet. After yanking the spear from the beast's head, Neiro fired it into the next bull's shoulder. When the pole snagged on a rock, the bull slammed to the ground – and the oncoming charge was halted.

Rock-solid and confident, Neiro menacingly raised his sword at the beasts. No wild beast matched his ferocity. Instead, they shook their heads, snorted unconvincingly, and nervously stomped their hooves. The herd wanted no part of Neiro.

Only one lone bull was poised to make a final run. Always first to attack, Uncle set his sword and charged. He leapt onto the animal's head, drove his sword through the ribcage, and the giant crumbled to the ground.

Uncle swiveled to face the herd, but the attack was over. The beasts galloped to the plain. We were saved.

"Chase them! Kill them all!" Zolia wanted more.

Neiro turned to face her. "Great warriors never chase and kill, Zolia. They stand, charge, and fight. They win or die." He looked to Sister first, then to me. "Do my warrior women understand?" Uncle looked to the heavens. "Minerva knows I will protect her daughters until the day I die for them."

We left the huge animals where they had fallen and would send a few men back to do the butchering there in the field. Then we headed back to Cures.

Zolia led the way, dancing and giving thanks to the goddess Diana. Her movements chronicled our fight and the flailing torsos of the wild cattle killed by Diana's arrows and Neiro's sword. As we approached the town, crowds marveled at Sister's creative expression. I was not alone in the realization that Sister would win the Coelus le Terpsichore and one day be a feared warrior. The Sabine emphasis on winning emboldened Sister, quickly washing away her indiscretion.

Later, at home we made an offering to Minerva and gave praise for a victorious day. Father splashed blood from the kills on the altar. When our families assembled for the feast, we dabbed roasted meat in olive oil and garlic and savored Mother's famous artichoke-dipped bread. Naevius poured wine to his parents, who heaped praise on our savior. Sister and I made sure Uncle received everything he wished to eat and all the wine he wished to drink. We adored our protector.

After the feast, Neiro took us to the riverbank. Zolia sat to his left and I sat to his right. Our guardian pointed at the sky and lectured us about the gods of Sabinium. Distracted by her proximity to an accomplished warrior, Zolia made awkward conversation about whom Neiro would marry. When he blushingly declared his love for Passidena, the fetching daughter of Mettus Curtius, we were caught off guard.

"I know this girl. She weaves cloaks and jackets for our priests," said Zolia.

Neiro tickled her. "Zolia, you know everyone in Cures and everyone in Cures knows you."

"So, Uncle, does this mean Passidena will soon bear your children?" asked Sister.

"Time will tell, Zolia." He smiled at us. "I have you two daughters. Do you think there is time for more?" Taking a small knife from his belt, Neiro carved the letter R into his right forearm and then the letter Z on his left. Zolia and I tore cloth from our dresses and dabbed his blood.

"Hear my pledge. As long as I live I will protect Minerva's daughters, my sisters and cousins both. These initials are a blood covenant. Minerva favors my daughters. I am the protector delivered by their goddess."

We rested our heads on his lap and tears of gratitude flowed from my eyes. This man, our cousin and father, would always be our one true warrior.

Chapter 11: Vibulena

Children of Cures were taught that the town's founder was Modius Fabidius, the son of Quirinus, the Sabine god of war, who was born to a young woman from Reate who, while dancing to sanctify and honor Quirinus, had become so frenzied that she entered his shrine for sanctuary. Noticing the woman resting her head on his spear, Quirinus asked, "Woman, what troubles you?"

"While I was dancing, my mind became light and my knees weak. I saw myself birthing a demon's son, so I sought refuge in your shrine. I mean no offense. I only wish to close my eyes and calm my infirmity."

Convinced of her faith, Quirinus offered the woman his blessing. "Woman of Reate, your faith exceeds the others. I shall bless you with my offspring. Just as you discovered my spear, so shall our son create a place for all who believe in him."

When the impregnated woman gave birth to the God of War's son, she named him Modius Fabidius. As a man, the son of Quirinus became an exalted warrior. To immortalize his legend and commemorate the divine union of Quirinus and his mother, Modius assembled his followers, created our town, and named it Cures, for "spear."

At the time of year when spring changed to summer, the people of Cures hosted an annual festival honoring our founder. Neighbors from other towns joined us for dance, painting, flower arranging, and other festivities. Townspeople and our neighbors brought food for all, and a grand feast was hosted in the town hall.

The festival of my eleventh year was exceptional. Our family carried four roasted oxen, fifteen lambs, and two cows to the feast. Some families brought fruits, wine, and homemade delicacies. The offering was magnificent.

As the people of Cures had enjoyed an uncommonly prosperous year, the mood was filled with excitement. The citizenry were bedecked in their most elegant garments. I chose my black tunic with red embroidered flowers, and Sister wore her white tunic with purple trim.

"Be careful, my daughters. Stay away from people you do not know," Father warned, as we rushed to the exhibition center where stage performers and dancers entertained the crowds. Zolia was enthralled by the dancers but I savored the performers, like the magicians who blew fire from their mouths and powerful stone-throwers who heaved giant rocks.

One old poet captivated clusters of women with readings from piles of skin parchments. The ladies melted before the poet's recitals of love and passion, but the readings were beyond my experience and of little interest to me. Turning away from the bard, I faced a refined woman wearing a silk tunic with an elegant black pearl necklace.

The woman's grace accentuated her peaceful painting style. When she turned to me and asked, "Does the golden-haired princess wish to see my painting?"

I was spellbound. The artist led me to the front of her canvas, where a crane with grass in its beak fed a frog. Next to the frog, a snake chewed a yellow flower. To me, the mesmerizing scene was picturesque but confusing.

Sensing my consternation, the lady asked, "How, young girl of Cures, do you interpret my work?"

"Your work is beautiful, but it confuses me."

The painter stood back from the canvas, tilted her head to one side, placed her hand on her chin, and squinted at her work. "Hmm, confusing, says she. Why? The color, the frog, the snake, or the flower?"

"Well, cranes eat frogs. Snakes eat both frogs and cranes, but your crane feeds your frog and your snake chews your flower. What does this mean?"

"Ah, it is good you understand the way things are. But I paint something the world will see in the future, not as it is today."

"Are you a visionary, a stargazer, a goddess, or a wizard?" I queried.

The beautiful woman laughed. "No. Just an artist who has visions. This painting is one such vision. Tell me, blonde beauty, do you have visions you could express through painting? Do you see things others should see?" The beauty's directness unsettled me, but she gently lifted my face so that our eyes met.

"Sister Zolia dances like a goddess. Uncle Neiro is the strongest warrior in town," I blurted.

"Ah," said the painter. "That is what your sister and uncle do. What do you know?"

"I cook. Wash clothes. Help my mother. Work on the farm with my father. My life is so plain people call me 'Domus'."

"Ah, you have skills, young black top. These skills make me jealous of you."

"Really? But I do not dance or paint. I am not gifted."

"Do not be so sure. I will teach you. Then, we shall see."

"You would teach me to paint?" I pleaded.

"Yes. But in return, you will teach me to cook, wash, clean, farm, garden, and herd the cattle."

This was my chance. I smiled approvingly. When the artist introduced herself as Vibulena from Falerii, a town ruled by Etruscan kings on the other side of the Tiber in Falsci, I was enchanted. While we conversed, we became oblivious to the festival, completely absorbed in our conversation. Vibulena had much to say about the world and conceded that she had heard prophecies about the daughters of Minerva.

Chapter 12: Proculus Maxim

After two years of development and expansion, Roma was poised for greatness; yet the king was uneasy. Proculus Maxim, a close friend to King Romulus, asked, "What bothers my king?"

"Our orgies wear on my city. Our prostitutes must go. Roma's children need real fathers and real mothers, or she will fail. Our Roman penises outnumber our proper wombs. For Roma to survive, this must change."

Proculus considered the king's concerns and made a suggestion. "We will approach our neighbors and ask for intermarriage. We can persuade them. Roman wives will be granted citizenship so they can become proper mothers."

Romulus agreed and summoned his senators to debate the proposition. "We will approach our neighbors, make an alliance, and ask their daughters to marry our men," the king informed his senators.

"Will this end our famous brothels?" asked one senator.

Romulus shrugged, "It is time Roman children know their fathers."

The senators laughed until one suggested, "Begin with our Latin neighbor, Caenina. After all, Alba Longa is a mix of Latin and Trojan blood. Now we need Latin women."

Not long past the winter solstice, a Roman delegation approached Caenina amidst great pomp. Wearing white and black tunics and playing harps, trumpets, and drums, musicians led a column of a hundred infantrymen who held banners inscribed "League of Friendship." The king's personal ambassadors donned their finest togas and arrived in rich chariots, with the singular purpose of procuring wives for Roman husbands.

The unannounced arrival confused the locals, who presumed an attack was underway. Soon, Caeninan warriors surrounded the Romans and prepared an assault.

A Roman delegate stepped from his chariot and calmly approached the crowd. "Why is Roma here? What is this?" the Caeninans asked him.

The delegate began to speak. "We represent the great nation of Roma. We come in peace to solidify an alliance with the good people of Caenina. We offer security, new avenues of trade, and great prosperity in exchange for your daughters and unmarried women who will mother Roma's future."

When the proposition sank in, most Caeninans laughed. One man shouted, "Are you insane? Our daughters will never mother children of Roma. Leave and take these other jokesters with you!"

A second Roman senator approached the crowd. "Why are you rude? Be polite. We are your neighbors and need your help. Our proposal is serious. You should not disrespect us. We represent King Romulus. Will your king speak with us?"

King Acron of Caenina and his guards met the delegation at the city gates. "Does King Romulus ask our daughters to marry Roman rapists?"

"Yes. This is our request from Roma."

Acron raised his frame. "We mean no insult, but no woman from Caenina will ever marry a Roman whoremonger."

"How can you say this? The women will be citizens of the Roman Empire. They will be treated as Roman wives, not prostitutes," explained the senator.

"Daughters of Caenina will never participate in Roman orgies with your unclean and profane men. Your request falls at the wrong doorstep," responded Acron. "You have our final answer."

"That is blasphemy and hearsay," said the senator. "You do not understand."

"Enough!" Acron shouted. "Everyone knows Romans painted Palatine Hill with their penises for seven days and seven nights."

"Philanderers! Filthy Romans! Leave Caenina!" the crowd shouted, while Caeninan soldiers banged their spears. "Leave! Never return!"

Acron motioned to his soldiers. "Show these Romans away from our gate." Townspeople chased the Romans, and Caeninan women spit on the vacating column. It was a dark day for the failed emissaries, who knew that the king awaited their report.

●●●●●●●

Chapter 13: Délitéscere Talentum

The artist took special pride in her painting of tanned skins of sheep, camel, and wild buffalo. Her impressive collection of expensive brushes made from the hairs of wild Mongolian cats, Greek squirrels, Mesopotamian hogs; her purple dye from the Phoenicians; and her expensive blue dyes from Afghan caves intrigued me.

"Vibulena, where did you acquire such fine brushes? In Cures, we only have brushes made from goat, hog, and ox hairs. Yours are much more delicate and made of fine hair."

"I am a traveling artist," she answered. "I have been to many empires and am blessed with friends in many lands."

Vibulena lifted a camel skin from her leather bag, inviting me to paint. My gawkiness was clear. I gripped the brush like an artist with broken fingers. "Ronica," began the painter, "imagine a picture in your mind. I will hold your hand to paint the brain's image."

"A yellow flower! I shall paint a yellow flower." As Vibulena guided my hand, a long-stemmed flower with petals and nectar began to emerge. The sensation overjoyed me.

"Do you suppose my flower, in the painting of the crane and frog, influenced your vision?" she asked.

Artist

"I think so, but may I add more to your crane-frog painting."

"Really! How would you do that, Ronica?" she asked, surprised at my boldness.

"We should have a bee, a hummingbird, a baby, and a river around your flower."

Vibulena stepped back to eye her skins from a different perspective. "I agree, daughter of Minerva," she said enthusiastically. Again she guided my hand, but this time her touch was so delicate that my body and soul opened to the canvas as we drew our bee and hummingbird. Vibulena let go of my hand and, without realizing it, I was painting without assistance.

When finished, I shouted, "There it is! We did it!"

"Not we," Vibulena said. "This is you, Ronica. Your painting. You should be proud. Someday, you will be a fine artist."

"How is this possible? How did I do this?"

"It is said that the daughters of Minerva achieve remarkable feats. What does this picture mean to you?"

"Our flower honors the provider god. The bee and hummingbird are nature. The child stands for humans and the river signifies our plentiful resources."

Vibulena's face lit up. "Yes, young Ronica, you are indeed a true artist who embodies the spirit of Minerva. You are blessed with what we call krymméno talénto."

"Krymméno Talénto? What does this mean, Vibulena?"

"It is Greek for 'hidden talent'." My mentor was clearly more than an artist; she possessed education and knowledge to match her elegant demeanor.

From around the corner an unusual man with long hair, dressed in a full brown robe with orange decor and a black pearl necklace, approached us. His fish-like sandals stood out. "Vibulena, who is this nymph?" he asked, in a voice that had both the ring of a woman and the tone of a man.

"Gino Pesna, meet my new friend, Ronica, one of Minerva's daughters." The man's curious feminine and masculine qualities put me off momentarily.

The unusual person stood on tiptoes, placed his cheek in the palm of his hand, and strummed his fingers like a woman. "Do I put you off, yellow top?"

"You are… quite beautiful," was all I could muster.

Vibulena sensed my unease. "Gino is your friend, Ronica. He would never hurt you. This is one man that will always stand at your side."

Zolia spotted us and strode over confidently. "What goes on here?" she asked. When I showed her my painting, the Crusader was impressed. "Once again, my sister, the Revolter, proves to be the most talented sister in Cures."

"You are blessed with beauty!" Zolia admired my artist, then turned to Gino. Her eyes narrowed in recognition. "You are a eunuch, are you not?"

This word was unfamiliar to me, but apparently known to Zolia. Vibulena cautioned Sister by saying, "How do you know such things?"

"I dance. I know eunuchs serve the king's court. Their dances are notoriously comical." Zolia studied the artist. "You look well-traveled… an adventurous, modern woman of our time."

Vibulena was amused. "You and your sister interest me, Zolia. Do you think your family would allow us to stay, teach Ronica, and learn housekeeping and farming skills in exchange?"

"Ronica, this painter and her eunuch are your friends. This is for you to decide."

My answer was obvious. We gathered up the painting supplies and led Vibulena and Gino homeward. Zolia danced all the way and I noticed that Vibulena observed everything Sister did. I knew Zolia liked the attention.

At first our parents seemed unsure about our guests; but as we came to understand our new friends, everyone relaxed. Vibulena was from a wealthy, royal family in Falerii. Many suitors had pursued her but she was more interested in travel and art than marrying. Vibulena would take time to find her match.

Gino was born impotent and asexual. His family were terracotta sculptors and made fine statues in Veli, but he had declined sculpting in favor of his first passion: dance. As a servant, he had helped many wealthy Etruscan families. Gino and Vibulena had shared a love of art since their early years.

That night, I prepared beds for Vibulena and Gino in our guest room. The festival noise prevented sleep so I took Vibulena to our farm, where we lay in the open meadows contemplating the night sky.

"Where do you suppose the idea for your picture came from?" she asked. "You really should be studying at the art school here."

"You inspired me, Vibulena. Art teachers in Cures do not teach creativity. They teach structure, which has no appeal for me."

"Hmm," Vibulena said. "Would you like to travel with me and learn more about the world?"

Flattered, I blushed. "Oh, yes! Thank you, but no. My oath is to stay home and care for Zolia and my parents."

"Then your artistic skills will be wasted. You have such potential, Ronica."

"Vision comes from inside, not from experience," I answered.

Vibulena faced me, resting her chin in the cup of her hand. "You are quite bright, Ronica. Yes, you can see the world from one place. People are similar regardless of where they live."

"Thank you, Vibulena. You have awakened what was subdued inside me. I will learn to paint pictures that reveal these feelings."

"Ah, then we have an agreement. I shall teach you to paint and you will teach me to cook, wash linen, fish, and farm. How wonderful!"

As we stared into the sky, I realized my senses were heightened. "Why are the stars not scattered around? They seem in a single line, do they not?"

"Ronica, when you travel high enough in the sky and reach a particular point, all the stars are in a single line," explained my mentor, as my mind soared to the planets.

The next day, we returned to Cures to meet our relatives. Vibulena and Gino observed life in town with interest. All the young men eyed Vibulena and were anxious that she visit their homes and sample their wine. Vibulena was receptive to meeting as many people as reasonably possible.

From our hosts, Sister and I received pomegranate juice while Vibulena and Gino were given wine in fine sparkling silver cups. Vibulena was polite but vigilant, never overdoing her welcome and usually accepting only a few drops of the grape.

When Zolia questioned Vibulena's reserve, the artist warned, "Watch the grape, you daughters of Minerva. Never surrender to a man for a cup of wine," she chuckled. "But, think twice when a bag of gold is at your feet!"

Zolia and I burst out laughing. "Salvé, Artist," Zolia said. "You are a witty one."

And so our tutoring began. During the day, I taught Vibulena gardening, housekeeping, farming, fishing, and cooking. My student was smart but unused to physical labor. Yet she declined assistance, saying, "My mind, body, and energy must learn to bend in all directions and draw from the strength and rhythm acquired after a day of tiring work."

Her clean, delicate hands blistered and quickly soiled. I was puzzled by her curiosity about my domestic skills. On our second afternoon, the artist said, "For a long time, I believed housekeeping and physical work were off limits to me. But when I saw your first picture of the flower, I realized that art and the hard realities of life should come together. Art needs the insights which you have and which I lack. My newfound powers of observation will make me a better artist. So you see, Ronica, my dirty hands will make me a better artist."

My infatuation with this talented woman, who understood full well the intricacies of womanhood but who could only cook fish broth with spinach, expanded with every revelation.

Zolia was delighted with Gino, who taught her the dances of eunuchs. Within several days, my brilliant sister was dancing better than Gino and had become so enamored with his uniqueness that she began imitating his walk, his speech, and his body language. While Zolia was a quick learner, her new affectations made me uneasy.

One morning, Gino asked Zolia how she liked his eunuch dances. "Your masculine-feminine dances interest me because they are from both sides of the human persona."

Gino laughed, "Zolia, were you a man I would love you to death."

"Ha, Gino. Then we shall be best friends, for I am a woman."

Our family came to accept Vibulena and Gino. When it was time to depart, Vibulena gave me fine brushes and several animal skins. Gino presented to Zolia his black pearl necklace. In exchange, we gave our new friends one pure gold coin that contained an imprint of Quirinus on one side and Modius Fabidius on the other.

We excitedly accepted Vibulena's invitation to her home for the early winter festival in Faleri to honor Juno Quiritis, whom many Sabines believed to be the first wife of Quirinus, and the eternal bond between Falisci and Sabinium. The festival in Faleri would be our first trip away from Cures.

●●●●●●

Chapter 14: Ovid and Scaveola

Over time, Zolia developed a crush on Ovid. He was the son, three years her senior, of a neighboring farmer. Ovid was also a dancer but, unlike my sister, he was not a warrior. He sought to become a triumph dancer, one who blessed the soldiers when they left for battle and then celebrated their return. Zolia's attraction mystified me; but rather than question Sister, it seemed best to let her latest pursuit play out.

Cousin Naevius was Zolia's usual dance partner. Like Ovid, he practiced to be a triumph dancer. Not long after the hunting incident with the wild cattle, Zolia and Naevius asked me to attend a performance. I eagerly accepted their invitations to introduce me to their friends, who promptly derided my domestic training by calling me "domus" or "housekeeper."

Zolia took offense and threatened to fight any boy who dared tease her sister. "How dare you talk to Ronica like that!" she shouted at Scaveola, leader of the catcallers. "If Ronica would teach your mother how to prepare meals, you would not be so weak. Everyone in your family starves in misery!" This was Sister's swipe at Vlpia, Scaveola's older sister and a dance competitor for Coelus le Terpsichore.

The stakes in this local dance competition were greater than the usual bragging rights, because the losing team would be forever prohibited from competitive dance. Because Naevius was needed to provide music on his lyre, Scaveola and Vlpia were paired against Zolia and Ovid. The challenge was to imitate Quirinus, the god of Sabine wars, in a test that was as much about endurance as artistic expression.

The winner would be the couple who danced the longest while maintaining constant contact between partners. Three of the dancers delivered stirring interpretations of Quirinus, but Scaveola was not as practiced as the others. As his confidence waned, his stamina followed. Soon his arms, hands, and legs shook like a lizard's.

From the start, the harmonious synchronization between Zolia and Ovid mesmerized me. My mind quickly ventured to the future and the day they would wed.

Vlpia's high-spirited dance paralleled Zolia's, but Ovid would surely outlast Scaveola. At twilight, both couples sensed that elimination was approaching. Vlpia tapped her last morsel of energy, dancing as lightly as an arrow in the air. Scaveola tried reining in the arrow, but his weak hands surrendered to exhaustion. He lost Vlpia, who staggered back and tripped on a rope.

In a flash, Zolia sprang away from Ovid and then caught and stabilized her competitor before Vlpia tumbled from the stage. Zolia's quickness stilled the crowd. Ovid and Scaveola marveled at her speed and balance. Sister broke the stunned silence. "This dance is a draw. Nobody wins. Nobody loses."

Scaveola knew he and his sister had lost, and he burned at the affront. "No, Zolia. This will not work. You and your dancer friend are the victors."

"Scaveola, I broke your sister's fall. You would do the same for me. Call it a draw."

The Crusader's declaration inadvertently degraded Scaveola, who would rather lose than suffer Zolia's concession. In a heated moment, he challenged the winners to a duel.

"Oh, so the bad dancer wants to fight? If that is how you want it settled, Ovid will fight you," offered Zolia.

But Ovid was a dancer, not a sword fighter, and Scaveola was a promising warrior. By Cures tradition, the loser would not be permitted to touch a sword again. This meant little to Ovid, but everything to Scaveola.

The combatants used wooden swords from the school. After they had donned armor, helmets, and shields, the fated duel began.

Scaveola easily dislodged the sword from Ovid's hand, flinging it to the ground. Aware that Zolia fancied Ovid, Scaveola sought to belittle the dancer. Every time Ovid picked up the sword, Scaveola knocked it away. Soon the stronger boy held the weaker to the ground and declared his victory by pretending to pierce the dancer's heart.

Outraged, Zolia rose to Ovid's defense. "Worry not, my dancer! I will have revenge." Assuming a combatant's stance, she screamed at Scaveola. "Fight me, bully! Show me there are men in your family after all!"

Shocked that Zolia dared challenge him, Scaveola turned scarlet with anger. I rushed to my sister. "Zolia, control yourself! You have won the day. We should walk away. Scaveola is a fighter, not a dancer."

Eyes ablaze, she pushed me aside. "This bully boy taunts

us, Ronica. We are Minerva. If he goes free, the town will call you 'domus' and me 'dancer' for eternity. Is that what you want? The Crusader fights for us!"

Zolia's ferocity was so imposing that I could only muster a weak, "Finish him."

Sister was the smaller battler. She compensated for her lack of size with skill and with quick, fluid movements. Every time the muscular boy came close, she jabbed and kicked him. "Zolia, you are the bravest girl in Cures. Forget the dancer. You are meant for a warrior like me."

"I will never marry into a genderless family, bully boy. In our home, men are men and women their equals. We respect each other, dancer, warrior, farmer, or housekeeper. You will rue this day."

Scaveola lurched forward, striking Zolia's wrist. Her sword flew to the ground. The aggressor pushed her down and placed his sword to her heaving chest. When he peered into her flaming eyes, Scaveola saw that the Crusader was not finished.

Grabbing a handful of sand, Sister flung it into his eyes. The blinded warrior staggered away. Zolia leaped up, coiled, and head-butted her prey to the ground. Lifting his fallen sword, she prodded his chest three times. "Dead! You are dead, bully boy!"

Zolia had won! Scaveola had lost. Flushed in victory, Zolia declared, "Had these been real swords, this would be my happiest day."

Cnaeus Augur and Uncle Neiro had witnessed the duel and rushed to intervene. Neiro pulled Zolia off Scaveola and helped the boy to his feet, and then scolded Zolia. "You are a dancer, not a warrior. You overstep your bounds and insult our neighbor."

Zolia bowed. "I apologize, Uncle Neiro, but this schoolboy insulted Ronica and my friend, Ovid. I had to defend them."

"She threw sand in my eyes!" yelled Scaveola.

"Zolia!" Uncle stated. "Cures warriors never fight like cowards."

"Uncle, the bully is stronger than me," she countered. "To defeat my enemies, I must use every trick and every element of surprise."

Neiro considered her. "Hmm. Could it be that Minerva's younger daughter teaches me something?"

Neiro tried to boost Scaveola. "This is but a game, young fighter. Forget the sword. Concentrate on your martial arts."

The boy replied with conviction. "I vow to never touch another sword in my life. This I swear in the name of Quirinus." I realized the irony that what had started as a dance had ended in a sad, life-changing travesty.

"What have you done to our warrior?" Uncle asked Zolia, who met his gaze but walked away in silence.

Cnaeus Augur approached her. "You are fine, little Minerva. You are fine." While we walked home, Neiro ignored Zolia but Cnaeus held Zolia's hand. "Zolia Minerva, you fought well. You were born to be a great warrior. One cannot fight their destiny."

"Thank you, Cnaeus."

"Enough, Cnaeus!" Neiro steamed. "Encourage her no longer. This is a dangerous game."

"Neiro, your Zolia merits encouragement. You must be patient with Minerva's daughters."

"Zolia needs discipline, not handholding. When the warrior's discipline breaks down, serious mistakes are made."

"These are righteous sisters from the heavens. They know how to conduct themselves. Only Minerva can instruct her daughters."

That night, Zolia promised to never pick another fight. In the still of the moon, she sobbed to me, "I am victorious. Why am I sad?"

I wrapped her in my arms and listened to my heart. My sister was indeed the Crusader.

Chapter 15: Ronica

With the domus now focused on becoming the finest artist in Sabinium, my days were filled with drawing and painting pictures at the expense of my household responsibilities. When questioned about my newfound passion, my response never varied; "Dēlitēscere talentum."

I was powerless to return to domestic work, which infuriated the Crusader. One afternoon, Zolia came whistling home from her dance class. At least once every few days, she wore her most sinuous red tunic to the evening dance – but my new calling had caused me to neglect washing her favorite tunic.

Zolia burst from her room shouting, "Ronica, my red tunic is filthy!"

"Forgive me, Sister. I have been busy."

Zolia studied me. "Perhaps. But I see you were not too busy to wash your own clothes. What happened to mine?"

"Young sister, I am an artist now. My art requires my time, as dance requires yours."

Fearing a storm, Mother offered, "Worry not, my youngest. I shall wash your robe as soon as our midday meal is served."

Zolia whisked Mother's response aside, preferring to chastise me. "Domus, you were once a good and caring sister. Since meeting the artist, you are transformed for the worse."

Heat rushed to my face. "I am no longer your domus, Zolia. And I am not Scaveola! You are old enough to care for yourself!"

Mother interceded, scolding Zolia for the first time in months. Sister ran back to our room, where each of her tears pierced my heart.

Mother asked me about Scaveola. When I sobbingly recited the details, Mother confronted an indignant Zolia. Suddenly, Mother's slap resounded through our home. Zolia stormed outside, screaming, "I will never talk to either of you! Never touch me again!"

Mother's heart ached for her reaction and we chased the dancer. Mother apologized but Zolia focused on me. "You are my center. Now you break my heart." She ran to the farm, seeking comfort from Father.

That night, Mother and I had the house alone and lay in her big bed. But each time I drifted into sleep, a vision of Zolia haunted me. I arose to paint the Crusader standing on beds of clouds and raining tears on the ground below, where I lithely danced above the flowers. Zolia was with Father, but the painting returned her love to me.

When Father and Zolia came home, he admonished Mother. "Never again strike Minerva's daughters. If a serious problem arises, advise me and I shall disarm it."

Zolia sulked for days, spending her time with Father or by herself. When she finally did return to our bed, I climbed in behind her, rubbed her face, and stroked her hair.

"What does my sister do?" she asked.

"I care for Little Sister," I answered

Zolia pivoted to me. "Now that you are the greatest artist in Sabinium, do you still love your sister, Ronica?"

Zolia's moment of doubt startled me. "Please suffer my new skill," I begged. "Know that my warrior dancer will bask in my love until my last breath."

Zolia kissed my forehead. "Ronica, you are not Domus. Just my caretaker and artistic sister. I am sorry for my selfishness."

When we awoke, I showed the Crusader my painting. She was pleased but troubled. "Sister Ronica, do you want to be a dancer? Why do I cry when you dance? Or do you celebrate my crying by dancing?"

Flabbergasted, I tried to see what Zolia saw. "When your tears fall, I listen even more closely. In the painting, I only dance to halt the rain."

"You are the sweetest sister in Cures. How would I live without you?" We understood that another pointless misunderstanding had passed and that we were two ends of the same pole.

Chapter 16: Romulus

Romulus was stunned to see his mission to Caenina return empty-handed. A fiery senatorial debate concluded that the Roman approach was flawed. Romulus and his strategists set plans to solicit Antemnae, an ancient Latin town north of Roma, with a better offer.

Late in winter but before the spring, another Roman contingent departed to present a scripted case. But the people of Antemnae were aware of the Caenina incident and stood ready. When the Roman delegation appeared at the town outskirts, elders awaited them.

"Do you know why we come?" asked a Roman senator.

"We have heard from Caenina. Your proposal is absurd."

"We regret our past mistakes," the senator asserted. "But, Roma has only men. We need women."

"We understand your urgency," an elder responded. "Had your orgies not been so public, perhaps some fathers might have considered your offer. But, as it is, there are no single women here that will accompany you to Roma."

"Perhaps you answer too quickly," said the senator. "We promise your women citizenship. They will not be treated as prostitutes but as wives. Most will be wealthy beyond their dreams."

Ghosts

"Like our neighbors, we do not trust Roma or its leadership. Romulus's orgies will haunt the city forever."

"Who killed Remus? Did your king kill his brother? Who could trust such a man?" a citizen yelled.

"Who dares spread such gossip? Remus was killed by Celer, not Romulus," Fabius lied. "The Babylonian disagreed with King Remus and became wild with rage. He hammered the king with his spade and fled to Etruscan territory."

"Refugees from Roma say the ghost of Remus haunts Palatine Hill."

"Gossip about Romulus and Remus has no place in our offer," insisted Fabius.

The elder measured his words. "We disagree. There is no reason for a man to murder his blood. No matter the dispute, it should have been settled. The daughters of Antemnae cannot marry men who follow such a brother. The curse of Remus will always be upon Roma. This heinous crime is made worse because the victim was a twin. In this village, we worship twin gods."

❖ ❖ ❖ ❖ ❖ ❖

Chapter 17: Juno Quiritus

When it came time to travel to the festival of Juno Quiritis, Naevius joined us. We set out in Father's wagon. Zolia and I sat next to Father, who managed our six horses. Naevius squeezed between Father's legs. The horses were spirited but Father handled the reins.

The Tiber highlands and valleys were ripe with green grass and blooming wildflowers. Our journey was festive as travelers, traders, soldiers, and food suppliers joined the festival goers. We offered greetings to all. Zolia was effervescent and joyful.

Gino met us at the town gate. We bounced from the wagon and ran to hug him. As he led the wagon to Vibulena's house, we walked at his side. Zolia and I laughed at our unfamiliarity with the many foreign tongues heard along the way.

Gino explained, "Here we speak Faliscan, a combination of Latin and Etruscan mixed with many Sabini words." Sister and I recognized our linguistic shortcomings and knew we were far from Cures in more ways than one. Faliscans welcomed us with tulips, bluebells, convolvulus, lunaria, and roses. Before long, we held entire gardens in our hands.

Though we were covered with flowers, Vibulena recognized us and rushed to welcome us. "Where is the most charming flower on earth?" my artist asked.

"Seek and you shall find, my mentor," I answered, shifting the flowers away from my face.

Vibulena lifted me. "How goes my best friend?"

"Never better," I smiled. "I work on my Dēlitēscere talentum every day."

From under her flowers, Zolia called, "Salvé, Artist. You did not say this was flower city. These bouquets are too heavy for me!"

Vibulena laughingly relieved her. Zolia straightened and dusted her tunic. "Why do your people try to make Minerva's youngest daughter a flower girl?"

Vibulena shook her head. "At festival time, we simple folk give flowers to women and children who come from distant places. It is our greeting, not a belittlement, Zolia, dear."

"Maybe so, but no person offered water. I do not want to die of thirst with these rootless flowers at my side."

"Zolia! You are rude. Just ask for water and it is yours," I snipped.

"Do you mean to annoy me, Revolter?"

Gino intervened. "Yes, Zolia. How thoughtless we are! Come. Water is at the house."

Maids carried water to Sister. When Vibulena's parents came to greet us, Zolia gulped the water and added, "Water on our side of the Tiber is tastier."

Vibulena's mother measured Zolia. "This black-haired beauty must be the Zolia we hear so much about." She allowed Sister to absorb the compliment. "You see, young maiden, Cures water is sweetened with sugarcane. This is plain water from our family well."

"Do you dislike sugarcane?"

Hearing Zolia continue her impertinence, I whispered desperately to her. "Behave yourself here, Zolia. We are guests. A cordial guest rates a cordial host."

Vibulena's palace had strong pillars, carved stone walls, silver flower vases, Persian carpets, animal-head trophies, and statues of different gods in every room. Riches, paintings in silver frames, and impressive antiquities were spread throughout the palace.

My mentor introduced us to her parents and two siblings: a younger sister, Selian, and her younger brother, Isidorus, who was one year my senior. His eyes devoured Zolia and me. His bulging pants left little doubt he fancied us both.

Travelers from Africa, Persia, and Judea stopped at the house for lodging. The home was a beehive of excitement. Vibulena shouldered the lion's share of responsibility, arranging rooms for weary guests. As busy as she was, she saved the rooms with her favorite art for us.

Our every wish was answered. While we enjoyed a scrumptious meal, Mother busied herself telling the cooks her favorite recipes. Father and his companions joined Vibulena's father and uncles for hunting, drinking, and games of chance. Soon we were so busy that Zolia forgot to complain.

Finally our intimate threesome headed to the school of arts, where the artist taught aspiring artists. The school was alive with creative energy. On the way, Zolia's striking beauty and jubilant chatter endeared her to all.

To honor my new pursuit, Vibulena painted a picture of my face set between bouquets of fresh flowers. Before she finished, she drew Zolia holding a silver mug of water. I giggled my delight at the irony.

"Your first yellow flower was the brilliant masterpiece that changed my life. Today, you painted a hundred more flowers. My mentor's spirit spins with creativity."

Vibulena kissed me. "Dear friend, that is the point. Surely, you know you are my essence."

Zolia had heard enough. She scratched herself obnoxiously as she eyed the painting. "What is this?"

"You see, Zolia? I drew you too."

"This painting makes no sense!" Zolia said. "The flowers are suffering and sad. Why do you not hear their cries? And my sister poses amidst their agony? And me? Why would I enjoy water from the mug rather than give the flowers their elixir?"

Speechless, Vibulena measured Sister's wrath. It took a moment before she could respond. "Zolia, how observant you are! You should be an artist."

"Art imitates collections of memories and experiences that are best left as originals. I could never paint fantasy, like you. Fantasies can be dangerously misleading."

I wondered at Zolia's wisdom. What did she know? What was Minerva saying?

The festival of Juno Quiritis was majestic. We dressed in elegantly draped togas. All young and unmarried women tied their hair like vestal virgins. Zolia's long braid gave rise to her splendid femininity. Men wore long white togas with gold and silver edging. The elders sacrificed lambs, birds, and rams in honor of their goddess. Streets filled with music and dance as Zolia and Naevius enthusiastically joined the festivities.

Vibulena was a vision. Men from near and far flirted with my friend, who smoothly brushed them away. I had never seen another woman draw as much attention as Zolia.

Meanwhile, Vibulena's brother, Isidorus, busied himself as my protector. His affection was exhausting but I tolerated him for Vibulena, who wished we would wed. The boy was torn between two orchids: Zolia, dark with intrigue, and me, the domus. His attempts to reconcile the conflict were laughable.

After honoring Juno Quiritis, another religious tribute was slated for Feronia, goddess of wildlife, fertility, health, and abundance. It would be held in early winter, about one moon cycle before the winter solstice. The famed temple at the base of Mt. Soracte, near Capena, was the venue. Zolia insisted upon joining the legions of performers who danced tributes to the goddess. As always, Sister's nimble movements and flexible body set her above the rest.

Another festival, Hirpi Sorani or "The Wolves of Soranus," was scheduled in several days. Soranus was the Sabine's dark god of death and the underworld. This festival would be held on Soracte's highest ridge and pay homage to the devil's wolf servants.

Vibulena detailed the history for us. Before the ceremony of Hirpi Sorani was initiated, followers worshiped in the sanctuary of Dis Pater, a temple built into the mountain. One day shepherds were burning their dead when wolves suddenly sprang from the woods, plundered the entrails from the fire, and ran away. Incensed, the shepherds gave chase; but the wolves successfully hid in the dark.

Lupus

Later the shepherds happened upon a cave and, assuming the wolves were inside, rushed in – unaware that the cave contained pestilential gases. All the shepherds suffocated and died. Fear ripped through the town, where the fate of the shepherds was attributed to an underworld curse.

To placate the gods, the mourning residents adopted rituals that imitated wolves. From that time on a chosen group of followers, who claimed to be descendants of Soranus, declared themselves Hirpi Sorani.

Vibulena's rendition captured our imaginations and we became eager to participate in the fete. At Acqua Forte, a natural spring, we cleansed our feet and legs. When we arrived at the cave's door to the underworld, everyone bowed to us. Our saffron-colored tunics and togas were well received by the priests, who donned wolf skins and wolf headdresses.

A statue of Soranus marked the altar, which was set behind a large rectangular pit filled with blazing pines. Priests performed ritual wolf imitations until the flames subsided to glowing embers.

Two high priests rose before the fire. One priest, bearing food, unhesitatingly stepped onto the embers and walked into the fire. Worshippers rejoiced and other priests danced and howled like wolves. The spiritual fervor for Soranus peaked when the priest emerged unscathed from the smoke and flames at the far end of the pit. The worshippers saw that their god protected his congregation. The priest approached the altar and deposited his harvest.

Then a second priest transported a vessel of water across the embers and calmly made another deposit. The priests kept going back and forth until clothes, gold, silver, swords, armor, empty vessels, and pots were piled at the altar. After the final deposit, the priests performed a purifying ritual for the community and a sense of gratitude filled the air.

I was lightheaded but Sister's eyes were fixed on the fire. "How could the priests walk across the fire unharmed?" I asked.

Zolia juddered her hips, quivered her legs, and raised her arms to the sky, declaring, "I will dance on the coals."

"What?"

"I want to dance in the fire."

Vibulena moved next to the Crusader. "Zolia, sometimes your zaniness astounds me."

"Zany? Not me. I will test my dancing skill on the heat of the fire."

"But you will be burned," Vibulena said.

"If the priests could survive, so will I. They are men. I am woman."

"The gods protect their feet."

"And Minerva protects me… and Ronica."

My heart sank. I knew too well Zolia's determination. With help from Gino, we persuaded Zolia to wait until the following day when the embers would be cooler.

We stayed the night and, late the next morning, Zolia performed in the ashes. She raised her joined hands to the heavens. "Holy god Quirinus and son Modius Fabidius, bless us! Show Soranus your power."

Sister balanced on one foot and pirouetted before her god, who carried her to the wolf of Soranus. She portrayed

Quirinus presenting her with his spear, which she plunged into the wolf's skull. Zolia danced into the underworld where, in exaggerated gestures, she found and killed Soranus by opening his chest and removing his heart.

She bowed to Quirinus before presenting him with the dark heart. "Thank you for the mighty spear, our god. I have killed the underworld god and all his wolves. This ritual has ended."

Suddenly a voice bellowed at us. "You worm! How dare you imitate killing Soranus!" screamed a priest assigned to check the pit.

"How dare you threaten Minerva's daughter!" retorted Zolia.

"How do I dare? I witnessed your scornful dance. You are disrespectful, child. Your foolish dance resembled a crazed bitch." The priest ridiculed Zolia with a gyrating rendition of her dance. "The high priest must know you are a non-believer."

Zolia scooped ashes from the pit and tossed them in the incensed priest's face, who began yelling his fury at her once again.

"First you insult the god Soranus and his messenger Hirpus. Then you insult his priest, who now curses you so that a wolf will tear your body to pieces and spread you across Mount Soracte! There, Soranus will torment your soul until your last breath. Oh, Soranus! Tell your servants in Hell this non-believer deserves no water, food, or clothes!"

The priest wiped the ashes from his face and stared at Zolia. "This is the curse that I swear will become your reality," he hissed.

Vibulena pleaded with the priest to closet Zolia's indiscretion. The priest relished our artist's favor, and he agreed to close the matter.

On our way home, Zolia was quiet. Vibulena questioned her, "Why did you dance? What made you perform such a dance?"

Zolia was preoccupied, considering the priest's curse. "Why do gods wait to judge and punish us? After death, it is too late. Human bodies decay. Our bones fall apart. But underworld dwellers regain their bodies and spirits? If we regain our body and soul, how many times will this occur before life's journey is complete? The ceremony for Soranus was farcical. I imitated killing the underworld god and his messengers because that is what Minerva would want."

Vibulena touched Sister's shoulders. "Why are you always in the middle of trouble and controversy? This is where bad things can happen, Zolia."

"Salvé, Artist. The heathen priest's curse is nonsensical. Without food and water, Soranus and his peasants could only torture me a short while before I would die. The priest's manmade curse is meaningless. Open your eyes and think about how ridiculous this is."

●◉❉❈◈●

Chapter 18: Return to Roma

Nearing the gates of Roma, humiliated senators slumped to the ground. They knew King Romulus must be told that the death of Remus had tarnished their efforts. As word spread from the chamber to the streets, Fabii followers of Remus rioted and pressed for the truth.

Infuriated, Romulus sat in court with his trusted advisers. With bulging eyes and flaring nostrils, the king announced, "This day, I shall reveal the truth to Roma." Then he rose and strode from the chamber to confront his agitated subjects from a balcony.

"Brothers and fellow Romans, listen to your hearts and judge me accordingly. Before I became king, I was a humble shepherd who chased robbers from this very hill. Now my hill spills over with crime. I have been tolerant and patient with the vagabonds who have flocked here.

"Prosperous nations are built with wise men and the heirs of kings, not with bandits and murderers. In Roma, you are not judged. I give you hope. Here, the living live. For these reasons and others, I, the protector of Roma, deserve forgiveness for my sins.

"I constructed your asylum believing that if you were

an exile, Roma would be your sanctuary. Where else are you so welcome? Roma opens her outstretched arms to shelter and protect you. Here you can mend your misfortunes and begin life anew. You need run no longer. The abundance of Roma spells opportunity for her free men.

"Yes, I invited runaway and outcast women from all corners of the world for you! Now I seek honest wives for you."

The king saw the city listening. He held himself higher before concluding.

"I have a vision of our empire of forbidden people. Remus disapproved of my vision. He scorned my ideas. My tireless love for all men was so great that I buried my brotherhood and removed Remus from this world.

"You are men and women of Roma. Let whoever wants to judge me now stone me to death. I shall be happy to see my brother in heaven."

The people of Roma fell silent. The king's loyalists shouted encouragement, "Hail, King Romulus! Hail the King of Eternity! By his hands, we live. Long live Roma!" With their cascade of cheers, the death of Remus was quieted and the relationship between the Roman king and his subjects was solidified.

After our happy time in Falerii, we returned to Cures secure in the knowledge that we had good friends who accepted Minerva's daughters for the women we were and would become. Vibulena teased about Zolia's positions and demonstrations, but she was clearly fond of Sister. We made plans to exchange visits for important festivals in our respective hometowns.

In my fourteenth year, I received a note from Vibulena:

Dear friends Ronica and Zolia,

This year, I shall travel to a distant land in pursuit of new art and culture. Regrettably, I shall miss Modius Fabidius and our festivals in Falerii, but you are always welcome to stay at our home.

You and Zolia will forever be as clear as the moon and stars in my mind. I think of you always. Please accept my latest rendering of my two inspirational sources of entertainment: Ronica, the Revolter, and Zolia, the Crusader.

Unequivocally, Vibulena.

Vibulena had painted us in yellow tunics with white shawls over our heads. Our hands were intertwined. In her rendering, we looked more angelic than we were.

"Ronica, your artist's feet and mind never rest," Zolia said.

Minerva's daughters stayed their course for two years. While we matured, I concentrated on my artistic talent and Zolia practiced to win the dance prize. We became women, but we continued behaving like young, protected girls – a popular topic with our parents. Mother was astonished that we outgrew our fascia so quickly and when we began to wear mamillare, men unabashedly stared at our expanding busts. Grown men started calling us curvaceous, a description that embarrassed me and infuriated Zolia.

Now that we menstruated regularly, we were ill several days a month. Mother encouraged us to stay home but Zolia was not to be deterred. Despite feeling chafed under the yoke, she was determined to dance through her discharge. Mother insisted Sister stay home to rest, but Zolia would have none of it. "Why must we stay home when our cycle erupts? Do our goddesses stop protecting us until their menstrual cycle ends? Why should Minerva's daughters be held prisoner?"

"Zolia, why do you rebel? Do not humanize our goddesses. Be respectful. Gods are immortal, above menstrual cycles."

"Ah, then they should have created us in their images. Why make us weak? Goddesses have breasts, we have breasts. Goddesses nurse their children, we nurse our children. If they do not menstruate, why do we?"

Zolia had answers for all Mother's objections. Eventually, Mother tired and Zolia began to dance during her cleansing period. But, nature would have her way. One afternoon, while dancing, Sister's blood began to drip, staining her white tunic. Zolia cowered in a corner, weeping in shame. Ovid rushed to comfort her.

To his dismay, Zolia pushed him away. "Stay back. I am cursed. It… it is my monthly discharge. My tunic is bloodied."

"Could you wear my tunic?"

"And what will you wear, Ovid? Your subligaculum? You will be ridiculed."

"Better me than you," joked Ovid.

Then Zolia suggested they stand back to back and dance their way home, but Ovid had to promise never to look at her stained tunic or mention this accident to anyone. Together they fashioned a highly interpretive dance that included mythical beasts, wolves, and gods and goddesses. When bystanders asked about their dance, Zolia would reply, "This is our 'way-back-home' dance."

Indeed, Sister and Ovid were the talk of the town. Several elders complimented their dancing, but others guessed they were showing their mutual affection.

When they reached home, Zolia faced the house and Ovid faced away. Mother came out to see what foolishness Zolia was now engaged in. The Crusader whispered to Ovid, "Thank you. You are more than a friend. When I run into the house, do not look." She flew into the home. Ovid's heart pounded but he closed his eyes and stayed motionless until the door closed.

Zolia cleaned herself, put on a new tunic, and was sitting near her window when Mother found her. "Daughter, tell me what happened."

Without looking at Mother, she said, "My discharge soaked my tunic."

"You had no protective cloth! Zolia, you put a stain on our reputation. You must always be prepared."

Miffed, Zolia mustered her defense. "Did Juno and Jupiter not know their menstrual intercourse would cause Vulcan's malady?"

"Daughter, cease slandering the gods!" Mother barked.

Zolia walked to her. "Mother, why do you try to rule me?"

"Stop, my daughter! With problems like these, seek help from another girl. Not Ovid."

"Girls make me uncomfortable."

"You trust this boy more than another girl? Sometimes,

you do not think things through. Your impulsiveness is a dangerous habit, daughter."

"Mother, trust has no gender."

When I arrived home, Mother explained Zolia's accident and remarkable remedy. I stood motionless, staring at Zolia, who said nothing and brandished a naughty smile. "I only wanted Ovid to understand we menstruate."

●✻✻✻✻●

Chapter 19: Crustumerium

It was with renewed confidence that King Romulus approached Crustumerium, another ancient Latin town north of Roma. This entourage was led by Proculus Maxim, whose favor with the king was undisputed. But Crustumerium knew of the insults by other towns and wondered why Romans approached.

Late in the winter, as the cold damp days dragged on, Crustumerium's soldiers and their king met the Romans on an open field in front of the city.

"People of Crustumerium, hear us in the name of our god, Jupiter," Proculus announced. "We come to make an alliance."

"Alliance? Who with?" asked the Crustumerium king.

"Between the people of Crustumerium and Roma!" Proculus answered. "We offer goods, weapons, and wealth in exchange for your daughters and unmarried women."

"Crustumerium does not ally with thieves, murderers, child molesters, and criminals," proclaimed the king. "In our land, these people are treated as criminals."

Proculus hesitated. "It is true that we regret some of our actions. But we seek a new, honest way of life with an emphasis on family."

"Maybe so. But it would be an unlawful sin against our gods and dangerous for us if we made an alliance with Roma. If we offer our daughters in marriage, our neighbors will unite in war against us as a land of lawbreakers and also against the deviants of Roma. This we cannot risk."

Proculus assured Crustumerium that Roma had sufficient wealth to care for new women and their families, a claim the king disputed. "The wealth of Roma comes from dirty deeds."

With the Roman case rejected, the delegation became outcasts. When asked to leave, the senators attempted to save the mission and overstayed their welcome. The townspeople heaved stones and garbage at the troops, who skulked away into the dusk.

❋ ❋ ❋ ❋ ❋ ❋

Chapter 20: Gracian

One hot day, Zolia and I went to fish in the Tiber. We splashed into the river to refresh ourselves. We were chatting and joking when the water suddenly waked.

In an instant a python wrapped around me. I struggled to reach shore but my right hand was trapped by the snake. Zolia caught a floating branch and banged the mighty python's head. Dazed, the snake loosened its grip long enough for Zolia to position the branch between the reptile coils and my body. "I will run for help!" she screamed.

I could not breathe. I gasped for air but my life was ending in the crush of the python. The branch was the only thing keeping the snake's brute force from drowning me. The snake circled me tighter, taking me below the surface.

My mind was drifting away when a hole opened and the water parted. Suddenly, a long knife flashed and severed the monster's head from the body. My savior sliced the snake's coils and raised me to the surface, where he exhaled air into my lungs. Grabbing my arm, he swam me to shore.

Spent, we lay on the grass gasping deeper and deeper for air. Is this real? Am I in heaven? I wondered.

Serpentis

My savior ran his hands up and down my arms, legs, and torso in search of broken bones. I was shaken but in one piece. His massage brought my body wondrously alive. Aroused from head to toe, I murmured deliriously, "What are you doing to me that makes me so alive?"

"Thank you, Quirinus, for saving this maiden," said my protector. "This is your lucky day, young beauty." Before I could ask, he declared, "I am Gracian from Reate. We are new to Cures."

My mind and body were in a faraway paradise, but I had to respond. "I… I am Ronica from Cures. You saved my life. How shall I ever thank you, my savior?" His fingers touched my face and another warm blush rose within me. "I like that you held me tight and made me warm. Thank you."

Zolia returned alone and was relieved to see me in Gracian's arms. "Thank you, stranger! My sister will not forget you." Sister sensed that my fear was gone, replaced by something more. Gracian had me in a place I had never fantasized about, one I did not want to leave. But Zolia's presence made Gracian uneasy.

"Now that your sister is here, Ronica, you are safe. I must return to Father." My liberator smiled and was away, giving me one last glance at his muscular torso before he disappeared into the woods. I was empty but could not let Zolia see.

Sister stared at me and tipped her head. "Did your handsome savior kiss you, Ronica?"

Waves of heat surged from head to toe. "A kiss I shall not forget! I am weak but strong. I am loved and I love. What is wrong with me? A snake brought my savior to me. How can this be?"

"Perhaps, Sister, the snake was a lucky charm? Why did he not attack me?" She laughed. I saw our kiss was on her mind and would not easily be forgotten.

After a few days, my efforts to run into Gracian were finally rewarded. Since my life was saved, I arose early, bathed, and brushed my hair every morning. I doted over colorful ribbons and tightened my mamillare to be more voluptuous, more desirable.

On the day we met again, I looked my most feminine. His presence was blissfully unsettling. I could control neither my blush by day nor the passionate sensations that wracked my body at night. Gracian excited me in a new way and I flirted unmercifully.

My savior was seventeen, one year my senior. His two younger sisters were named Muluia and Baia. Like other strong men in Cures, he would be a warrior. His father traded pearls, a favorable profession. I saw a young man but heard the voice of a carnal man. My feelings were powerful and I sensed he was similarly smitten.

Before we separated, I invited Gracian and his family for a midday meal. Zolia's animated versions of my rescue had keyed curiosity in Mother and Father and they were anxious to meet the town's newest family and my snake slayer. Thankfully, Sister omitted that I swooned in his presence, a fact she revisited whenever we were alone.

On the day of our gathering, Zolia stopped teasing long enough to help prepare the meal – a miracle in its own right. Father had permitted me one plump lamb for the occasion. My preparation included Mother's perfect spices and a few secrets of my own.

Our families connected marvelously. Gracian was polite and Zolia behaved with uncommon reserve. Our fathers shared their interests while our mothers strolled in the garden, talking discreetly. I escaped with Gracian to the farm, where we held hands and brushed against each other. Each caress ignited a volcano at my deepest center. I felt myself a joyous, delirious, trembling woman for the first time in my life. Gracian would be my love, my life.

The next day at the market Zolia and I met Orania, the wife of Pomponius and mother of his three sons. Her fourth child was due soon. The family enjoyed a reputation for high spirituality and prosperity. Although a longtime friend of Bionca, Orania always treated us as younger sisters.

I inquired if she hoped for a boy or girl. "It is time for a girl. Three boys is enough! If my daughter could be like you, Ronica, or like sister Zolia, it would please me no end."

"What names have you chosen?" asked Zolia.

"Popillia for a daughter. Numa Pomponius for a son." Orania smiled up at Ronica and at Zolia. "Minerva's daughters, would you bless my child for me?"

Together, The Crusader and the Revolter placed their hands on Orania's pregnant belly. "Minerva, give this child wisdom to live in safety always," I said.

"Minerva, give this child strength to protect itself always," Zolia said.

As we blessed Orania, the baby kicked, prompting the mother to say, "Perhaps my newborn will be as stubborn as Zolia."

Zolia posed with hands on hips. "Why does my pregnant friend tease me? Am I to be judged?"

"You know, Zolia," Orania began, "Bionca shares all your misadventures with me." She paused. "Even the Juno and Jupiter episode when the young man came to your aid."

Sister and I exchanged a look. "So, did Mother tell the whole town my private story?"

"Your mother only lightens her burden with me, as we have since childhood."

After our farewells, Zolia asked, "What crossed your mind when the baby moved?"

"That I was pregnant with Gracian's child."

Zolia stopped short, threw her arms in the air, and shouted, "Domus, you are in love!" She sighed. "I admit it! I felt the same thing, except for Ovid."

"We are blessed with special men in our hearts," I concluded.

On our way home, Gracian rushed to join us. "Ronica, can we talk?"

Zolia sped ahead so we could be alone. Gracian's eyes burned straight to my heart. "Yes, my savior, I shall always have time for you."

"I saw you blessing the pregnant woman." He stammered, searching for words. "It set me thinking. I… I feel we are destined to be together. Since the river, I have been unable to eat or sleep. You fill my spirit, but I am half finished. Ronica, dearest girl from Cures, will you marry me and make me one again?" He handed me flowers from behind his back.

I welcomed the flowers but felt weak with excitement. I feared I would fall to the ground. My heart pounded and my most private place flooded with passion. I had to leave.

"Gracian, is this a fairy tale? If I stay any longer, I shall crumble to the ground." I showered him with the special smile I had practiced many times since the river. "I, my love, am yours, but if I do not leave, I will wrap myself around you and ravage you." I turned, clutched the bouquet, and ran for home, where Zolia paced before the door.

"What happened? Did he kiss you again?"

I buried myself in the fragrances of the flowers. "Sister dear, I shall marry Gracian. I promised myself to him. He is my beloved."

Zolia stood dumbfounded, simultaneously smiling and sobbing. "Oh, Ronica, your man is a good man. This day, Mother Minerva is pleased."

My emotions and senses flamed for days. All I could manage was painting my beloved. My brush stroked his hair, face, chest, legs, and groin. With each throbbing sensation, I came to realize this was my moment, my opportunity to share this enjoyment of life.

Chapter 21: Zolia and Ovid

It was only natural that Zolia would become serious about her own romance. Never patient, Zolia would not wait to ensnare her mate. One day after dancing with Ovid, the boy overflowed with desire. Without warning, he embraced Zolia, kissing her tentatively at first but deeper as the kiss lingered.

Gathering herself, Zolia stepped back. "Ovid! What is happening? What are you thinking?"

"I am not a child, Zolia. I know what you suffered that day you needed me. You are woman. I am man. What is happening between us is destined. We are young but my love for you is powerful… too powerful to be ignored."

Zolia melted. "Ovid, you only needed to ask for a kiss. It will always be returned."

"Do you love me, Zolia?"

"I may be young, but I know women never admit this emotion first." She laughed, turned, and ran to school, leaving Ovid frozen in time and place.

Goddess Luna perched bright in the sky and love-struck Zolia bathed in moonlight radiance. As Ovid wondered about his role, Sister suggestively danced her thanks to the goddess Luna.

The elders who observed her performance commented, "Minerva has found a man for her daughter. Luna will witness the consecration this night." Zolia was at her happiest, a flower in spring, blossoming before our eyes. She tried to conceal her joy but, like me, she was weak with passion.

"Ovid kissed me," she kept repeating.

"At least you did not wrap your legs around each other," I added.

"Sister, how can you joke about such things? Tell me what you know. Is this what you and Gracian share? You sound experienced, Ronica."

"What happens between two lovers is theirs. Only theirs. Can we agree?"

"Yes, Ronica, but who will teach me?"

When it was time, we exchanged presents with our suitors. We would always have their gifts to remember our loves and they would always have ours.

Gracian gifted me a bracelet of black pearls, and I happily presented my future husband a vividly colored necklace made of shells from the Tyrrhenian Sea. I stored my bracelet under my bed but clutched it every night. Each time I looked at the pearls, my love's face smiled back. I often kissed one pearl at a time. These were the steps on the ladder I would climb to the heavens.

Ovid bestowed upon Zolia a magnificent silver butterfly brooch. The piece was made from his family's treasured silver cup collection. Sister struggled to find the ideal gift for her betrothed.

Love

For Gracian's birthday I had planned to give him a spotted cuckoo, several of which had surprisingly migrated to our farm. I spent day and night setting nets to trap my prey but the cuckoos were abnormally wary. When I staged a cage with peach leaves, two birds – one male, one female – were mine.

I hid the birdcage in anticipation of surprising my savior, but on the day of his birthday the cage and the birds were gone. I frantically searched everywhere without success. At one farm I overheard workers say, "Zolia surprised Ovid with a cage with birds."

The Crusader had gone too far. Upon her return, I confronted her. "Sister seems especially elated today," I began, giving her a chance to explain.

After moments of silence, I continued. "Gracian's spotted cuckoos are gone. I heard from neighbors that you gave Ovid such a gift. How could you, Zolia? You stole my birds!"

Zolia played dumb, saying that someone else must have taken my birds. "Zolia, you assign blame too easily! You make excuses for everything. Take responsibility for your actions. You knew the birds were my gift to Gracian. You stole them for Ovid, the sissy dancer, and claimed them to be your gift!"

Sister charged me like a bull. Suddenly we were pitching vessels at each other. When I ran, Zolia tackled me and started choking me. I fought to resist her. "My suitor deserves the birds more than your snake man. I have nothing else for him!" she sobbed.

It was several days before we spoke, or slept in the same room. As usual, I came to feel sorry for Zolia. She was the younger. When I apologized for calling Ovid "sissy dancer," she kissed me, crying her apology for calling Gracian "snake man."

That night, I cuddled her, stroked her face and hair, and reminded her that we were sisters and never divided. No man would come between us. Men could only make us closer.

❧❧❧❧❧❧

Chapter 22: Cures

When the disgraced delegation reported to King Romulus, his reaction was harsh. The angry king realized that his shabby citizenry needed women more than they needed a conflict. Romulus was determined that Roma's tactic with the Sabini would be more aggressive.

"We will not play with the Sabini. They are unlike other towns and could attack without provocation. They will challenge our authority. We shall gather half our population and impress them with the magnitude of our force."

As the warmer days of spring took hold, I saw Roman banners flying and men on horseback approaching our city for the first time. The ceremony of the entourage was presumptuous, for the people of Cures had little fear and less respect for the Romans whose arrogant king led the parade.

Cures elders upheld our integrity, offering hospitality in the form of lime, pomegranate, and grape juice; cakes; fruit; and olives to the surprised guests. King Titus Tatius welcomed Romulus but, while the kings sat on a stone bench, all Sabini warriors, including Uncle Neiro, had daggers and swords at the ready.

Negotiation

Zolia and I peered through a window into the great hall and listened.

"Do you know why we are here, King Titus?"

Titus smiled. "Indeed, Romulus."

"We need an alliance with our righteous Sabini neighbors."

"The Sabini are friends with all nations. Why not Romans?" answered Titus.

Romulus sighed with relief and began speaking about his people, his nation, and its future improvements. When he raised the city's need for Sabini daughters and unmarried women, Titus asked forgiveness, explaining that the Sabini had once been Spartans in Greece. Known for their courage and strength, the Sabini had grown weary of Greek regulations and a group of Spartan men, women, and children had migrated from their homeland to this land of aboriginal tribes.

"Here, we took the best of both cultures and started to live a harmonious life. We developed our gods, language, food, traditions, games, dance, and art. Like our neighbors, we have no interest in intermarriage. We strive to preserve our heritage and bloodlines."

"Do the Sabini reject our mixed ethnicity?" asked Romulus.

"No, King Romulus. But intermarriage is not our way. We must remain true to ourselves."

Romulus persisted, promising that his men would make of our women honest wives and new Roman citizens. King Titus asked the town's elders and augurs their feelings. In one voice, they agreed with our king.

Then women of marriageable ages entered the hall and conveyed to Romulus their disinterest in Roman marriages. To appease the Romans, Titus suggested that, as our two nations came to understand each other, intermarriage might take place in the future. It was a condescending offer that we knew had no bite.

Romulus resorted to his last strategy, "Titus, I have half the men of Roma at your gate. Are you not intimidated?"

Titus laughed. "If we wanted to capture Roma, we would send one-quarter of our children to take the city."

"You are too brazen, King Titus," replied Romulus.

"I know my people, their training, and their heritage," Titus responded. "Do you?"

Romulus and Titus exchanged icy stares until Romulus was convinced the Sabine were unlike other neighbors. Titus broke the silence. "Why not enjoy an early meal before you return to Roma?"

"We have been treated well and will leave Cures peacefully," said Romulus.

Sabini guards eagerly escorted the Romans to our city gates. On his way out, Romulus stopped to face Titus. "I am pleased that we have at least one ally."

"We stand shoulder to shoulder, Romulus. Let time pass." So the Romans left with their honor intact.

PART II :

Chapter 23: The Deception

In his chamber, Romulus tried to decide if Titus Tatius had insulted Roma. As elders, senators, and military leaders debated the events in Cures, the king rose from his throne and toppled a table, casting glasses, jars, wine, and water across the room.

"Enough! The Sabini spat in our faces and wiped it off with silk." The chamber fell silent while Romulus stormed the room, ripping drapes from chamber windows, kicking chairs, and shattering anything he could against the walls. When the king returned to his throne, his eyes blazed, his jaw was set firmly, and his fists were clenched.

An elder gingerly broke the silence. "Romulus, please hear me out. Everyone in this chamber shares the trouble in your heart. Lead us and we will follow."

Retiring to his throne, Romulus turned to his legion commander, Hostus Hostilius. "Do you believe Sabini children could capture Roma?"

Another elder interrupted. "No, my lord, Titus was out of line. Order a strike and our legions will face the Sabini in battle."

"We must abduct the unmarried women in our neighboring towns," declared Romulus. "The time to kill Sabini will come."

Hostus Hostilius exhaled agreement. "My king, if war is our path we must be sure of the outcome."

"Does my general have doubts?"

"Sometimes fear and uncertainty make for better preparation. If we fight, we must triumph. Roma will never enter a battle without strategy and surprise."

Romulus appreciated his general's candor. "Well said, Hostus. We must plan. Our targets will be the women of Caenina, Crustumerium, and Antemnae." With this decision, the chamber ignited with opinions until King Numitor asked his grandson, "Why not the Sabini?"

"Can we handle all our enemies at once, grandfather?" Romulus asked.

"We should be less concerned with the number of enemies than with the number of marriageable women Roma requires. As you know, Sabini women are treasured for their beauty and talents."

Hostus Hostilius supported Numitor. "My sword does not know the difference between Sabini and other warriors. Our strength will be the surprise."

The advisers began mapping a devious plan to abduct the women from four neighboring towns. Using Neptunus Equester – a false Etruscan god that Romans did not worship – as Roma's Trojan Horse would appease the neighbors, allay their suspicions, and disguise Roma's intent.

Gods

Romulus perpetuated the ruse by ordering the construction of a temple to honor the false god. Dates of the surreptitious celebration were decided and Romulus ordered this to be the grandest of all festivals.

To ensure that word reached the corners of the territory, Roman dignitaries accompanied by beautiful women wearing twisted togas and ruby necklaces were dispatched to officially invite neighboring tribes. The entourage rode gold-plated chariots that allowed the women to distribute luscious cakes to town residents.

Chariot drivers wore sharp leather uniforms of the militaris. Ox-leather invitations, inscribed in purple ink and signed by Romulus himself, were presented to town elders. The territory was impressed and welcomed the new festival for Neptunus Equester.

The towns of Caenina, Crustumerium, and Antemnae received the first invitations. When Roman messengers arrived in Cures, we put aside any lingering hostility and extended our usual hospitality. We enjoyed their cakes and enthusiastically accepted the festival invitation. The ambassadors assured Cures that there would be horse races, chariot races, sword duels, art contests, dance competitions, magic shows, and a fire display; in other words, something for everyone.

Like most Sabini, we were excited about the festival until Vibulena's Gino unexpectedly appeared at our door and uneasily asked for Father. "Corradeo, Vibulena asks that Ronica and Zolia stay home during Neptunus Equester. The festival is a guise. The Romans will attack those who are lured to Roma. All people of Cures would be wise to stay home."

"Gino, are you sure of this?" asked Father.

"The Romans scheme something deadly. We do not know the details. Vibulena has married a rich Roman senator. She hears that Romulus has a devil's plot. My mistress insisted I warn you."

After considering Gino's information, Father rushed to meet with King Titus and the elders. "Leaders of Cures, we should not go to the festival. Roman scoundrels plan a dastardly attack behind a lavish diversion."

"Corradeo, forgive us but your sources are unknown to us. If we did not attend, it would be an insult," answered Titus.

"My king, Roma has no reason to celebrate the Etruscan god. Our friend, Vibulena, has no reason to discourage our attendance."

"If we do not attend the festival, the relationship between the Sabini and Roma will be ended. Besides, Romulus is not brave enough to challenge Sabinium," Titus decided.

Though Father was widely respected in Cures, his plea was rejected and the elders decided to proceed. When Father arrived home, he was angry. "Cures may go to the festival, but my daughters will not! Something smells foul in Roma."

As the festival approached, excitement in Cures grew feverish. We resisted the temptation; but when Zolia considered the dance competition and I mulled the art competition, our enthusiasm revived. Zolia wanted the ivory-coated golden sandal for best dancer and I wanted the golden box of fine brushes that would be awarded for best painting.

We decided that Romans merely wished to impress their neighbors with their newfound wealth and riches. Surely this was the true purpose of the festival. Not even Romans would taint a festival honoring a god, false or not.

Against Father's wishes, Zolia and I planned a deception. For our scheme to work, we needed Mother, who agreed on the condition that a Cures warrior accompany us as protector.

We chose our cousin Naevius but, when we asked, we were surprised to find he sympathized with Father. Our initial invitation was declined.

But Zolia worked on Naevius's masculinity. "I did not know you were a coward who only wears a sword to cut fish and fruit. Admit it, cousin. Romans terrify you."

"What? The dancer of Cures knows Uncle Neiro trained me well. See this!" Naevius jumped, rolled, maintained his balance, and handled the sword so accurately that a bee would not escape his swing.

Zolia whistled her admiration. "Naevius, you are impressive. What a protector you would be!"

Naevius chuckled. "Ah-ha! All Minerva's daughters need do is ask, and I am at their service."

At first, Sulpicia, Naevius's sister who was betrothed to Brocchus, rejected our invitation. But, when Naevius agreed to escort us, Sulpicia changed her mind.

"I would be the better protector, girls," Mother teased Naevius.

Naevius pretended surprise. "This family lacks respect for men. Can the women in this house possibly doubt my skill? If so, I shall fight Corradeo to prove myself."

"Ha, Naevius! Before you fight Corradeo you must fight

me, for Sabini women are more feared than their men. My daughters and I fight men with one arm behind our backs," joked Mother. "But children can defeat a Roman, so I suppose you will do."

Our excitement for the competition outweighed our judgment. But, as our plan came together, we still needed to escape Cures without Father's knowledge. Mother solved that problem by agreeing to use her temptress powers on Father. She encouraged Corradeo to sleep in the farmhouse the night before the festival.

"Come, my husband. We will go to the farm and spend the night under the stars," Mother suggested. Our parents enjoyed each other so many times that Mother almost canceled our trip. But, when morning arrived and Father headed to the fields, Mother joined us in time to depart.

❀ ❀ ❀ ❀ ❀ ❀

Chapter 24: The Abduction

During the hottest time of the summer, Naevius and Sulpicia arrived at our home in their horse-drawn cart and wearing their best outfits. Naevius had a dagger in his belt where his sword was sheathed. When Mother arrived, we departed for the festival of Neptunus Equester.

Along Via Salaria, men and women were in high spirits. Father's fears seemed unfounded. Outside Roma, we came upon a flat road built of clay, chalk, and gravel. "Do you suppose these roads will one day reach Cures?" Naevius asked.

"My son, this is how Romulus flaunts his wealth," answered Mother. "Who knows what ostentatiousness lies ahead?"

At the city gates, men showered us with flowers. Zolia laughed that Roman women did not do menial work "like our domus." Roma was alive with energy. Soldiers were dressed in leather brooks and braies, elders wore expensive togas, and young men were decked in pastel tunics. The city was festive beyond anything we had ever seen.

We stabled the horses and visited the temple for Neptunus Equester. The statue was unfinished but a small pillar stood next to the sculpture. As priests sacrificed bulls on the altar, we offered prayer to Neptunus and asked that he bless Roma. I prayed that Roman men would find women. Mother gave the priest coins before we went sightseeing. We marveled at how quickly Roma had become such a magnificent city. Our reservations seemed behind us.

Minerva's daughters had never seen such giant citadels, voluptuous statues, rich gardens, and strong stone roads. Jugglers with wooden balls; men walking on spikes; dancers; artists; horse racers; arm wrestlers; and magicians prompted Zolia to ask, "What paradise have we come to?"

One magician showed us an empty box before reciting a magic spell. When he opened the box, he presented me with a bouquet of red roses which I eagerly accepted and placed the flowers in my companion's hair.

Naevius entered a three-circuit horserace. We cheered loudly but, in the last lap, he was nipped by a bald rider on a white horse. For his second-place finish, Naevius received a silver plate with an imprint of King Romulus.

During the awards, a man with a shaven head introduced himself as Proculus Maxim, the victor in Naevius's horserace. As he chatted idly about defeating Naevius, the man's eyes stayed fixed on our bust lines. Growing uncomfortable, we excused ourselves.

My mind was on painting. I found the festival for the artists and entered the competition. My work, "The Fûturûs Fámliás of Roma," featured handsome Roman men with pretty wives and happy children. The citadel rose high above the backdrop of Roma's five developed hills. Spectators enjoyed my work. Their favorable comments gave me assurance.

Proculus Maxim suddenly appeared behind me. "Ah, Ronica from Cures. Those are Roman families in your painting."

"Did you guess from the citadel or the landscape?" I inquired.

"No," he said. "I guessed because the men's faces were so stern."

His answer puzzled and impressed me, but Zolia ended the conversation with the "voyeur" who quickly offered us wine. Remembering Vibulena's warning, we ignored his offering. Several Sabini women were not as prudent and over-indulged, though not to the excess of women from Caenina, Crustumerium, and Antemnae.

For Zolia's dance to Neptunus Equester, she rode an imaginary horse into an imaginary sea, pretending to splash water on the heads of Roman men with her elegant hands. Then she sternly placed her hands on her hips, spun, and kicked water on their faces. Her flippancy enchanted the Romans, who whistled their approval.

Sister's flirtatiousness infuriated Mother, who summoned her from the stage where Romans reached to touch her. Mother led us away but not before we were told that all prizes for art and dance would be awarded later in the evening.

All afternoon, we enjoyed tasty cakes and herbal soup. Wherever we went, Proculus Maxim stayed within reach. Even when the voyeur complimented Zolia for her dance, Sister would have none of him. Her curt words led Naevius to warn Proculus to leave us alone.

At the festival's peak, King Romulus stood on a balcony observing the celebration. To our amazement, Proculus stood beside the king. The square had a nervous energy. Something felt wrong. Roman men ogled women and seemed unusually aroused. Zolia grew edgy and suggested we leave; but when Naevius reminded her about the prizes, Sister wavered.

When soldiers summoned everyone to the citadel for the awards, tensions were high. When a distinguished elder rose to address the crowd, we were so focused we did not realize that Romans encircled us. From his balcony, Romulus lifted his hand and let fly his red handkerchief with a wolf imprint.

"Look! He signals someone!" Zolia screamed.

Romans smothered the square, rushing into the crowd and grabbing any young woman they could catch. While fights between visiting men and Roman kidnappers broke out, we were ensnared in commotion and loud noises. Fearful women punched the Romans, but young women were no match for bullies who preyed like vultures snatching mice. Innocent women from the hill towns were brutalized in place. Mothers, brothers, and fathers fought valiantly for their daughters but the vultures outnumbered the innocents.

When Romans came to capture us, Zolia and I stood in the center of the crowd. Two men rushed us. Naevius grabbed one by the throat and Mother jumped on the other's back. Zolia smashed a rock against the brute's head. With blood pouring down his face, the man shook off Mother, who crumpled to the ground.

The scoundrel snatched Zolia by her mane and pulled her toward a house. I bit his hand until he released Sister. When the man wheeled to strike me, Naevius smashed a stone into his face, toppling him like an apple from a tree. We rushed to help Mother, who clutched her twisted wrist.

"We should have listened to your father," she repented. "Quirinus, please save us!"

We found Sulpicia cowering in shock behind the statue of Jupiter. We started our escape, but Zolia stopped. "We must not run. We are Sabine! We must help our neighbors." When Naevius protested, Zolia yelled, "Fine boy, you go! I will fight by myself!"

"Who should we help?" asked Naevius.

"Those children, Naevius! Look at the children."

Innocent children separated from their families were darting dangerously between skirmishes. Smaller children were pressed to the ground, crying for help.

We deposited Mother and Sulpicia behind a mighty oak and ran to gather as many children as we could. Many were wounded. All were in shock. Because we carried children, Romans mistook us for mothers and ignored us.

When baton-wielding Roman scoundrels rode their steeds into the crowd, the violence intensified. These men had a plan. Their prey did not. We kept pointing children to the tree. While Naevius protected a chubby infant, a Roman soldier struck them with a baton. Naevius absorbed the blows but refused to drop the child.

Zolia grabbed a fallen sword and severed the soldier's hand. Nearby soldiers heard the pig squeal and turned on Naevius and Sister. We ran to the oak. "We must be away!" Naevius commanded. "There are too many!"

Two boys and a girl joined us. "Who are you?" I cried.

"Germanus and Valens," answered the older boy. "This girl is Lucilla." We explained that the Romans would not hurt them and begged them to help the other children.

"Good, but you are in the greater danger. Run. Save yourselves!" Germanus shouted.

The boy's courage inspired me. We should have put young children on our hips and pretended to be their mothers but instead we fled.

At the stable, we were surprised that our horses and cart were intact. We managed to get two of the horses harnessed and hooked to the cart, and then sped away until a dozen Roman soldiers blocked our path.

Resistance

"Here are the sisters! Get the artist! Get the dancer!"

When they demanded our surrender, Zolia spat her reply on the leader's chest. Naevius handed her the reins, unsheathed his dagger, and leaped from the cart. Romans charged him but Naevius ducked, stabbing the lead soldier in the chest.

"Brave boy of Sabinium!" shouted Mother. "Kill them all!"

Zolia and I screamed encouragement. Another Roman came at us. Naevius lunged at him, cut his nose, and sent the Roman rooster away. But Naevius was cornered. Vultures jumped him, took his dagger, and bound him like a trophy. Naevius kept shouting for us to flee.

As Roman horsemen climbed onto their mounts, we sped away. Zolia drove like Neptunus as Mother, Sulpicia, and I fended off the attackers that dared climb the cart.

We dashed into the hectic crowd. Roman pigs were everywhere. Zolia screamed warnings to clear a path and men and women ran for their lives.

We saw Roman thugs indiscriminately throwing young women over their shoulders or dragging them to their lairs. I caught a fleeting look at the children behind the tree. "Ride faster, Zolia! Ride!" Germanus yelled.

"Be brave, my children!" she shouted, to the fearful faces of the innocents.

Our horses had taken many arrows. By the time we neared the bottom of Palatine Hill, they could barely stay afoot. When one toppled, the other followed. The cart crashed, throwing Mother against a tree. We smashed into rocks and fell unconscious.

Our nightmare had begun.

※ ※ ※ ※ ※ ※

Chapter 25: The Cell

I awakened in a limestone-walled cell. A swaying curtain covered the solitary window. A corner kitchen was filled with vessels.

Zolia rested on my stomach. Beneath us, a thin layer of sheepskin was spread across the floor. Our hands and feet were bound. Ropes anchored our hips to a solitary pillar. Zolia awoke, studied our surroundings, and murmured, "Roman filth imprisons us."

We had lost Cousin Sulpicia. Mother and Naevius were missing. We scrambled to untie the ropes, but it was fruitless. Zolia was searching for her silver butterfly brooch when the voyeur, Proculus Maxim, showed his face.

"Welcome, my ladies of Cures. Did you rest well?"

"Salvé, Roman. Untie us. We must go home." Zolia spat at the man.

"You may remember me. Proculus Maxim." The beast bowed to us. "Again, I welcome you."

"You are a kidnapper, nothing more! Untie us!" demanded Zolia.

"Understand this, dancer. This home is your home and a good home it is. Settle yourself. Look around. If you need something, ask me or your guards and it is yours." Proculus walked to the door, smiled, and left.

In a short while, the monster returned with two guards. Zolia demanded her lost brooch but Proculus shrugged her off, saying the king expected us at an assembly. When the soldiers untied the ropes, Zolia was already plotting an escape. The guards tied my right leg to Sister's left and pulled us away. Zolia worked the rope but we were bound like slaves, surrounded by Roman scoundrels.

At the king's citadel, Romulus posed arrogantly on his balcony. Next to the rooster stood a buxom girl in a blue tunic. Like us, the woman was bound. With Romans proudly parading their captives, we resembled cattle at an auction.

Zolia nodded to fellow dancers Myra, Ona, and Eligia, and I smiled at my art friends Lide and Messina. Despite the terror lining their faces, the sight of them gave us hope.

Romulus stood above the crowd. "Welcome, women of Roma, our future. I apologize for our ruse. What is done is done. Know that your families are safely gone. No one was harmed." He paused. "You only need look around to know why we kidnapped you. Roma has no mothers, no children of her own."

"Liar!" Zolia whispered. "Do not listen to this wolf, Ronica. There are no women because Roman penises are like their brains: dead."

Romulus opened his arms to include his hostages. "Love us well. We did not take you to make you prostitutes. Be our wives. Mother our children. You are citizens of Roma with the same rights as any Roman. All you need do is cooperate and breed."

The king swelled his chest. "Forgive us. Our sin is that we love you. Try to understand us and you will be rewarded."

The Romans applauded thunderously. Zolia and I exchanged quizzical looks. Was this man insane? Could Roma be so sick?

Romulus lowered himself to one knee before his hostages. His subjects imitated their king. Were they all insane? Romulus saluted his captives. "Our bodies are filled with love. We understand you need time to adjust, but those who accept this situation will be ahead of the game and live happily ever after in our wonderful city."

Zolia shook her head. "See these fools, Ronica. What kind of king begs women? Kneels to hostages? This is a sly fox, not a king. It is no wonder Romans have no women. Who wants them?"

Romulus turned to hold forth his captive, Hersilia, a girl from the town of Casperia in Sabinium. Romulus released her rope and kissed her hand. Hersilia rubbed her wrists, saying, "King Romulus, the conversion you ask is too fast. Moments ago we were with our families. Now, Romans corral us. We need time."

The king accepted her response, smiled, and waved the crowd away. On our way to the cell, we spotted Sulpicia and rushed to her. Cousin was the prisoner of Natta, who allowed us a few words.

"I need to go home," whispered Sulpicia. "I want Brocchus, not this pig."

Back at the cell, we were reconnected to the pillar. Zolia prayed for our cousin until our captor arrived.

Proculus sat on a bamboo chair before us. Cocking his head, he asked, "Do Minerva's daughters understand they are here to please me and bear my children?"

"We will never please you. Your seed would foul our wombs," Zolia snapped.

"We shall see, Dancer of Cures."

"Other Romans only have one woman. Not even the king has two," I volunteered.

"Ronica, the smart, inquisitive one. It is you I love more than your sister. If I had to choose, you would bear me one hundred children. You should know that because I am a special friend to the king, I am permitted two wives." Proculus laughed. "This allows the sisters to stay together. You will thank me when we share my bed and your wombs savor my seed."

"You make me sick, voyeur. The thought of the stench of your seed poisons me. I must relieve myself," said Zolia. "My bladder is bursting." Proculus had the guards lead us to a public latrine. Inside were five rows of ten stalls each. We waited for two adjoining stalls to empty.

We heard women whispering their fears. One woman asked, "What happened to the Cures sisters? Have the Romans raped Minerva's daughters?"

Zolia and I gasped. "Rape us? Is that their plan?"

"Your master is the worst," the woman warned. "Two wives? What an ego!"

Back at the cell, guards brought lamb stew and bread. We attacked the meal. Our first day passed amidst misgivings.

By the third day, our lack of exercise dimmed our appetite. We felt soiled and knew we smelled of body odor. Proculus instructed the guards to let us bathe and then presented us with fine tunics. Clean and with fresh clothing, our bonds could not detract from our elegant appearance. We were briefly refreshed but fear was now our constant companion.

That night, Proculus lay on the floor feigning sleep. Several times I awoke and caught the monster staring at my body. Zolia felt the same uneasiness. Our only defense was to turn our backs.

Chapter 26: Proculus Maxim

Despite our rejections at every turn, the voyeur kept asking us to marry him. Zolia explained that we had suitors in Cures. Proculus pouted like a child and tried to tempt us by extending bits of freedom. Although our hands were cuffed, we were disconnected from the pillar. Our waking time was spent circling the cell, imagining our escape. Guards took us to wash and visit the latrine whenever necessary.

We were surprised when Proculus escorted Gino and Vibulena to the cell.

"My dear friends!" Gino said, embracing us.

Tears streamed down Vibulena's face. "Why did you come?"

"Salvé, Artist," Zolia barked. "What brings you here?"

"I live here, Zolia. You know that."

"Of all the men you flirt with, why choose a Roman dog?"

"This man is my choice, Zolia." Vibulena tilted her head to peer into Zolia's eyes. "Crusader, I am your friend, not your enemy… and not the reason you are here."

"Artist, you are part of this Roman kidnapping. You pretend to be true, but you are one of them. I never want to see you again."

"Look into my eyes, Zolia," Vibulena said. "I love you more than my own sisters."

I saw Zolia's anger and tried to ease the tension. Vibulena told us her husband was a powerful senator who had the king's ear. She promised to present our case. Her words gave hope to me, but not to Zolia. Before they left, our friends promised to visit again.

During one visit, Vibulena reported she had met with Romulus and requested leniency. "Women are already reluctant to marry us," he replied to her. "If I set the sisters free, there will be repercussions."

While Vibulena struggled to explain why Proculus was allowed two wives, Zolia lost control and rained hostility on her until our guards arrived to take us to the king's court. This would be our only chance to plead our own case.

Romulus started by telling the gathering that Proculus having two wives was unacceptable and causing trouble. Many Romans still had no women at all and had complained. The king turned to face us. "You sisters from Cures have a choice. One of you can marry any other Roman man, or you can stay together with Proculus. That is the choice. You must decide."

We were stunned. "Now, after some fifteen days, you want to separate us? This is insane. There is not one Roman, much less two, we would marry," said Zolia defiantly.

"My offer answers the request of your friend, Vibulena. Your case is an exception that must now be accepted or rejected. Roma is a place of laws."

"Laws! Are you serious?" Zolia steamed. "The artist said

she would talk about our release, not about other grooms. She betrayed us. If I am untied, I will kill her.

"We are Zolia, the Crusader, and Ronica, the Revolter, the daughters of Minerva. We cannot be divided by any earthly force, especially by a bald voyeur or any other Roman scum!"

Romulus studied Sister. "So, you are the brave one, the cart driver, right? You are unlike the rest. Whom do you want to marry? If you choose my friend Proculus, I shall warn him to sleep with one eye open."

"No Roman king or other citizen can split the daughters of Minerva. Our people are coming for you. You do not have time to rape and breed. You should prepare for war."

Sister's brashness startled the king, who sat taller on his throne. "Dancer, your tribe wants nothing to do with Roma or with you. You and your sister will marry Proculus. There is no way out. Now, waste no more of my time."

In our cell, Zolia spewed hatred for Vibulena. Who could I trust, my mature friend or my brash sister? Before we could talk, Proculus burst through the door, delighted we had returned. "My wives have returned to me. Now I know you want me! I love my wives and they love me."

"Roman! You are an idiot," barked Zolia. "No matter how long you imprison us, we will never love you. One day, you will pay for your sins."

As the days wore on, we fell into a routine. One evening, we were summoned to the court so their king could boast about the conquest of the Sabine woman. While forced to witness Hersilia's marriage, Zolia fidgeted.

After the ceremonies, the king awarded prizes from the

festival that seemed a lifetime ago. Zolia refused to accept her ivory shoe and I declined the paint box with brushes. Other women received their prizes. We fleetingly saw Sulpicia but she averted eye contact.

When we returned to our cell, Proculus was waiting. "My two wives have won the competition! Our family is famous!"

"We did not win for you, idiot. We are not your wives. Not your family. We are just your captives. You are crazed!" said Sister.

Proculus grabbed Zolia's tunic and shook her. "Why are you like this? I have been kind and gentle with you. My friends tell me to rape you. I have not. I warn you, Dancer and Artist: Do not push me."

Chapter 27: The Grape

Like many Romans, Proculus eagerly consumed the grape. In his stupors, he invariably rambled on about romance or wrote ridiculous love poems that sounded more like a whimpering schoolboy than a master. When he passed out on the floor, we were cautious but believed him harmless and silly. When he left, we laughed at his antics.

Our only outside interaction came at the latrine, where women from Antemnae, Caenina, Crustumerium, and Cures lingered to gossip. Once we met a Crustumerium girl who had married a Roman. I asked how this could happen.

"One night, he offered wine," she began. "Soon, everything blurred. I became lightheaded. He had his way with me. One time became two, three, and then more. After that, we made love whenever his penis was sober enough. I decided to be honest and married the goat."

Zolia and I were stupefied. We reasoned it was the wine that felled her. We agreed to never sip Roman wine. We suspected this was why Sulpicia shunned us. Each time she came to the latrine, she shied away.

One day, Zolia waited and caught her by surprise. "We are your cousins and sisters! Why do you avoid your sisters?" Zolia demanded. Sulpicia could not face us. Sister throttled her. "Die now or tell us what has happened." Sulpicia coughed, but Zolia squeezed harder. "Answer me, Sulpicia."

"Zolia! You abuse me like Romans. Take what you want."

"What say you, cousin?"

"I am abused and raped, Zolia! I am defamed and you shout at me. Must you remind me I am married to Natta?"

In the beginning, the Roman had treated her well. One night, he came home reeking of wine. He wrestled her to the bed. She begged him to stop. She told him of Brocchus, but the Roman was unstoppable. He forced himself into her vagina, taking her virginity and self-esteem. The next day she sat naked in the corner, crying uncontrollably.

The animal apologized and begged her to accept him. Again he plied her with wine. The more she drank, the less she resisted him. Having already lost her virginity, she surrendered again. Sulpicia yearned for Brocchus, but every time she accommodated Natta her past fell further away.

In the latrine, there was so much talk of rape that Sister and I came to appreciate the fact that Proculus had not violated us. Sulpicia's story put us on edge but, for the next two months, Proculus was content to impress us rather than rape us. By this time, one-third of the abducted women were married to Romans. The stories from the latrine intensified. We encouraged our friends to resist the beasts, but each day someone was lost.

Gino was our only visitor. Once he asked how we resisted Proculus. Zolia explained our loves were in Cures and our Roman captor had no allure for us. She begged our friend's help. Vibulena still worked to rescue us but Gino was unable to do anything. Zolia continued to question Vibulena's sincerity.

As more marriages took place, Romulus ordered that women in the custody of their kidnappers could be untied. After six months, there were two types of women in Roma; those who accepted their captors and those who did not. We would never surrender and busied ourselves with escape plans and guessing when our families would rescue us.

A story about Hersilia circulated the latrine. Romulus had shackled her for three days but did not rape her. Instead, the pig kept reminding her that his wife would be queen of Roma. The king laced her food with stimulants to arouse her. When she finally dropped her subligaculum to the floor, Hersilia let him fondle her breasts, suck her nipples and probe her vagina before discharging his seed into her. All the while, she repeated, "Queen Hersilia, Queen Hersilia." Even though her heart rejected the way Romans had acquired their wives, our Sabini sister replaced her cherry with a crown.

Talk of stimulants made us afraid to eat. We were sure Proculus would resort to this. The scoundrel kept finding excuses to brush against our bosoms or bump our bottoms. He apologized but his mind was an open book. In one of his drunken stupors he mumbled, "If only one woman was in my house, I would fill her with my seed. Two sisters are impossible."

When half the kidnapped women married, the future of Rome was secure. With children in mother's wombs, Romulus stressed that Roman men must give precious care to their impregnated wives. The king encouraged women to accompany their husbands to festivities. These farces infuriated Zolia, who said the Roman king was the devil personified. Yet we dutifully took our places next to Proculus, the perfectly contented and vain peacock.

Proculus was always ready to impress us with his story. He had been a Greek sailor when he heard that Romulus, his childhood friend, had founded a new kingdom. He had come to Rome to help his friend. We doubted this, but it was better to indulge his self-serving story than suffer rape. We tolerated his vanity while pouring encouragement – and more wine than he could tolerate.

As women's bellies expanded, the days grew shorter. The trees shed their tired leaves and winter arrived. Roma had no social activities during the cold season, so Romulus staged regular dinners. Masons had built a spacious kitchen where necessary vessels and utensils were kept. The granary was stocked with foodstuffs. Cooking for such a crowd was challenging, but preparation started early.

Zolia never worked in the kitchen. Instead, she wandered around complimenting the cooks. Finally one kitchen helper asked, "Why do you not help us, girl? What makes you privileged?"

"I am Zolia, the dancer. I do not cook, kitchen wench! Your job is to cook. Mine is to eat and dance."

The lady pointed her spatula at Sister. "If you dance, then dance. It might relax us. At least you will help pass time."

A singer from Antemnae sang a song praising her gods and goddesses. Zolia rose on her toes. Bending her body like branches of a tree, Sister flitted her fingers across the faces of the cooks and danced around the kitchen. Our cooks cheered. She placed her hands on the workers' hips and moved their bodies to the song. By dinnertime, she had won their hearts.

But her dance reminded her that Cures would soon hold the winter dance competition. She begged Proculus to let her compete, promising to return after the dance.

"Do you think me a fool?" he growled.

Zolia became angry. In the kitchen the next day, she curled up in a corner. I explained what had happened. The cooks offered their support but Sister's suffering persisted. One unknowing cook asked, "Why does the princess of dancers not dance? Your dancing is the only joy in Roma. Dance for us, not for Roma!"

Ona, Zolia's dance partner, added, "We know your dance is magic, princess of Sabinium. Do your magic." Zolia stood, started to dance, and lost her frown. Myra and Eligia joined her. The kitchen was energized and spirits lightened. For many days, Zolia's dancing relaxed us.

Gradually, small doses of freedom came our way. As improbable as it seemed, we made friends. Drusa, a singer from Antemnae, and our friends from Cures often exchanged visits. None of us could understand why our warriors had not come for us. Were we forgotten so easily?

We were shocked to learn from Drusa that Sulpicia was pregnant. In Roma, pregnant women had to marry and Sulpicia had wed the Roman scum, Natta. Her wedding was the final insult. With the Crusader's patience exhausted, she charted our escape.

Chapter 28: The Blessings of Picus

Romulus believed gods must bless the mothers of babies in the womb. At an assembly, he announced a new celebration. "During the winter, the Blessings of the Picus will be the only festival. Mars will send his messenger, the woodpecker, to bless the wombs of the women who carry Roma's children."

"Perhaps the woodpecker will steal the babies before they have to live in this filth," whispered Zolia. We left the meeting convinced that the king was insane.

Romans quickly set about preparing for the festival. When it was discovered that no Roman priests knew the ancient rituals, Romulus sought Etruscan priests. But when the king's emissaries arrived at Etruscan territory, the natives beat the Romans senseless. Using their knives, the tribesmen carved "rapist," "coward," "thief," or "cheat" on the backs of the emissaries and sent the hated Romans back to Romulus tied to donkeys. The irate king swore that Roma would have revenge.

Romulus ordered excavation of a mammoth fire pit, but his more puzzling order demanded that every Roman man and woman contribute one subligaculum to the ceremony. Just two days past the winter solstice, the festival commenced and wine flowed liberally. The kitchen offered sumptuous lamb, ox, and goat meat.

After the feast, Romulus ordered the collected undergarments brought to the pit. "By offering these subligacula, we will protect our reproductive organs. We give these to the God of Mars and his messenger Picus to ensure the continued flow of our offspring." With his proclamation, the undergarments were thrown into the fiery pit. The priest recited prayers. As the undergarments burned, cheers rose from the throng.

Zolia and I scoffed at the king's stupidity. Our suspicions of Roman ignorance were again confirmed.

Watching the undergarments burn, Zolia shrugged. "Romans have no brains. The gods should show them mercy by removing their heads and throwing them in the fire."

❂❂❂❂❂❂

Chapter 29: The Escape

When the festival dispersed, we returned home. Proculus was elsewhere and our guards were asleep in front of the citadel. We saw our opportunity and quietly crept away, using trees and bushes for cover.

At the city gates, fourteen inebriated guards snored in drunken exhaustion. We quietly passed under the arch and were scurrying downhill toward the highway when shouts suddenly surrounded us. "Lide has escaped again! Find the wench!"

Out of the dark, torches and dozens of men came rushing toward us. Proculus was with the jackals. He screamed, "Where do my witches run? Shackle the witches! Take them back. We will find the missing Sabini and deal with my wives later!"

"This is our time to go!" Zolia yelled at Proculus. The beast clenched his fist and smashed Sister to the ground.

"No more! Stop! Stop beating her! We will go back!" I yelled.

"Yes! You will return. You have no choice. When we find the other Sabine witch, you will see how Roma treats escapees," the monster barked. "My wives will soon beg for mercy!"

The soldiers tied our hands and pulled us to the citadel. Other soldiers had found Lide and roughly dragged her bound body into the square. A crowd gathered to witness our fate.

When Romulus came to inspect his captives, he glared at Lide. "Ungrateful wench. You escaped the first time and I pardoned you. You are not pregnant. What good are you?"

"You sick lunatic!" Lide shrieked. "I will never bear children by the pigs of Roma. You and your Roman penises disgust me. Your only brains are in your subligaculum. End this torture. Be done with me!"

Romulus flushed with anger. "I gave you one chance to live. I treated you with leniency. You betrayed me."

The king faced the crowd. "Men of Roma, what shall I do with this empty womb who insults your king?" Romulus jerked Lide's head up by her hair. "You will repent for the rest of your life. Strip her!" Romulus ordered.

We moved to shield Lide, but soldiers pushed us away. Lide crouched to cover her nakedness. The way Roman dogs leered at her naked body, I feared they would rape her in place. After the king ordered her thumbs chopped, two soldiers produced a finger-cutter and stretched her fingers.

We screamed in protest. Lide fought, but the men were too strong. Her screams and the sound of severed bones penetrated the night. She fell to the ground, writhing in bloody nudity. I wavered but not Zolia. She stood to face Romulus, who eyed us with anger.

"I showed you love and compassion," he barked. "I allowed you to be together. In return, you show me hatred. I gave respect, you slapped my face. I showed trust, you betrayed me. Hear this, Roma! From this day forward, any woman who tries to escape will suffer their thumbs hacked away.

"This law commences tomorrow. The wives of Proculus are my last exception. They will be bound until they are married and conceive children for Roma. Only then will I be convinced they are worthy of freedom."

The soldiers shoved us into our cell. When iron shackles bound our legs and wrists, Proculus stormed into the cell. "Tonight you witches were lucky. That's the last of it."

He yanked Sister's hair. "Zolia, you are trouble."

Proculus slapped my face. "Ronica, you are smart enough to understand. If you two keep this up, I will hurt you in other ways."

"What kind of creature beats women?" Zolia screamed. "Is this what makes the eunuch's penis hard?"

Proculus slammed his fist to her jaw. "You wretch! Never speak to me like this again! I am not a schoolboy from Cures."

The monster kicked me in the stomach. "I have been too kind. Now, it ends."

Chapter 30: Assault

Everything changed. Fear was the food we swallowed, uncertainty the fluid we drank. The next day, we could tolerate neither. When Proculus inquired about our appetite, I answered, "We are not hungry."

He tapped Zolia's hand, telling her to look into his eyes. She turned away, rubbing her sore jaw. "Why do my Sabini goddesses not love me? Wives must respect their master."

"We are not virgins," Zolia blurted. "My suitor is young and virile, not old and corrupt. We have been together under the moon, under the barn roof, on the pasture grass, anywhere he wanted."

"You do not fool me, young wife! When we invade Sabinium, I will shear the boy's testicles with my dagger. Then you will have your eunuch."

"Ha! If you go to Cures, Uncle Neiro will have your head for what you have done."

Proculus grabbed her hair, driving her head into the pillar. "Your family is dead. I am all you witches have left." He laughed, slamming the door.

Crumbled against the pillar, Zolia sobbed, "He is the beast we suspected."

At the king's hunting dinner, an elder named Crispinus asked Proculus how he pleasured himself since the failed escape of his two wives. While elders guessed the erotic perversities two sisters in one bed could perform, Proculus drank himself into a tantrum.

"Which sister do you prick first? The young one? Or the one with big breasts?" Crispinus asked. "Do you put your pole in one and your finger in the other? Do they lick your spear until you explode?"

Proculus smashed his fist onto the table. "Enough! Stop! My wives will attest my penis the best in the five hills." Flinging his goblet against the wall, he scooped a flask of wine and stormed away.

Drunk and staggering, Proculus dispatched our guards and crashed into our cell. With the man's rage focused on us, we huddled against the pillar. The lush plopped on the floor, offering us his flask. We sipped cautiously. "Drink more, my wives. Tonight, I defile you and put smiles on your morning faces!"

Confident he would fall asleep, we poured the drunkard more wine. But when the flask was empty, he was still awake with fantasies dancing across his eyes. "Zolia!" the beast barked. "One night with me and you will forget your boy."

"Proculus, if I hurt your feelings, I apologize." Zolia offered.

Proculus exploded off the floor, yanked Sister's hair, and slapped her cheek. "Hurt me?" He pulled a key from his robe and disconnected her shackles.

Zolia fought like a wildcat, pushing, punching, and swatting the monster. I tackled his legs and begged him to stop. He punched Zolia's head and bound her hands with his belt. The monster lifted her and threw her onto the bed.

When I screamed for help, Proculus left Sister and flew at me, raining punches at my face and stomach, anything he could hit. "I loved you first, Ronica. Be still or your sister dies tonight."

Zolia staggered off the bed. Proculus smashed her to the floor. Sister gasped for air. "You run? Did you run from your cherry picker?" He tossed his silver dagger on the shelf and cast aside his clothes. The monster pushed his face at Zolia, kissing her and licking her face like a crazed animal.

He ripped away her tunic and lunged at her naked breasts, savagely biting her teat. Zolia shrieked and kneed him in the groin. The unfeeling monster punched her stomach and pinned her down. When he sank his fingers into her vagina, Sister shrieked in shock.

I begged him to stop. "Be quiet, wench! Or I will kill this viper and be rid of her!" Proculus pushed his face onto her womanhood and laughed like a maniac. "Ha, Zolia! I smell your virginity."

"Stop, Proculus! Stop! Leave her! Take me instead!" I begged.

The monster wedged Zolia's knees apart and brutally drove his penis inside her. "Monster!" I yelled. Zolia shrieked and struggled to throw him off, but he kept thrusting into her. Blood oozed down her thighs and poured onto the bed. Sister writhed in agony and sin. "The virgin witch is spoiled!" the monster barked.

Everything was gone. The rapist had deflowered Zolia. I had not saved her. As we sobbed, the monster wiped her blood on a cloth and placed it in a jar. Closing the lid, he stood over Zolia.

"Tell your Neiro about this! Tell him how you will never forget your first penis. Ask him where he was when I raped his virgin niece!"

Zolia stared up at the monster. "He will come for you, rapist!"

"Wife Ronica! Your soiled sister repulses me. Watch how Romans deal with repulsive women." Sensing the demon's perversity, I buried myself in prayer.

The monster flipped Zolia onto her stomach. Instinctively, she locked her knees together. Like a dog with a scent, the rapist moved his face up and down Sister's back. "Now, Dancer! Be a good wife and show your husband how wide your anus will spread." While Zolia held firm, Proculus smashed the back of her head.

"See how her vagina goes between her legs like a snail inside its shell. But her anus pops up like the mouth of a volcano."

The rapist plunged his penis into Sister's ring. Zolia screamed her horror. When her leg shot to the side, the monster pumped into her. Sister's head reached for space but there was none. It seemed an eternity before the rapist crashed in a drunken stupor.

Zolia crawled away from the monster. I lowered her head onto my thigh and covered her abused and naked body. My heart quaked. The unconscionable monster had despoiled her. I prayed to Minerva to give Zolia strength.

The rapist awoke sometime later. We could not face him. He seemed unaware of his crime. Zolia still quivered on my lap. This Roman devil was a rapist, like his king, and unlike any Sabine man.

"How is my young wife?" he asked. "I am sorry for what happened. I overdrank. But you have both failed me. It is your obligation to please me."

His ignorance did not merit a response. The silence infuriated him. "Wife! We will be a family!" My mind blocked his words. "Say it!" he screamed.

I stared at the floor. "We will be family? Is that what you want to hear?"

Zolia avoided my eyes and would not face the rapist. I yearned to comfort her. She pulled herself up next to me. Tears swelled her eyes. Proculus dressed, picked up his jar with the cloth, and stumbled out the door.

I stroked Zolia's hair, but she shook her head. I asked if she would bathe. "No water can cleanse me," she said. "I am soiled forever."

That night, our fears came true. The drunken rapist came to the cell with more flasks of wine. Handing one to each of us, he demanded we drink. We locked our hands in denial.

Proculus kicked Zolia and pressed his foot against her head. "Slave whore! When your master says drink, you empty the jar. Now, suck my toe!" She refused. Proculus jerked her hair and forced his toe into her mouth, pressing it so deep she gagged.

The monster turned to me. "Drink everything, Ronica. Empty the jar." Seeing that Sister's only relief would come at my expense, I swallowed.

Before he loosened my shackles, he tightened Sister's chain. My stomach heaved with wine and tension. The monster's ugliness stood naked before me. His body was so ugly, I closed my eyes and prayed for Minerva to give me strength.

"Ronica, it is time we have sex." I pulled my tunic tighter. "You are a gentle wife, not like your whore sister. Do not make me beat you. Undress yourself and we will enjoy each other."

I froze. I hated him. Zolia eyed me between strands of her hair.

"If you do not remove your clothes, I will." With that, the monster pushed me flat on the bed. When he stroked my neck, I nearly vomited but rallied enough strength to push him to the floor. The rapist laughed wildly. "Sabini women are miserable lovers. This is what I shall tell my friends."

From somewhere inside, my Sabine voice returned. "If you touch me again, my father and Gracian will kill you!"

"Ha! Yesterday, Neiro. Today your father and Gracian, another boy. Bring these fools to me." His hand wrapped around my throat. "Behave! Do what I want. Enjoy my Roman penis!"

"Monster!" I shouted.

Proculus slapped me. My eyes welled. "Monster spear, you mean! Two witches from Sabinium deflowered by the same penis! How will Sabinium like that?"

"Roman son of a whore!" Zolia yelled.

"The young wife begs for more? Tonight, my whore-wife waits and watches while I pick her sister's cherry. Not to fear, young wife. You will lick your sister's juice from your master's cock soon enough."

Survival

The monster tore my tunic away. Zolia moved toward me but the chains stopped her short. She screamed, distracting the rapist. He stuck the silver dagger near my eyes. "Keep that up, whore-wife, and I will gouge her eye!"

The rapist cut away my undergarments. I could not hold him off. I felt his member rip through to my core. I shrieked. Zolia banged her chains and growled like a lion. Blood and my virginity streamed down my legs.

Suddenly, the monster tensed. His semen burned into me. "Jupiter, thank you! Two virgins in two days. I am the luckiest man in Roma!" The monster wiped my blood with another cloth and closed it in another jar.

Shocked, weeping, empty, I lay on the bed.

"Do the cloths remind you of your whore mother?" Zolia snipped.

Proculus kicked her face. Blood shot from Zolia's nose, but she laughed back through her tears. The rapist lifted the jar with my pride, hope, and virginity, and slammed the door.

Sister and I huddled, sobbing until our sorrow and energy drained. We were damaged, but not broken. We had survived.

Chapter 31: Gloating

The next day, Proculus instructed us to clean and dress. Our faces were battered, our bodies reeked of the rapist and his wine. We looked and felt like harlots. The monster led us to the washroom, where women took one look and whispered about our unimaginable plight.

Vibulena stormed past Proculus and into the washroom. One look proved her worst fears. "What happened?"

Zolia shot her a look. "We took Roman sperm, like you." The Crusader lunged at Vibulena's face and thrust it into the water basin.

"Zolia, I am here to help!" Vibulena said.

"Vibulena is not to blame!" I yelled.

"Every time she comes, she asks, 'What happened? Are you all right?' She is Roman, Ronica! Like them."

As I described what the rapist had done, Vibulena listened in horror and Zolia broke down in tears. Flushed with rage, our artist instructed us to meet her outside. While we helped each other wash, I tried to replenish Zolia's hope. But our spirits were drained and we were only going through empty motions.

When finished, Vibulena ignored the guards and led us to the citadel. She barged into the king's chamber. "King

Romulus!" she snapped. "I demand justice for the rape of these women."

The king and his elders stopped their meeting and stared at us. Vibulena described our torment. Romulus summoned Proculus, reluctantly questioning the rapist, who denied everything.

Zolia faced Vibulena, "Why do you bring us to the wolf that planned our abduction? He has no morals. He is scum like the rest of Roma."

Queen Hersilia flew from her throne to slap Zolia. The chamber fell still. "Never speak to my king like this."

Zolia turned to Vibulena. "Thank you again, Artist. As usual, you make things worse."

Soldiers escorted us to our cell. When the rapist returned, he screamed at Zolia for insulting the king.

"Insult the king of rapists? Impossible. The man's existence insults all women."

Proculus pounced at Sister. I jumped on him and pulled at his belt. His fists flew, but we held him off until the monster grabbed a lash. The struggle stimulated the animal. He whipped Zolia and chained me to the pillar.

With Zolia nearly unconscious, Proculus mounted her and raped her from behind. Before he climaxed, he withdrew his penis and sprayed her face. "Smell my seed! Whore!"

I was powerless to shield her. Sister awakened and crawled to me. I wiped the blood from her lashed, abused body. We sobbed through the night. While I stroked her hair, she stirred.

"What are you doing?" she asked.

"I care for my sister."

"Does Ovid still love me?" she whispered.

"Ovid will always love you, my Crusader. Gracian will always love me," I added.

Zolia rose to a squat and urinated on the floor, then fell into my lap, staring aimlessly at the window. Sister's wounds were everywhere, but we surrendered to exhaustion. In the middle of the night, a satchel with ointments flew through the window. I crawled to the package and began applying the ointments.

The next night, the drunk returned. "Ronica," Zolia pleaded. "I cannot survive this monster again."

Proculus wanted more of her. I interceded by offering to accommodate him if he agreed to leave Zolia alone. He untied me and led me to the bed. I undressed and lay down with my legs spread.

The monster rode me like a racehorse but he could not finish. My vagina became dry and every lunge stung. Each of the devil's thrusts drove Gracian further into the background. Horror swarmed over me.

When the rapist finished, he declared, "You are wenches but I love you. Now we are a family."

❦ ❦ ❦ ❦ ❦ ❦

Chapter 32: The Sisters

The rapist left us alone for several days. I saw that I could manage him better than Zolia could. To steal time, we told him we were menstruating, which he believed to be the devil's work.

Soon Proculus decided we should work in the kitchen. He presumed it was a punishment, but the workers sympathized with us. As I worked, Zolia coiled up, holding her hands on her stomach. She rested by the fire and did not communicate.

All our coworkers understood rape and urged Zolia to dance to help cope with the misery. Somehow, she found the strength, and the dark mood in the kitchen lightened.

When the monster uncovered our menstruation pretense, he was angered. "You witches lied to me about your cycles," he fumed, dragging Zolia across the floor and beating her. When he tore away her tunic, he stared in disbelief at the proof of her new cycle. Repulsed, he kicked her in the groin and stormed from the cell.

His childlike solution was called "unum subligaculum." He would allow us one subligaculum. Only the sister who menstruated could wear the protection. I urged Zolia to wear it for many days so she could recover while I serviced the fiend. I pretended I was not being penetrated by a devil and honored my pledge to help Sister at all costs.

We learned that Proculus struggled to balance his love of wine and his virility. His weaknesses gave us strength.

Zolia learned to taunt the rapist. "Tonight is my turn to pleasure your penis, Master Proculus," said Zolia slyly. "Maybe I can breathe some air into the lifeless worm. Please try to last longer this time." Sister seductively twisted her beautiful body, slowly removing her tunic and unwinding her inner garments.

The monster bulged with anticipation. When Zolia stroked him with her hand, I thought he would burst. He tore off his clothes as she moved to the bed. When he pressed his mouth against hers, Zolia reached down and rubbed his penis, stroking him vigorously and groaning to his satisfaction. The monster harmlessly grunted and discharged. His semen spewed onto the floor.

Before the monster could recover, Zolia grabbed his flaccid member and ridiculed him. "This is all you have for me, rapist! My Ovid would laugh at your puny size." Zolia recognized the monster's vulnerability was his ego. For days, she masturbated Proculus until his penis was raw.

When the monster finally left, I lay next to Zolia and stroked her hair. "My sister has changed," I said. "What are you doing with Proculus?"

"I do this for Gracian," she said.

"For Gracian?"

"For thirty days, you slept with the monster to protect me. I saw his weaknesses. Now I will make sure you do not fall for the monster the way our friends have given up hope and succumbed to their Roman rapists."

My heart cried out to her. I kissed her face over and over.

As the rapist bragged about his conquests to his friends, he came to understand that we avoided the post-sex intimacy his friends described. We grasped the rapist knew little about sex, romance, or arousal. He was an animal, with basic instincts. The monster's idea of intimacy was to tell dirty, childhood secrets. He lacked the sense to see that his ideas of romance bored us.

Laughably, he attempted to make himself more interesting by telling us about his days as a pirate – not the sailor he had bragged about before. As a plunderer of Greek ships, he had acquired enough wealth to buy his way to Roma, where Romulus shielded him from the Greeks.

His bribes endeared him to Romulus. He even tried to bribe us with pirated diamonds, but Zolia and I entertained our latrine friends by throwing the rocks in the fouled waste buckets.

Chapter 33: Spolia Opima

In the end, after many months, the King of Caenina led his army into Roman territory. Romulus led his own army against the invaders. After the Romans killed the King of Caenina and routed his army, Romulus did not hesitate to counterattack.

By the dark of night, Romans surrounded Caenina. At dawn, the army stormed the city, slaying a hundred more Caeninan fighters, pillaging the town, capturing young women, killing unmarried men, and looting the town's gold and silver.

When the plunder was brought to Romulus, the king celebrated his victory by building a quartz altar to honor Jupiter Fetrius on Capitoline Hill. On a fine day in early spring, the citizenry was ordered to attend the temple's consecration. The ecstatic king promised the spoils of Caenina, "Spolia Opima," to thirty hand-picked families, who would receive their bounty when their firstborn arrived.

Soon greedy women flirted with the devil's king, flattering his ego by suggestively shimmering their breasts and swiveling their hips whenever he was in sight.

Zolia and I stayed true to ourselves and true to Sabinium. Roma had deflowered us, but not corrupted us. We still prayed that King Titus would rescue us. Our strong minds, good upbringing, and strong survival instincts were our best defenses against the atrocities of Roma.

We knew vengeance would come.

Chapter 34: The Lashings

Sister and I developed strategies to tame the rapist and his penis brain. Masturbation remained our best defense but we began to play Proculus for the egomaniac he was. A compliment here or there bought us sweet time.

Meanwhile, the unmistakably pregnant bellies of the women of Roma were sprouting. Half the women had transformed themselves into wives whose newborns would soon arrive. Friendships between female resistors grew, and as our shared confidences became more personal we helped each other.

Zolia had grown as a person and as a woman. I was different but, for better or worse, I was unsure. In the still of night, we still cried, but we divided our sacrifices. Our friends maintained we were the most beautiful women in the city of devils.

As older sister, I protected Zolia by letting Proculus have his way when Zolia's masturbation came up short. When I could not tolerate him, Zolia bore the brunt. We removed ourselves so far from the sex that it was cold and meaningless.

We encouraged Proculus to drink, which inevitably induced more pirate stories. We licked his face, whispered in his ear, and rubbed his feeble pole until he spilled out.

One night when Proculus persisted, Zolia let him push his puny brain into her. Throwing her head back, she raised her chin and released an unmistakable laugh. The monster halted. "Why does my dancer wife laugh?"

"Master rapist, I apologize. For a moment, you reminded me of Ovid, the boy who had sex with me on the farm," she stated. "I thought a pirate more man than a virgin, but alas, I am mistaken," she laughed.

Zolia only saw the rapist as a monster with an ego and a penis. His interests were self-gratification and posturing for his image. This is why deflowering us had special significance to him. We had learned to soothe his ego and appease his penis without any connection to our souls.

Our bodies were still shackled most of the time, but we greeted Proculus cheerfully and did little things to boost his ego. We sensed he was becoming bored because he kept fantasizing about new escapades.

One was a "doubles" experiment. Zolia and I were to make love to each other. Usually, when he imagined repulsive ideas, we would tickle his penis or ask him pirate questions. When his penis brain was satisfied, whatever escapade he imagined was forgotten. The only risk to our defense was his wine consumption, which made him slightly unpredictable.

On one drunken night, he insisted that we fulfill his "doubles" fantasy. When our usual tricks could not satisfy him he exploded with anger, slapping Zolia and pushing her onto the floor.

"Stop! Leave her alone!" I cried.

"What does your mother look like, Ronica?" he asked.

"She is very beautiful," I said.

"Would you like her in your bed?"

"Never talk about our mother, rapist," Zolia said.

"You are Sabine whores so your mother must be the queen of whores."

I saw that Zolia hid something in her hand behind her back. "Master, we are your family. Why fight about childish things? Tell us what you want. Let us pleasure you."

"Come, young wife. Kiss your husband's pirate penis."

"Ah! The pirate penis," Zolia edged toward him, tempting him by flicking her tongue in and out of his mouth. The rapist teetered on the edge of a drunken sleep when Sister flashed his dagger from behind her back and slashed the monster's face from his left eyebrow past his nose.

Blood exploded from the wound. As Zolia raised her dagger to slit his throat, the rapist squirmed beyond reach. I lunged to hold him so Sister could finish the attack, but my chains restricted me. Zolia's face was drenched with his blood, but she held her dagger tight. The monster screamed for help.

"Rapist! Know that your face looks like your whore mother's vagina," Zolia spat at him.

"Whores of the earth!" Proculus hissed. "You sliced me!" He wiped his face with his sleeve but blood was everywhere. Vengeance spilled from his black heart. The monster grabbed a nearby spade.

I tried to work the chains as Zolia heaved plates and vessels at the monster. He lunged at us but we spun away. When I kicked his groin, he buckled, but Zolia could not finish him.

Guards pounded on the locked door. Another watched from the window until several soldiers smashed into the cell.

They commanded us to stop but we wanted it settled. When the soldiers grabbed the rapist's spade, we saw an opening and rushed to attack but the soldiers pushed us back.

Zolia had disfigured the rapist. Our brand would scar him the rest of his life. Whatever would happen next, I was proud of my Crusader.

Two men stitched the rapist's face with animal sinew. With each stitch, he howled with pain. "Faster! Faster!" Sister yelled, encouraging the healer to pull the stitches through more painfully. Proculus stared at her with hate in his eyes and death in his mind.

Eventually, the soldiers carried the wounded rapist away.

Other guards surrounded the cell, but for three days we heard nothing. Our food arrived as usual. We used the latrine and bathed regularly. We knew our reckoning would come and busied ourselves steeling for the future. When I asked Zolia what had inspired her, she answered, "He insulted our mother. Thinking of her made me realize we had surrendered too easily. This is a fight we should already have had."

After forcing us to endure the wait, Romulus summoned us to his chamber. Our reckoning had arrived. With a cloth patch covering his face, Proculus sat next to his king.

When Romulus asked our version, I provided vivid details of the ongoing rapes and abuses. To my surprise, several elders seemed sympathetic. Queen Hersilia scolded Proculus before a raging debate took place.

Yet in the end, we had no say. It was as if we were not in the chamber and our suffering did not matter. Because we were unmarried, it was decided we should be judged as slaves and that Zolia had attempted to murder a Roman. Under Roman law, slaves had no rights. Zolia's precedent was dangerous. In this backdrop, Romulus pronounced our verdict.

"The slave attempted murder against her Roman master. The slave will receive forty lashes. The slave helper will receive ten. Roma shall witness the thrashing as a reminder of our caste differences.

"Because Proculus is disfigured, the sisters are bound to marry him. They are to be shackled for the rest of their lives. They are prohibited from public events and festivals. No person is to speak with them.

"If either wife attempts to injure her husband, she will be hanged in the square before the citadel. These judgments are irrevocable and can only be absolved by me."

For the span of several heartbeats, Zolia was silent. "You have no authority over us," she finally said. "You deceived us and all the women of Roma. We are Sabine, not Roman. If Sabini judge us, so be it, but your words mean nothing to Sabine."

"I am king of Roma, the city where you reside. Until you marry, you are slaves. Outsiders with no rights and no privileges," Romulus fired back, waving his soldiers to take us away.

We were dragged to the square where a gathering swelled. I was tied to a stake, my tunic ripped from my back. Each lash cut to the bone. The scorching pain set my skin afire. When I fainted, the next strike snapped me back. Sheer agony followed every snap of the whip. After the ten, they cut the ropes. I crashed to the ground. My back was all I could feel. A pregnant woman covered me and helped me to the side.

Like a warrior, Zolia stood to the post. As the soldiers tied her, the Crusader did not resist. Her body squirmed with each snap of the whip, but her mind seemed elsewhere. The Crusader never looked away from Romulus or his stooge rapist. Her eyes welled but she would not cry. The rapist and his king saw Sister would not surrender.

After thirty lashes, her legs caved and the ropes could not support her. Her peeled flesh lay on the ground around her. The warrior raised herself. "Roman whips are as weak as the penis of pirate Proculus. Finish it!"

The executioner stared at her filleted back and handed the whip to another slave driver. No person wanted to administer the last ten lashes. Roman men and women turned away from the sight.

One Roman slave driver administered the final blows and cut Zolia free. Sister lay on the ground, scarred and drenched in blood. A woman passed her a covering. The Crusader lifted her head to Romulus. "I spit on Rhea Silvia's womb. Her son shames all men!"

The king raged with anger, but Sister owned the crowd. Romulus swirled his robe around him and hurried away, the pirate at his side. A soldier put Zolia's covered body over his shoulder and carried her to the cell. Another held my arm. Along the way, Romans apologized. "You are braver than any man. The mother who weaned you is blessed."

In the cell, blood oozed from Zolia's back. The cloth stuck to her wounds. When I removed it, the flimsy flesh ripped away. We had no medicine. As I prayed to Quirinus, another leather satchel with ointments flew through our window.

In her sleep, Zolia murmured Ovid's name. I marveled at her bravery. No abuse would deprive us of our dreams.

Chapter 35: Vengeance

When Proculus returned to our cell, a blood-stained cloth hid his face. His posture reflected suffering.

"Your sister did this to me!" the monster began. "She scarred me and insulted my king. The young whore needs a lesson!"

The pain from our lashings meant nothing to the rapist bent on revenge. Zolia slept on my lap. Her back was raw and my less intrusive lashes screamed for relief. Agitated by excess wine, searing pain, embarrassment, and the realization that he was scarred for life, Proculus would not be deterred. He savagely grabbed Zolia's crotch and tossed her onto the bed. When Sister landed on her shredded back, her eyes drifted away.

"You can never be trusted!" shouted Proculus, tying her hands. Sister's weakness aroused the monster and before I could protect her, the rapist lifted his robe and plunged his penis into her unconscious vagina.

Over the next two days, the pirate indiscriminately violated Sister's every orifice. When he thought about his ugliness, he interspersed rape with beatings, hair yanking, and ejaculating on Zolia's face, stomach and back.

Anchored to the pillar, the sight of Zolia's body overwhelmed me. The monster's semen, spit, and blood caked

Sister's skin. Most of the time she was delirious and when she awakened, Zolia was forced to lick blood from his scars.

I cried, begged, and banged on the pillar like a crazed person but my pleas fell upon deaf ears. To punish her further, Proculus cut off her food and water. With no other remedy, he would kill her through attrition.

When Proculus finally left, Zolia was overcome with fever. I applied ointment and shared my food but there was no comfort for her battered, scratched breasts, blood-soaked vagina, and raw anus. I prayed to Minerva we would die as one.

At the peak of despair, another satchel filled with ointments, fresh food, water, and small doses of hope sailed through the window. While blessing our unknown shepherd, I fed Zolia and applied the herbs and ointments to her wounds.

After Zolia's fever broke, a guard escorted us to the kitchen for our routine visit. No workers dared speak to us. Sister rested by the fire. I silently cut meat and prepared bread.

I smiled at my distraught sister but, when she looked away, I trembled with fright. What were these beasts doing to Minerva's daughters? Yet Zolia wore her shame with resolve even when her raw back and arms prevented her from feeding herself. Only Ona volunteered to help.

When we returned to the cell, Proculus awaited us. He held forth the leather satchel, demanding the donor's name. "Minerva," I replied. The guards covered the window with iron bars and a dark shutter. We were now disconnected from the outside world, devoid of natural light.

Before our tormentor left, he warned he would return after a dinner party. There, the ugliest sinner in Roma, Sawtooth

Villius, ridiculed Proculus's face. Villius's nickname came for his mouth's uncanny resemblance to a saw blade. "Proculus, my friend, your young wife gave you quite a thrashing. Your gash makes you the new Bogeyman of Roma!"

The monster stormed into the cell. "You whores have made me the new Bogeyman of Roma." His eyes burned at Zolia. "You, wretch, will know how it feels to be a spectacle!" The monster pulled out his dagger and shaved her head, laughing like a possessed devil. "Ha! You are a shaved sheep, the Bogeywoman of Roma!" He tossed strands of hair into Zolia's face and kept taunting her.

I feared Sister would reward him with an angry reaction, but instead she flashed her tormentor a magnificent smile. The monster stopped in his tracks. "Why do you smile, witch?" he screamed.

"Ha! Yes, I am a witch… whose hair will grow back. Your Bogeyman scars are permanent. No free woman will ever accept you. Rape is the only remedy for your puny cock!"

Proculus swiveled, throwing his full weight behind violent strikes at Zolia's face and body. Sister kept smiling until falling unconscious. Her face was covered with contusions. Her lips bled. But Zolia had stayed her course and given me hope. We would live another day, fight another fight.

❋ ❋ ❋ ❋ ❋ ❋

Chapter 36: Resistance

I wondered at her resilience and feared Sister was approaching her limit of physical and mental abuse. Yet that night, she breathed peacefully and slept through the night. I caressed her head and smoothed her back. "Your kisses are sweeter than my hair, Domus. Kiss me more," she whispered.

The only way Bogeyman would tame Zolia was to starve her to death. A guard watched to ensure I did not share my food or water. I always held my last gulp for Zolia, but the Crusader was starving. After two days, she fainted.

When the monster arrived, he goaded her. "Is the young wife hungry? Is the young wife thirsty?"

"I need water."

"Fear not. I am here to quench your thirst." He placed his dagger at my throat and commanded that Zolia serve him fellatio. Too weak to argue, Sister sucked his penis until he squirted down her throat. The monster lifted the water vessel and poured the contents onto the floor. Zolia crawled to the spot and licked the water. When he threw food morsels, Sister crawled to what she could reach. The Crusader lived like this for days.

Chapter 37: The Mask

Proculus acquired a red iron mask to hide his shame. Our only comfort was that he looked the creature he was. Only his eyes and lips were visible.

In his frustration, from the depths of his dark soul, the masked monster contrived a challenge fight against my abused and feeble sister. If she defeated him, she would be freed. The monster knew Zolia could not resist, just as he knew her fragile state put her at his mercy.

Zolia's back had not healed even though her spirit had rebounded. She accepted the challenge. From the start Proculus pummeled her, throwing her to the floor, kicking her, and slapping her back. When she lay crumpled in a corner, he said, "Tell me, loser. Other than a good beating, what do you enjoy?"

"Dance," Zolia muttered. "I dance."

"Your dancing days are over, whore!" Proculus pinned Zolia's stretched frame against the stone and bashed her right kneecap so a loud crack echoed the cell. Zolia screamed her shock.

"Your hair grows back but not your knee. Good luck dancing on one leg, harlot! Your whore knee is the price for my scars."

"You crazy monster. You deserve the face you have. Your friend is right. You are the Bogeyman of Roma!" I exploded.

"So the other Cyprian has a foul mouth like her sister! When was the last time you pleasured my pirate penis, Ronica?" The monster smashed me against the wall and mounted me so many times everything blurred.

My anger would never subside again. I stared into the monster's eyes and laughed as loud as I could, just as beautiful Zolia had done. "You will never please another woman, Proculus. You are the ugliest crocodile in the world. You have no idea how to please a woman."

The rapist may have expected this from Zolia, but not from me. I cried out so the guards could hear. "The rapist looks like a hyena's ass!" One of the guards laughed, further agitating the pillager. Proculus shoved three fingers into my anus and bit my breast.

"His penis is soft!" I yelled to the guards, who snickered. "All the Bogeyman can do is beat women with his soft penis."

Zolia joined in. "Guards! Look! Behold the miniature pirate penis." Terrified the guards would tell others, the rapist dressed quickly and left the cell.

At some point, Vibulena and Gino arrived with a healer. We lay on the floor, half-naked, covered only with a torn blanket. Proculus swept back into the cell, trying to intercept Vibulena. "Woman, you have no right here! The king has spoken. No person can talk to the witches."

"These women did not appear for work in the kitchen. Romulus instructed me to interview them. Let's be clear, Proculus. You do not teach me the law of Roma," Vibulena said emphatically.

Vibulena and the healer examined my bruises and my battered face. I wrapped myself tightly in a blanket, shielding my inflamed anus and puffy vagina. "Proculus broke Zolia's leg," I offered.

Sister lay motionless, unable to respond to their questions. The healer and Gino gently lifted Sister onto the bed and tended her wounds. Vibulena insisted that I describe what the monster had done. When I painted the rapist's profile, Vibulena's rage mounted.

"Was it you who threw us the medicine?" I asked.

She fidgeted nervously. "What medicine?"

"The same medicine you give us now," I answered.

"Hmm, Ronica. That will be our secret." My mentor said she had painted our whipping scene. When she realized how we lay in the dirt after the lashings, she became so incensed she burned the painting and swore to Juno Quiritis to never paint again.

The healer and Gino wrapped Zolia's shattered knee and bandaged her leg. If Zolia was permitted to heal, she would walk again, but with a limp. As Proculus had vowed, her dancing days were over.

"You are right, Sister. Vibulena is kind," Zolia said that night. I smiled and let it rest.

The next day Vibulena reported our tormentor's behavior to the king, who argued Sister had agreed to the fight.

"If Zolia had done the same to Proculus, would you be here?" the king asked.

"This monster beats and rapes defenseless girls. If this is Roman law, Roma would be safer with no laws," Vibulena argued.

In the end, Romulus expanded our routine and ordered the window opened for light and air. When you have nothing, small comforts give hope. Guards took us to the kitchen, but despite her crippled leg Zolia remained in chains. She leaned on me for support. Pitying our predicament, a few coworkers gave us solace. As we followed our guards back to the cell, Zolia said, "I can never dance again. I am crippled."

Proculus was the worst woman-abuser in Roma, a reputation that we suspected inspired him. He drank more and came home less regularly. After one bash, he surprised us by arriving in the cell around midnight. The monster could barely walk and slurred his words through his repugnant mask.

Half-spitting, he faced Sister. "Salvé, 'Fellatio,' how is your crippled leg?" laughed the rapist. "Zolia, from this day forward, your new name is 'Fellatio.' After I told my friends about your luscious sucking, they suggested this."

The monster presented Zolia his penis and demanded she lick him. He put his dagger to my throat and Zolia sucked him until he came. "From this day forward, your only responsibility is to take my penis in your mouth and play with my sack while you suck my seed into your heart. This is what crippled dancers do."

The monster turned to me. "Ronica, I hear you can cook. From now on, you will cook for us. Zolia can suck me while you prepare the meal. You will pleasure my penis when we are finished. Do my wives understand their jobs?"

To validate his authority, he fondled my breasts, took me over his knee, and spanked me. He stuck his penis in my face but I masturbated him until he was so raw he begged to stop. His mask hid his scars but not the horror of the beast.

When he left, I massaged Sister's head. "What are you doing?" Zolia asked.

"Seeking the source of your courage and strength."

"Fellatio weakens my morals," she answered. "Do you think Ovid can love a ravaged cripple?"

"Yes. Ovid will love you and carry you on his shoulders."

We planned that if Proculus molested her again, Sister would bite his pole to cut it off, regardless of the consequences. Zolia agreed but, with her deteriorating resolve, she seemed more ready to die than to fight.

With the arrival of spring came hope and bursting bellies. Roma left winter behind and began to bustle. Proculus let me cook undisturbed and avoided Sister.

At first, I prepared delicious meals. The beast ate well, drank his grape, and then tried to rape me. I lost interest in cooking and served fouled food. I would let him play his game but he would eat spoiled food.

When Sister asked me what he did to me, I answered, "What is the difference between an evil penis in the mouth, vagina, or anus? It comes from the same devil."

❀ ❀ ❀ ❀ ❀ ❀

Chapter 38: The Butterfly Brooch

One night, Sawtooth Villius barged into the cell. He reeked of wine. The closer he came, the more rotten his foul mouth.

"What does Bogeyman want?" I asked.

He ran at me, clasping his hand to my thigh. "I will give Minerva's daughters a proper servicing." The creature suddenly jumped on me, rubbing his stiff member against my groin. Zolia pulled at him until he punched her in the stomach. As he lifted my tunic, Proculus came from behind and yanked him away.

"Proculus, you have two whores. I have nothing. At least let the young one suck me!"

The pirate waved his dagger, warning his friend to leave. Zolia and I huddled in the corner. Proculus closed the door. "See how I love my wives. I punished my friend for misbehaving. You are lucky to have a husband like me."

Zolia squeezed my hand, making a comical face. "Thank you, master, for the scripted show. Your bad acting is only topped by your horrendous lovemaking."

"Master, does it bother you that Sawtooth Villius is better looking than you?" I laughed. "He is probably a better lover, too. Should we rate our rapists and report to the king of rape?"

Proculus removed a small cloth from his pocket. "Do you see this, Fellatio?" The monster unwrapped Ovid's silver butterfly brooch.

"That belongs to me, rapist!"

Proculus dangled the brooch, daring Zolia to try for it. Instead, she begged. In exchange for her best fellatio, he said Sister could have the brooch. Clinging to her last wisp of hope, she satisfied Proculus by caressing his penis. A dangerous precedent was set.

Over the next several days, the rapist ravaged her from top to bottom, but always withheld the brooch. Finally, when he was spent with her, he said, "Young whore, tonight is the night I will take you out under the moon and return the brooch." I sensed betrayal but kept silent.

Proculus and his torchbearers took Sister to the darkest place on the river. He waved the brooch before her and Zolia's face filled with promise. As she reached for the piece, the monster flung it into the river. Zolia flew at his neck, but he fended her off. She limped to the water's edge and searched for while Proculus mocked her to his guards. When Sister returned to me, she was bruised, scratched, and demoralized.

Zolia's eyes glazed over. "Everything is gone. There is nothing more to lose. I shall cry no more."

❂❂❂❂❂❂

Chapter 39: Roman Newborns

Outside the cell, the first crop of babies was being born. Most of the abducted women were married but Romulus issued a final edict that all women must marry or be treated as slaves.

The king ordered one of us to wed the rapist. His verdict triggered wagering among Romans as to whether the rapist would marry "fellatio Zolia" or "anus Ronica." Smart bettors wagered it would be neither.

Believing me easier to manage, the rapist proposed on bended knee, an offer that only sparked laughter from us. Realizing my rejection was intractable, he threatened to kill Zolia with either his penis or his dagger. But the Crusader had drawn her line, insisting she would rather die than see me marry the monster.

Proculus arranged a slave's wedding. When I refused to wear his new white toga, he threatened to break Zolia's left leg. As a slave, I was bound with a rope. Two soldiers were assigned to guard Zolia, who remained in the cell.

"Never marry the deviant with the ugliest face on earth!" Zolia yelled when we left. Her guards snickered but Proculus led me to a small temple of Jupiter, where the wedding would take place. The sight of the Roman elders, priests, and the king of rape caused me to laugh aloud.

"So, Roma's finest thinks there is a wedding today?" I asked. "Does the monster rapist seriously believe a daughter of Minerva would marry a pirate?"

Traditionally, the bride and groom exchanged grain straws and flowers. The monster tried to bribe me with a bracelet, which I accepted, fully expecting to deposit it in the latrine. In return, I presented him with a replica of a small, straw penis fashioned by Zolia. Proculus seethed but several elders roared approval.

As the audience prepared to settle their wagers, a priest ordered my rope removed and asked if I was ready to exchange vows.

A shroud descended over me. I stood motionless, clutching flowers and straw. Elders yelled for me to proceed and Proculus resorted to another threat. "If you do not step forward, Sawtooth will violate your sister and slit her throat."

I knew I could not marry the beast. I loosened my hand and Minerva cast away the straw and flowers.

"Do you not fear for Zolia?" Proculus asked.

"When you threw away the brooch, you sapped her hope," I said.

The priest addressed Proculus. "No person can force another to marry before the gods."

"It is good that in this evil land a person cannot be forced to marry against their will. But it is wrong that the king encourages rape," I volunteered. "Even if I chose to marry this rapist it would not be legal, for you are no more than a jester to the king of rape–not a priest of gods."

Zolia's spirit was in me. I pivoted sharply and walked away from the evil filth toward the cell. When I entered, the soldiers were confused. I moved to the Crusader and hugged her. "Today I was brave, like my sister."

Proculus stormed in. "You dirty witch! You cannot treat me this way."

I put the soldier's spear to my throat. "Then, kill us, penis brain! If you were a man and deserved a wife from Cures, you would fight Uncle Neiro in a duel. But, no, you are nothing more than a shadow man."

"Do you whores understand you are abandoned?" Proculus asked as he stormed from the cell.

"You spoke well today," Zolia said. "I adore my domus, but the monster is right. We are alone. We must fight for ourselves."

"Minerva gave me strength and courage. She will again."

"Is that so?" Zolia raised her brow. "Please ask Minerva where she has been since our abduction. No god, goddess, man, suitor, father, mother, brother, or sister came for us. Yet you still have faith. It is the domus who is brave. Blind, but brave."

Chapter 40: The Vision

That night, a vision of a man walking by my side came to me. His hands were soft and tender. Roma's streets were empty and the city was clean. The man blessed me just before a goddess led him into the mist. I awoke sharply, but the same puzzling dream returned every night.

With the heat of summer Queen Hersilia birthed a daughter, who was named Prima. The king hosted a large celebration, to which we were invited. The monster presented us with new violet tunics. We were sufficiently recovered that heads turned when we entered the chamber. The elders and the king sat on chairs of granite at a long stone table.

Hersilia seemed different, politely asking us to bless her baby. We kissed the babe's cheek and held her to Minerva. Holding the baby, Zolia's eyes widened. "Hersilia cheats on her king. One day, you will see!" she whispered.

Even in this festive atmosphere, soldiers kept a wary eye on Minerva's daughters. Before dinner, Romulus named thirty families to serve as Comitia Curiata, Roma's decision-makers. These families would be entitled to assemble, hold court, decide religious issues, and settle family disputes.

After the announcement, Romulus distributed Spolia Opima and the festivities gained rhythm. Men enjoyed wine and generous plates. Zolia and I sipped the grape, momentarily forgetting our miseries. Roman songs were sung and men and women performed dances.

At the height of the party, King Romulus banged the table. "My daughter deserves the best dancer in the land. Who will dance for her?"

"Let the woman with the ivory shoe dance!" yelled one of the elders.

A great cheer arose, but the crowd was unaware of Sister's infirmity. Only our friend Ona protested. "Zolia's leg is injured."

"A dancer needs only one leg to balance her body. Zolia will dance for Prima," Romulus declared.

Zolia's love of dance overtook her common sense. She folded her arms as if cradling a newborn and raised the invisible babe to her breast to receive a blessing.

"Move your legs, dancer!" a spectator cried. Sister rested on her right leg but, while shifting weight, lost her balance and fell.

Foolish men laughed. Zolia rose from the floor like a daffodil from the soil. Her hands flowed elegantly. Her fingers begged Minerva for assistance. She bent her right leg and rested it on her left thigh, jumping like a sparrow. She circled the stone table, imitating signs of the gods with her hands. Sister astonished the audience. Elders banged the table. Women clapped in amazement.

A senator insisted that Sister dance on the tabletop. Romulus waved to guards to lift her. Zolia's tunic was torn from her fall and, because it was my time to wear the undergarment, Zolia's shapely leg, thigh, and most private parts were exposed.

Yet she danced from one end of the table to the king at the opposite end. But the torn tunic snagged, causing an early stumble. Ever the performer, Zolia floated across the table. Many elders craned their necks when they saw Sister wore no subligaculum. Then, shielding her nakedness, Zolia stood before the king.

"Brilliant, Zolia! A wonderful dance," proclaimed the king.

Zolia collapsed, falling to the floor. When she stood, her anger coursed. "Roman animals! Next time, ask your daughters to dance the table without subligaculum!"

Sister hobbled toward me but Proculus caught her, slapping her loudly. Zolia flew like a leaf to me. Her right cheek swelled.

I sat her on the floor and raced to Proculus, who was taken aback by my boldness. "The only thing you had not done was expose our bodies to other Romans. Today, you committed the final sin. You are a joke of a man. Take this." I removed my bloodied subligaculum and threw it in his face, then walked to the king.

"You are the scum of all nations. I know how you built Roma and what you are doing to keep it."

"What do you say, witch of Cures?" Romulus asked.

So that only the king could hear, I bent to his ear and whispered one word. "Malocanis."

Romulus slumped from his chair, wounded to the core and struggling to breathe. I turned and walked away. Everyone in the hall stared, wondering what I had said to topple their leader.

Zolia saw the fury in my eyes and rushed after me. "Revolter, your eyes glow with intrigue. What did you say to scare him?"

I turned to face the chamber. "If anyone touches my sister or me again, Roma will burn to ashes." We walked from the room.

The next morning no one approached us. The guards did not shackle us and Proculus stayed away. That afternoon, Romulus summoned us to the citadel where he nervously paced his chamber.

"Lady Ronica. Lady Zolia. My friends from Cures. Come sit with me." The troubled king shifted his focus to me. "Tell me, older daughter of Minerva. How do you know the name you mentioned?"

"Because, king of rape, Malocanis came to me in a vision."

"You have seen her? That's impossible. Where?"

"In my dreams," I answered. "Her face is burned into my memory, like a scarred carving on the wall."

"In your dreams? This cannot be. Perhaps you know her name, but not her face. Does Zolia share your vision?"

"I know the secret you have hidden from heaven and earth for a long time. Now you are exposed, Romulus."

"What do you think you know?" asked the king.

Without fear, I stared into the king's eyes and conveyed my vision.

> "Your mother, Rhea Silvia, was the victim of rape. Her affair with Silvanus was a fabrication, created to cover her shame. Your mother was abused and raped by

her father's brother, your great uncle, Amulius, who coveted her beauty and ravaged her against her will.

"After becoming King of Alba, Amulius locked Rhea Silvia in the temple, isolating her from the outside. Your incestuous father threatened to kill her, just as Proculus does to us. Amulius lived to rape his niece, but tried not to breed with her.

"Your mother endured his abuse for five years until she realized she carried the beast's seed. When she threatened to expose Amulius, he tried to silence her.

"Eventually, Rhea Silvia escaped the evil king. In hiding she befriended Silvanus, but dared not tell him she was impregnated. Instead, she told him Amulius wanted her dead.

"But Rhea Silvia spread the lie that Silvanus had fathered her child, leaving the innocent man deceived and in need of clearing his name. When he threatened to meet with elders, Rhea Silvia slew Silvanus in his sleep and told the town Amulius had killed her lover.

"Rhea Silvia birthed twins: you and Remus, two sons of a rapist. While fleeing your father, she realized her hopelessness. Before taking her life, she stood atop a hill and gave her twins to two innocent shepherds.

"The nervous herdsmen took the boys to Amulius, who realized they were his inbred sons and that their existence jeopardized his reign. Rather than lose his crown, the corrupt king chose to give the shepherds gold to dispose of you and Remus. The good shepherds put one-third of the gold in the vessel and set you and your brother adrift.

"That is when the queen of whores and witches, Malocanis, saw her opportunity. As a prostitute and brothel owner, the slut was hated by her community. One night, townspeople stormed her whorehouse, beat and burned her prostitutes, and destroyed the building. The witch of witches escaped with burns and a scarred face and was consumed with vengeance.

"As her flesh rotted away from her face and body, she plotted revenge against mankind. To perfect her evil, she traveled the earth, mastering sorcery from renowned sources like Aksumite, Assyrian, Chou, Nubia, and others. When she met the wickedest god of all hells, Vieranima, he took her powers to the most sinister level.

"These were the horrors she would unleash upon Alba in order to destroy the peaceful lifestyle of the kingdom of shepherds and all mankind.

"In one of her visions, the witch saw twins born to the Princess of Alba. Malocanis determined the twins would found her evil, murderous kingdom. Staring into her bronze mirror, she spotted the outcast babies and drove her ship ashore to harvest them.

"The witch solidified your fate by administering evil spells learned from Vieranima. You, your brother, and Malocanis bonded in mind and body, but she was cunning enough to know her plot could not unfold until the twins matured and gained trust.

"It was Malocanis who cast the spell that led Faustulus to the she-wolf's cave. Faustulus was a simple farmer and believed the wolf and woodpeckers had stolen you and Remus.

"Malocanis resurfaced when you were twelve and began poisoning your minds with stories of Rhea Silvia and Amulius. Through her demons, the witch knew your incestuous roots. Unlike you, Remus became uncomfortable with the dark side. Yet he protected you by not revealing your past or your connection to Malocanis.

"You brothers acted like brave shepherds, chasing thieves and burglars who stole property from the hills. The only thief you did not chase was Proculus, the notorious grave robber who was connected to the queen of whores, who stressed you should leave the grave robber alone. When your following grew, you killed Amulius, your father, and assumed the throne.

"Malocanis realized that the prophecy of the sow had to be fulfilled. She insisted that you and your brother start a new kingdom, but a bitter rivalry with your brother materialized. Because Malocanis favored you more than Remus, she trained you to seek the counsel of others in order to manipulate history to your favor.

"When Faustulus suggested casting the vultures, you schemed to win the advantage. While you and Remus waited on your hills for the birds, Malocanis doubled the number of Remus's vultures for you so Palatine would triumph. You became king and consecrated Roma with the gods of your ancestors.

"When Malocanis decided you would rule Roma, she plotted the abduction and rape of hundreds of virgin women to sustain your kingdom. It was through the blood and tears of raped mothers that Roma would be purified.

"But Remus consulted his gods and learned the life

story of Malocanis and her Hell god, Vieranima. The real disagreement between you and Remus was about Malocanis and the dark side. Tempted by riches and power and convinced of some sort of malevolent entitlement, you slew your own brother."

The king of rape's eyes widened, revealing his fear. I possessed the truth he knew could rid him of his power. Zolia sat motionless, shocked by my revelations.

"What else does the older daughter of Minerva know?" asked Romulus.

"You mean other than that you killed your brother and incestuous father, protected a pirate grave robber, and arranged the rape of hundreds of innocents by order of a malicious witch?" I waited, hoping for a reaction – an apology – anything. When it did not come, I started again.

"You are not a ruler, Romulus. You are nothing more than the witch's messenger. When you invited worthless people to your asylum and promised them citizenship, you added herbs and sprayed perfume on their noses to increase their need for sex so their minds could be warped by your orgies. You could not purify by blood, so you chose semen and fluids of scum.

"This was the plan of the evil queen of prostitutes from the beginning. On her behalf, you have sanctioned all men to abuse women because you endorse brutality and violence as a means to your end. You manipulated the guilt of Roman orgies to the advantage of Malocanis and her devil agent.

"You! You are the architect and administrator of the rape of Sabine! What you do not understand is that

Romans know you are too corrupt to differentiate right from wrong.

"Because your brother's spirit haunted you, you performed rituals to calm that spirit. After the witch consulted her dark gods, she discovered we were Minerva's daughters. To destroy Minerva's goodness, we had to be ruined and killed. You hosted dances and art competitions to lure us and other virgins to your web. Malocanis cast out demons to influence the virgins of the land.

"To abuse Minerva's daughters, you and Malocanis chose a man who dug a thousand graves and lived with corpses. Proculus came to Roma knowing he would abuse, torture, and finally burn us and our children to fulfill the witch's plot and ensure the evil empire's eternal survival.

"The final abuse would start when all men and women burned their subligacula. You took our defloration cloths to appease the witch, who burned them with sulfur, aromatic herbs, and incense to awaken demons from Hell. This is how Malocanis confirmed that we were ripe for sacrifice.

"Neither you nor your queen of whores expected Zolia to destroy Proculus's face, or for Proculus to break her leg. The witch did not think we could survive the abuses. Our fight weakened your power so, to repair your reputation, you connived to gain public support by arranging for Proculus to marry me. Even though this plan failed, you now wait for our babies so you can burn us all, thus completing your assault on goodness and on Minerva.

"With our deaths, you feed Vieranima, so that the

monster god from Hell will grant the children of Roma long lives. Malocanis will have her generation of people without morals in her murderous and misguided nation. They will reject gods, goddesses, and the laws of nature. You have assisted Malocanis in creating a Roman Empire that will destroy the human race."

I waited for Romulus to wonder if I would convey my revelation to others. "Did you believe Minerva would not assist us? Did you believe Minerva would allow Malocanis to destroy civilization so a man who killed his father and brother and raped hundreds of virgins could rule? Even you, the king of rape, are smarter than that!"

Zolia flew to me, hugging me and staring at the gasping king.

"You cannot kill us. You need our babies," I said. "We are off."

We started to walk away from the chambers, but Romulus called to me. "Goddess Ronica, I beg you. There is one last thing I must know. Will my blood and heir rule Roma?"

I closed my eyes and the answer came clear. "Never! The blood of Romulus will never rule Roma. The gods will never forgive you or your people."

The king sank to the floor. "Ronica! Ronica, I must know. Which god delivered this vision to you?"

I stared at the pitiful corrupt puppet. "The source of my visions was not a god, but was nonetheless an indisputable source. It was your brother… Remus."

Chapter 41: Preparation

"You have a gift!" Zolia exclaimed, on our way from the chamber. "Domus, you are the most brilliant sister on earth." As we walked freely to our cell, our positive gait made the Romans wonder about our meeting.

In the cell we sat on the bed, discussing how the king of rape might respond. Proculus rushed into the cell, gesturing frantically and providing Sister with an eagerly anticipated opportunity.

"What did you say to King Romulus?" demanded the masked man.

"Salvé, Roman," Zolia said cheerfully. "We are in conversation about your fate. Begone, fool!"

"Fellatio, you forget yourself. You cannot speak to me like that."

"I shall speak any way that pleases me, grave robber."

"I am a good citizen of Roma, not a grave robber. You are both ruined goods. No real men will have you!"

"Grave robber, were you intimate with skeletons in their graves?" Zolia asked. "Is that why Minerva's daughters are virgins? Only a dead man who slept with corpses bothered us."

"How do you know my past?"

"We have visions, sent by the gods." Zolia responded. "We see everything."

Proculus raised his hand to strike Sister, but she shrugged him off. "Never touch us again, grave robber! If you strike us, the king of rape will have your miniature testicles!"

Unexpectedly, Romulus entered the cell. Seeing Proculus threatening us, the king ordered his subject to desist and vacate the cell. Proculus argued but the king held firm, saying that if the pirate returned he would suffer.

With his tail between his legs, Proculus turned for the door. Zolia patted him on the behind. "Good luck finding a place to stick your puny penis. Maybe Sawtooth will accommodate you!"

For a long time, Romulus, the king of rape, sat in a chair conveying stories he thought entertaining. We could only wonder why men thought their life story made good conversation. His childhood experiences and favorite pastimes held no interest for us but we tolerated Romulus's bad manners. All the while, I knew the Crusader was plotting.

When Romulus left, he posted fifty guards around the property. We were not permitted to leave and no person would be permitted to enter our new house.

A guard who flirted with Zolia reported that Roma overflowed with gossip about what had happened between the sisters from Cures and the king. For the first days, we enjoyed cooking, dancing, singing, eating well, and sleeping soundly.

Thinking we had gained the king's favor, our guards tried befriending us. Occasionally I served meals and gave them food for their families. They thanked us for basic provisions. Despite their persistent questions, we remained silent about Malocanis and Romulus. At the same time, we knew the king of rape suffered from our vision.

Slowly, we gained strength. We washed our hair and wore clean robes every day, a change that thrilled the guards. Small rays of hope dawned but I realized Zolia's right ear was failing. The pirate's beatings had taken a toll. I seethed that Roma had deafened and crippled Sister, but dared not show my anger. Zolia's state served as a constant reminder of our suffering.

While we grew stronger, Romulus set a secret meeting with Malocanis in old Alba. His newest scheme called for our murder under the pretense of a failed escape. "It is too dangerous to let them live," Romulus told the whore witch.

"Slow down," Malocanis said. "We are close to fulfilling our dreams. We must be patient. We need the children."

The partners agreed that Malocanis would visit an ancient Lavinium town and seek answers from the Trojan Penates. We were to stay locked in the house. Unbeknownst to the witch, the rape king had his own agenda. The schemer wanted us dead, away from his city.

In the midst of this intrigue, a soldier who fancied Zolia whispered, "Your friends are here to see you."

Chapter 42: Gino and Vibulena

Gino and Vibulena snuck into the hallway. "Dear sisters, I overheard a conversation and I fear your lives are in jeopardy. The king plans to kill you next in just a few days, at the festival of Neptunus Equester," Gino said. "A dozen men wait to make it look like a failed escape. This is how Romulus will explain your deaths."

Before our friends crept away, Vibulena insisted we plan an escape. I began to pray but Zolia scoffed at my prayers for divine intervention. Romulus planned that Neptunus Equester would appease Roma's neighbors for the loss of their women, who were now impregnated with Roman babies.

Shortly after her first visit, Vibulena returned with herbal sleeping powders. She instructed us to mix them with the food we served our guards. She suspected that, during the festival, only two guards would be at the house. This would be the opportune time to execute our escape. Once the guards fell asleep, we would scale the wall and run to the woods.

I asked her to approach Sulpicia to accompany us. From that moment on, we busied ourselves talking and flirting with the unsuspecting guards. On the day before the festival Vibulena approached Sulpicia, who swore to secrecy but answered that her newborn child would slow our escape.

On the eve before our escape, Vibulena and Gino joined us for dinner. As Gino and I prepared the meal, Zolia and my mentor conversed. "Why do you dislike me, Zolia? What have I done?" Vibulena asked. "Is it because I love a Roman?"

"Do you love him, Vibulena?" Zolia asked.

"Of course. I understand you have been to Hell and back, but there is love in this world and I love my husband."

"Were you a virgin when you first slept with him?"

"No, I was not a virgin."

"Why did you choose this man over the others you bedded?" Zolia pressed ahead while Gino and I worried that either might explode.

"I wanted to marry a man I loved and who could provide for me. Sometimes the two do not go together. You never really know a man unless you have slept together. Intimacy is part of understanding each other."

"You see, Artist, Ronica and I have suffered because people like you think women vulnerable to male penises. Men tame our minds and bodies in the name of sex." Zolia emphasized her point with a shrug.

I was not sure I agreed. I wondered about the complicated implications of sex.

When it was time for our friends to leave, Gino hugged us. "You are my best friend, Zolia," he said, kissing her on the cheek.

"If all men were like you, Gino, marriage and sex would work."

Vibulena kissed me but stood back from Zolia. "Vibulena, you are a good and caring woman. Take care of your husband,"

Zolia offered. A solitary tear slipped down Vibulena's cheek before she and Gino left us alone.

"Sometimes, Sister, I do not understand you," I confessed.

"I wanted Vibulena to understand women's values and learn what is right and what is wrong." At night I curled behind my sleeping sister, stroking her hair and caressing her scarred back.

"What are you doing?" she asked.

"Trying to understand my Crusader sister. I am happy you trust Vibulena."

"I trust your friend because she passed my test," Zolia answered. "Revolter, Vibulena has sisters in Falscii. She never brought them to Roma to marry a Roman. The more men a woman beds, the weaker her mind becomes and the less she is true to herself. The artist's soul is pure, but not her body. Our souls are the reasons women never surrender."

Chapter 43: Flight

I kissed Zolia before we fell asleep. I wondered how Sister seemed to know so many things, but dared not press the issue. The preparation for our escape was filled with anticipation and regret. We were again entering the unknown.

Convinced of our success, Zolia charcoaled the wall with Death to the Grave Robber and stepped back to admire her message.

Vibulena was right. Only two guards remained at the house. I made pomegranate juice and mixed in Vibulena's herbal powders. After the guards enjoyed it, their eyes rolled back and their goblets clanked to the ground. We lugged them inside and confiscated their swords and spears. After we attached kitchen knives to leather flaps on our hips, we snuck away.

We passed several dwellings before a familiar figure faced us. "My beautiful slaves are stealing away from the den? You whores are done!" Proculus said, raising his sword.

Zolia lowered her spear and charged. Proculus slid to the right and kicked her to the ground. I dropped my spear and gripped my sword. Uncle Neiro's words came to me: "When you fight, watch their hands. Never drop your sword!"

Proculus and I swung our swords. I fought like a lioness. Zolia charged but the monster punched her back and smashed the sword from my hands.

Zolia signaled me to distract him so she could grab his dagger. I dodged and weaved and when he turned, Zolia sunk her kitchen knife into his gut and released a stream of blood. I bit the monster's hand and Sister swiped the dagger from his belt.

"The dagger is a gift from my father, whore."

"Only you would use your father's gift to rape women and dig graves? Did your father sleep with corpses, too?" Zolia spat.

Proculus smashed the butt of his sword into Sister's stomach and struck me on the head. After he reclaimed the dagger, he dragged us to the house. "If I finish you, my king will kill me," he fretted. "I will tell Romulus of your escape attempt. Then he will put an end to my misery."

Proculus had just began shackling us when Gino suddenly burst into the cell, jumping on the rapist's back. Gino barked for us to leave. Sister grabbed the fiend's dagger and we ran.

When I looked back, Gino held the demon's legs while Proculus stabbed him with a spear. Our friend held until the last drop of blood drained from his body.

Our chains clanked as we passed through alleyways. Two soldiers blocked our path. We stretched our chain horizontally and ran at the first guard. "Roman! You die today!" we screamed as we struck his chest, dragging him over the cliff. His tumbling momentum threw him down the hill until his head banged into a rock.

The second soldier threw his spear, but we ducked. Screaming louder, we charged, but the spear chucker disappeared in the dark. Zolia's leg and the chains slowed our flight, but darkness was the blanket that buffered us from Roman jackals.

During the night, we left Roman territory. Our new environs were unfamiliar. We were hungry and exhausted. Owls, wolves, and foxes howled in the dark.

I tried to fashion a spear from branches but Zolia would not let me use the dagger, insisting I use my kitchen knife. "His dagger should be purified. We must never use it. We will give it to Uncle Neiro to sever the serpent's head," said the Crusader. While we crafted two spears, we alternated uneasy naps.

The next morning we hunted small game, but the chains limited our movements and created noise. We resorted to berries and fruit. Though we ate well, we were always hungry.

We survived ten days scavenging fruit and shivering through the night. When dehydration overcame us, we fell against the base of a large tree. I prayed to Minerva that Romans would not find us; but, on the verge of fainting, I saw shepherds approaching and guessed that our lives were over.

To my surprise, I awoke in a limestone house where sculptures and oil paintings lined the rooms. Our chains were gone. A familiar-looking woman encouraged me to stay still. She tended my wounds with a gentle touch and cleaned my face with a warm cloth.

"Where is my sister?"

"Sleeping in the next room," said the shepherd.

"Where are we?"

"In Veii," she said. "My name was Larthi."

"You look familiar," I offered.

"I know you, Ronica. But, you do not know me."

Zolia's scream pierced the quiet. "The Romans have us!" She limped into my room, falling onto my lap.

"Be calm, Sister," I said. "We are in Veii, not Roma."

"Are you sure, Ronica? The sculptures are Roman." She looked at Larthi. "I know your face."

Our shepherd opened a chest and held forth a picture. Zolia and I stared incredulously at a picture of Roma in the background and Gino in the foreground. It was signed by Vibulena. Zolia sank to her knees, tears streaming down her face.

"You are Gino's sisters from Cures. I hope my son follows you?" Our report of Gino's passing caused such grief that Larthi crumbled to the floor where she and Sister wept together.

Gino's house mourned for two days. We felt shame for Gino's death. Seeing our grief, Larthi took us to his room and opened a trunk that held many pictures of us. Gino had told Larthi about his love for us. He called Zolia his favorite friend and predicted that one day he would die for his sisters from Cures. He had said a miracle would lead us to his home in Veii. Now we knew why Gino's parents treated us as daughters.

To help the family, I resumed my domus duties and cooked for Gino's family and their servants. Zolia spent time visiting sculptors and herding cattle and remembering Gino. We lived peacefully until the Antemnates invaded the Roman kingdom.

Surrounding tribes were in such confusion that Gino's father insisted we stay. Everyone in Veii celebrated the invasion until we heard that Romulus had mounted a surprise counterattack. Zolia and I looked at each other, knowing history was repeating itself.

"Roman men are united by their orgy mentality," Zolia told her audience. Everyone except the sisters from Cures laughed.

Romulus had deployed the same strategy used against Caeninia to defeat and ravage the Antemnates. After victory, the Roman king would offer Spolia Opima to Jupiter. All kingdoms, including the Etruscans, feared Roma. It was Queen Hersilia who persuaded Romulus to forgive the captive women and their parents and allow them to live in Roma. Romulus's popularity waned but the queen continued to gain favor around the empire.

We knew Malocanis and Romulus sought to capture and destroy us. The king of rape had appointed a special cavalry of one hundred troops to find us. When our location was mysteriously leaked to Romulus, he promptly dispatched his special unit with Proculus at the head.

When the Romans surrounded Veii, the masked rapist approached the people. "We are here for two sisters from Cures, Zolia and Ronica," Proculus told Veii. "They are escaped prisoners of Roma. It is unlawful to shelter them."

The townspeople denied knowing us but, that night, Gino's father suggested we leave and guided us to the woods.

He gave us swords, bows, and arrows. Larthi provided bags of food and prayed that Gino's spirit would protect us.

Gino's father directed us to Nomentum and then to Allia, only a short distance from Cures. Our mission excited Zolia, but her leg injury caused us to rest frequently. With swords, bows, and quivers strapped to our backs, we looked like warriors from heaven who had been to Hell and back.

Romans were everywhere. For protection, we used camouflage and traveled at night. One night, four Roman horsemen passed so close that we thought Minerva had blinded them. After many days, we came to the outskirts of Nomentum and turned for home.

When we approached Cures, we realized our menstrual cycles were overdue. Our incessant hunger and vomiting left little doubt we carried unborn passengers. Our restless minds suffered in eerie silence.

In search of peace, Romulus had tried to establish a treaty with the Sabini. They rejected his offer. Anticipating an uprising, Roman guards patrolled the Sabini border, limiting our movements. We hid in the woods for a whole eight days.

Zolia refused to be pregnant but vomited every day. The truth infuriated her. Trying to abort, Sister chopped trees with her sword and jumped and rolled on the ground. At one point, she prepared to stab her stomach but I restrained her.

We were confused and dejected. Our food supply was exhausted and the path forward unclear. Should we return to our family or kill ourselves? Would our suitors accept us with Roman children? I prayed for advice. Our exhaustion and hunger pushed us toward home but it was an uneasy decision.

We carefully navigated to the town's perimeter. But before we approached the gates, we saw townspeople arguing in the town center. We cautiously hid behind trees, observing the debate.

Five women, including Ona, stood on a stage. Another sixty women were corralled to the side. We recognized Drusa from Antemnae, two more women from Sabinium, and one Caeninan woman whom we knew from the Roman latrine.

Apparently, the five women had escaped Roma but now faced some sort of trial. The other sixty women were separated and being treated as refugees, not heroines.

When I saw Father, I wanted to run to his arms but Sister pulled me back. "Stay still, Revolter! Listen! Something is wrong here. Wait and we will see what comes next."

One elder announced, "These two women are seven months pregnant. One is Sabine, the other Caeninan. They carry Roman babies that must be returned to Roma. The mothers are unwelcome in Cures."

"We cannot send them away," said another. "They escaped. Romans hunt them like dogs."

A third elder yelled, "Let these women stay. We will protect them. Once they give birth, we will kill the babies and keep the women."

To our bewilderment, the town accepted this insane plan. The people of Cures hated Romans and would kill their newborns rather than let them live. Father and a few other men argued, saying it was sinful to kill innocent babies. But the majority prevailed. The two women were taken into the town. When born, their newborns would die. Father stormed away and headed home.

The sixty refugees were allowed in the town. Knowing her baby faced certain death, Zolia turned and walked away from Cures. I called to her, but she kept moving. Sister did not intend to go home.

"We have been abused for so long," I said. "It is time to go home."

"Not like this, Ronica. Not to a town of baby-killers."

"Do you not want to live with Ovid and have a happy family?"

"Not with neighbors like this."

"But, Zolia, you tried to kill yourself and your baby," I said. "What has changed?"

"My baby is my baby, Ronica!" she screamed. "I can do what I want. No man will dictate terms to me again!"

Chapter 44: The Plan

"Zolia! Sometimes you are so confusing. What other surprises do you have?"

"Ronica, Roman men treated us like pigs. They abducted, raped, abused, and whipped us. No one came to save us. No gods, and no goddesses, acknowledged our torture. We escaped on our own.

"Now our townsmen want to kill innocent babies for no reason? We grew up with these people. Has the world gone crazy? Women are not men's playthings. We do not exist for men's egos. We are humans, equal to men. If we allow babies to be slaughtered, the future of women and motherhood will be in question. Ronica, our responsibility is to retaliate, not surrender."

"What can we do?"

"We will give birth to our babies and raise warriors who will gain our revenge by assassinating Proculus."

"Zolia! Where will we live? How will we raise two children? The Romans want us dead!" I cried.

"I know you love Gracian more than I love Ovid. It is difficult for you to take on a mission like this. There will be no hard feelings if you leave, Domus. Go, live a good life with your love. My decision is made."

Sister turned toward the deep woods, but I blocked the path. "Are you sure this is what you want, Zolia? Our home is here. We are women. We cannot fight men and win."

"You say this, Ronica? You, who scared the king of Roma? Where is your bravery? Keep your faith. The men inside our town, including our father, never came for us. When alone in a bad place, a woman must fight for herself."

I sat on the ground, pondering Sister's wisdom. No man, including my suitor, had come to our aid. They cared not what we suffered. Zolia and I survived because we protected each other. We were alone and now the demon's flesh and blood was in our bellies. How would we love these babies?

"I will always love you, but I have chosen my path, Ronica. When I triumph, I will return with the head of Proculus. Until then, take care, my sister." Zolia kissed me and walked away.

Chapter 45: The Wolf

A powerful force overwhelmed me. Zolia's need to punish Proculus on behalf of the raped women of the world had new clarity. I hated what the monster had done. We were restoring ourselves, physically and emotionally, but the scars ran deep.

Zolia was right. Abused women bore their burden alone and had to fight for themselves. We were not the first women to suffer and, unless we acted, we would not be the last. I turned my back on Cures and raced to catch the Crusader.

"Why does the Revolter follow me?" she asked.

"What can a Crusader do on one leg? Admit it. You need me," I teased.

"You dare call me crippled? Defend yourself!" We chased each other like children running in a field. Spent, we lay on the grass, drawing strength from each other.

Many questions faced us. Should we go over the mountains or across the sea? We pondered until the sound of hooves startled us and we scurried to conceal ourselves.

A dozen Romans suddenly surrounded us. "The sisters are somewhere near here," the leader commanded.

Had we been betrayed? Who saw us? As we contemplated

the possibilities, lightning from the gods erupted, distracting the bounty hunters.

We slid deeper into the forest until Zolia's feet slipped on wet moss, sending her crashing into a tree. I moved to her unconscious body and shouted to the gods that we would not fail, not be denied. We would fight for all women!

When Zolia stirred, I cradled her to my bosom.

"Salvé, Wolf," she mumbled. "Why do you stare?"

"Sister, are you delirious?"

"Are you the suckling mother of the king of rape?"

"Zolia, wake up! You are dreaming," I sobbed.

Zolia pointed behind me. "See the she-wolf, Revolter?"

I turned to see two radiant eyes beaming at me. A wolf walked toward us. I waved my sword.

"Stop, Revolter! This wolf is good," said Zolia. The wolf toothed a corner of Sister's tunic and tugged her to cover. The Crusader gave me a knowing smile.

As soon as Zolia recovered, the wolf led us deeper into the thick woods. At a cave the wanderer raised her head, emitting a howl to announce our arrival. We followed her into the cave and were surprised at its clean spaciousness. "Look, Ronica! This wolf is a savior from the gods." We spent the night comfortably cuddled to our savior.

The next morning a rabbit lay at my feet. I patted Wolf Sister's coat and she snuggled into my body. Zolia suggested we name her "Romula," but after a revelation from Minerva I suggested "Fe Lar." Zolia smiled her agreement.

Our isolated cave sat east of Cures and offered a freshwater stream that flowed down the rock-filled mountainside. There was work to do but this seemed a safe haven. We immediately busied ourselves fashioning pots and plates from wood and stone. We carved water vessels and crafted a small bed for our new sister, who preferred cuddling between us.

My time spent learning from Mother helped us survive. I tanned animal furs and tied pieces with strips of bark for clothes. Zolia learned a few domus duties and our cave began to feel like home. We were nervously content.

Our challenge was harvesting food and water. Fe Lar helped but we sought bigger game, like deer and boar. When we made a kill, we cleaned, cooked, and gave thanks to the gods. Whenever we ate, we shared with our new sister.

We guessed we were six months pregnant. I prayed for healthy babies but it was clear that Zolia ignored her faith. I hoped it was temporary.

As a diligent sentry, Fe Lar warned us when there was activity. At the slightest risk, she would bite our tunics and tug. We gradually learned to communicate with our sister. Zolia fretted that Fe Lar had no friends, another trait we shared.

The spirit of Remus revisited me. I knew Malocanis was offering rewards to bounty hunters. In the battle between good and evil that now characterized our existence, Minerva seemed to have an edge but I worried that Sister was growing complacent. I should have known better. I often thought the Crusader a goddess in her own right. Like Fe Lar, Sister was fearless and comfortable in the forest.

Meanwhile, our babies kicked and moved inside us. The children reminded us of our humanity. We put our ears on each other's stomachs and listened intently, all the while longing to know the sexes of our unborn, nameless children.

With winter, new challenges arrived. Dark days and cold nights made it difficult to be outside. We stoked our fire and cuddled close, awaiting our deliveries.

One night, Fe Lar warned us something was afoot. When we moved near the entrance, we heard voices. "This is where Romulus said to search for the whores," said a soldier.

"How can he know?" another soldier asked. "There is cover everywhere. One quick look and we are away."

While the Romans searched a nearby cave, we quickly gathered weapons and snuck into the woods – and just in time, for the soldiers found our own cave where the pots, vessels, food, and bed would give us away.

We sank down behind a large rock until Fe Lar returned – and with her were a few other outcast wolves. When Fe Lar led her pack inside the cave and faced the troops, the wolves acted like the cave was their den.

When Fe Lar snatched a plate from one Roman's hands, the soldier said, "These wolves are related to Soranus. They steal entrails and goods from people to give to Hirpi Sorani, the god of Hell. If we bother them, we will be cursed. There's nothing for Romulus here." Assuming they had stumbled into a den of wolves that pilfered from humans, the Romans scurried away.

After the Romans left, one wolf lingered, rubbing against our sister. We watched as they licked each other's faces and danced. When Fe Lar returned to us, Zolia said, "She-wolf, you tricked the Romans. I like your cunning!"

But Fe Lar dropped two acorns at my feet, signaling that we must relocate. When the soldiers told the king what they had seen, Malocanis would want to inspect the items in the cave. If the witch touched the goods, she would connect them to us. We packed what we could and burned the rest before moving on.

Fe Lar led us several leagues away to another remote cave. We built a fire, lay on the dirt, and slept for great lengths at a time. When we awoke, Fe Lar seemed uneasy but we were settled. Situated between two narrow rock ridges, the opening to the cave was nearly invisible. Our new cave seemed safer than the old.

Almost immediately, our labor pains became sharper. Our days were filled with boosting our inventory of water and bemoaning our unborn packages. Wolf Sister proved an accomplished small-game hunter and brought us food. I cooked and the three of us shared meals without complaining.

* * * * * *

Chapter 46: The Irony

Zolia kept teasing about the gods putting us in such a perilous situation. "Do you remember when the priest at Mount Soracte cursed me and said wolves would tear my body to pieces? Now, a wolf saves us.

"Ronica, can you see there are no gods? Man invented gods, and priests perpetuate religion for their own survival. They are too lazy to do real work so they bully good people in the name of false gods."

My pain was too intense to debate. When my water broke, Zolia slid an animal skin under me for comfort. Sister knew nothing about delivering a child and I had little experience. I was afraid to push, afraid to hold. The pain kept rising until I wanted to explode.

Fe Lar understood our ignorance. With each contraction, the wolf placed her paw on my stomach and pushed, shifting the heaviness inside me. Fe Lar directed Zolia to reposition my body to an upright position with my head above my hips.

"Stop, wolf!" I said. "I cannot sit with this boulder in my stomach."

Zolia raised my upper body so I could rest against her and the pressure moved lower. I panted like a boar. Fe Lar dropped her head to watch between my legs. She placed her paws under my bottom and lifted. I placed my faith in her.

"Fe Lar will deliver the baby!" yelled Zolia. I screamed, grunted, groaned, and pushed so hard I thought my life would end. But no baby arrived. Fe Lar lifted for one final push. My insides ripped apart.

Wolf Sister crawled forward, licking the baby's head. "Good Ronica! Fe Lar sees the head. Push hard. Get this baby out!"

"I am done. No more pushing…"

"Pretend Romans are here. Push, Ronica. Push!"

I envisioned Roman faces and the horror of Proculus. My exhaustion disappeared, allowing a final thrust. My baby entered the world peacefully. I gasped and sobbed, nearly passing out.

Zolia laid me down and went to help Fe Lar. The baby was covered in bloody juices. Zolia's hands trembled. "Ronica, my wonderful domus, your baby is born." She stared at me. "What now?"

"Slap the baby, Zolia," I whispered.

Sister rendered gentle slaps until the baby cried. My baby was born at the time of year when spring was becoming summer. Fe Lar helped Zolia clean the newborn. Then Zolia cuddled the child and settled against the wall, next to me.

But when I awoke, Zolia was hysterical. "Ronica, what should I do with the baby's cord?"

"Cut and tie, Sister. Cut and tie." I said. "Do I have a boy or a girl?"

"You have a girl, beautiful like her mother." Zolia tried to be brave, but could not cut the cord. Her queasiness made me wonder if she was in labor.

"Bring me the child." Zolia held the baby close. I cut her cord, finishing it with sinew from a rabbit. My daughter's tender lips found my breast. Her determined sucking was curiously blissful and gave purpose to my filled breasts. Her innocent face calmed me. Unable to hold a surge of unidentified emotions, I sobbed through her entire feeding.

Two days later, Zolia's pains peaked. I was still recovering, so Fe Lar took the initiative. I wrapped my daughter and placed her in the corner for Wolf Sister to guard. Grabbing two pots, I set out for the stream.

My weakness and the dark made the woods treacherous. The stream seemed an eternity away but I filled the vessels and headed back. As I neared the cave, I heard cries from Zolia's newborn and rushed into the cave.

The baby lay on an animal skin, still connected by the cord. Most of the blood had been licked away. Zolia slept, oblivious to the baby's cries. The wolf hopped happily around the cave. I cut the cord, tied it tightly, and cloaked the boy in a fur.

He immediately sucked his fist. I nestled her son next to Zolia and moved to feed my baby. When Zolia awoke, she ignored the infant's cries. When Zolia turned her back, I barked for Sister to feed her baby.

"Is it a girl?" she asked.

"It is a boy."

"Who does he look like?"

"Zolia, he looks like his father," I answered, handing her the baby. "The child is hungry, Sister. Feed him."

Zolia pushed the boy away, refusing to acknowledge him. I placed the baby next to his cousin. Fe Lar barked and growled at Sister.

"Zolia, your son will die unless you feed him. He has already waited too long. This is why we are born! Will you act like the townspeople we left behind?"

"Are you threatening me?"

Zolia's ability to remove herself from reality had become infuriating. "Sister, even Fe Lar knows what you are doing is sinful. I will not stand by and watch this baby die. I am leaving for Cures." I lifted my daughter and headed out.

"Does my sister leave me with a wolf? You cannot betray me. Our plan is to kill Proculus!" Zolia's obsession never relaxed.

"If I stay, you must agree to feed your baby every time he is hungry. Without your son, how will we kill the rapist?"

She looked down at the boy, resolutely lifted him, and rewarded him her teat. The boy drank everything he could. After a few burps, he was comfortably full and closed his eyes.

From that day forward, when it was time to feed her son, I kicked Zolia's leg or tapped her arm to remind her. Fe Lar witnessed her stubbornness with undisguised disgust. When the boy cried, Wolf Sister tugged Zolia's tunic to ensure she paid attention.

Fe Lar often played with the boy. They enjoyed their time together. I came to worry that the boy would regard the wolf as his mother, for Sister rarely spoke and cried most of the time.

One day, Zolia's unpredictability surprised us yet again when she cheerfully addressed her baby. "Salvé, boy. How are you?"

Startled, Fe Lar stopped playing with the child and gave me a curious look.

"Why do my sisters mock me? I am mother!"

Later, I moved behind Sister and touched her hair. "What does my sister do?" she asked.

"I check the Crusader's hair. It grows well."

"You no longer care about me," said Zolia.

"That is not true, Sister," I reassured her.

"I do not know a better person in this world," Zolia said. "When you said you were leaving for Cures, my heart was broken."

"You need inspiration to love your son. I shall never be away," I volunteered, kissing Zolia's cheek.

＊ ＊ ＊ ＊ ✿ ＊

Chapter 47: The Children

"Eat and defecate." That is all our babies knew. Whenever they did either, they smiled.

Zolia afforded my daughter more affection than her son. In turn, I showered attention on her son, whose eerie resemblance to his father was sometimes disturbing. The more I observed him, the more I saw that he shared many of Sister's mannerisms that drew me to him.

We believed our cave was near Ameria. During the day, we stayed close. When spring brought fresh air, we celebrated. During the next year, we realized many times over that we were neither prepared nor equipped to raise infant children. Fe Lar often scolded and guided us.

As if to deny our attachment, we stalled naming the children. Eventually, when we could put it off no longer, I chose Vittoria. Sister had rejected every name I proposed for her son but when I suggested Silvestro, she hesitated. Seeing an opening, I said her son must be named either Silvestro or Proculus.

Following Sabine custom, I whispered "Vittoria" three times in my daughter's ear. When she giggled back, it was a good sign. When Zolia sternly whispered "Silvestro" to her son, the boy stared back at her, looking unerringly like his father. But, when I endearingly whispered, he laughed happily.

"See, he likes you more," Zolia said.

"No, Sister. Silvestro is sensitive. If you are kind, he will smile at you." The next day, when Sister called his name with affection, the boy smiled and grabbed her face and hair. But when Zolia was stern, Silvestro became hysterical.

The Crusader was more naive than me, but sometimes her ignorance was intolerable. Fe Lar became impatient with Zolia's ineptitude and chose to ignore her blunders.

Despite our weak parenting skills, the children progressed and soon mimicked sounds and words. They inspired each other and their babbling voices became music. Zolia sometimes said Silvestro sounded like his father. I warned her to stop saying such things, for fear the children might remember her slights.

Time passed. When the children were three, our love for them dimmed my hatred for Roma. Sister reminded me of a warrior coaching trainees. She tended to be strict and unforgiving, so I managed the children.

Our parenting was different. My role was to offset her strictness. I loved Silvestro and the boy reciprocated. He endured his mother's moodiness by turning to me. When Vittoria made a mistake, Silvestro assumed the blame. Their bond reminded me of the bond between their mothers.

Chapter 48: Fe Lar

Silvestro looked princely riding on Fe Lar's back and roaming the woods. One day Fe Lar stumbled, tossing her passenger to the ground. When we tried to help, we discovered her pregnancy.

"Salvé, Wolf Sister," Zolia said. "Do you know the father? Or are you Roman and bend yourself to all wolves in the forest?"

When Fe Lar howled her protest, Sister laughed. "You are a good wolf, Fe Lar. Tell us if the father is the wolf you rubbed against at the old cave?" Wolf Sister howled affirmatively.

Now was our time to care for our pregnant sister. We fed her, took over her chores, and heeded her every need. When her time came, Fe Lar birthed four whelps, three of which were males. Black circles and spots distinguished their faces but it was six months before we could tell the cubs apart.

The children loved the whelps. We named the males Polus, Silex, and Telum, and the female Luna.

As we counted the days scratched on the cave's walls, we knew the children were four years old. We were safe, the children were growing, and we had found degrees of peace in our work.

Chapter 49: Proculus

Silvestro loved swimming in a pond near the cave. Vittoria was not as brave but enjoyed wading. One day, while watching the children, we heard horsemen. Zolia, Vittoria, and I hid under an overgrown bush while Zolia frantically signaled the innocent Silvestro to dive under the water.

Twenty cavalrymen were led by Proculus. The mere sight of the monster sent shivers through us. Zolia showed Vittoria the monster's disgusting face but withheld any explanation.

I could see that Vittoria was wondering about this. "Who is the ugly man?" she whispered.

"The worst sinner on earth. The destroyer of our family."

Meanwhile, Silvestro stayed under the water holding his breath. I turned to Zolia, who pointed an arrow at Proculus. I pushed her bow down, reminding her that Vittoria and Silvestro would slay the rapist.

"My son will drown!" Zolia realized.

The rapist led his mount to the pond's edge for water. The monster's horse drank slowly. Without realizing it, father and son shared the same water. Then, much too slowly, Proculus turned and left.

Submergence

We quickly swam to Silvestro, who surfaced gasping for air. Zolia and I led him to land. Zolia wiped his face. "How did you hold your breath so long? You could have killed yourself!"

"My mother said to stay underwater. I obey the Crusader," he said, and Zolia sighed.

Sister doted on her warrior cub for many cycles of the moon. We constantly reminded Vittoria about the monster. Like us, she came to hate her father.

We never disclosed our plan that the children kill their father. Silvestro was distracted, and kept dwelling on how long he had stayed underwater and insisting he had not seen the monster's face. Zolia's narrow patience wore thin when he avoided the point of her exercise. Sister feared fate would prevent Proculus from being slain by his own seed. She often vented her frustration on Silvestro, scolding the boy unnecessarily.

As I witnessed their maturation, I saw that Silvestro was more disciplined than Vittoria and needed shielding from Zolia's uneven parenting.

Chapter 50: Silvestro

When the children turned five, Silex and Telum decided to leave. Polus and Luna would stay but we were sad, and in our quiet moments shared concerns about the day our cubs would leave.

One afternoon, Zolia and Vittoria went hunting while I stayed to cook. Silvestro played with Fe Lar.

"Fe Lar, are you sad because your sons left?" he asked. Fe Lar put her nose to his face. "I know you care for your whelps," he said, patting her.

The wolf lay down and Silvestro rested his head on her belly. "I would be happy if you were my mother, for Zolia does not like me. Will you be my mother, Fe Lar?" Wolf Sister howled approval. "I would happily sleep on your belly rather than with my mother."

The boy's conversation pulled my heart. Zolia had to know of Silvestro's feelings. When Sister and Vittoria returned, I sent the children for wood so we could talk mother-to-mother. Sitting on a stone outside the cave, I lunged at Zolia as my frustrations with her mothering spewed out. She pushed me back and we rolled off the rock where she held me down.

"Why does the Revolter attack the Crusader?"

Abandonment

"Your scolding hurts Silvestro."

"This is about Silvestro? Why? Did he complain?"

I relayed what I had heard. Zolia neither responded nor reacted. I refused to speak with her. That night I slept with Vittoria and Silvestro, leaving Sister to herself. After a few days, Zolia became vacant and melancholy. During daylight she went to the woods and stayed until sunset. When Sister returned, she was silent.

One night, I rubbed her hands and touched her hair. "What are you doing?" she asked shrilly.

"Where is my sister's kindest heart?"

"I cannot believe you let Silvestro come between us."

My guilt overwhelmed me. What had prompted me to interfere?

Zolia turned serious and asked why I loved Silvestro and she did not. She wondered if my sex with Proculus had somehow created a soft spot for the little children.

"I have a soft spot for Silvestro, just as I do for Vittoria. So should you. Their father is a monster but the children are innocent. Do not blame them for the dastardly acts of Malocanis, Romulus, or the pirate rapist. We survived. These children are our reward. They deserve our love."

Zolia considered my answer and said she wanted to rebuild her relationship with Silvestro. She stood up, woke the boy, and took him outside under the moon. The dancer pointed to the sky. Zolia put Silvestro's feet on hers and began dancing in the moonlight.

The commotion awakened Vittoria. We sat next to each other, watching the motherhood melodrama unfold.

The boy was alight with joy. Sister was determined to teach Silvestro to dance and fight in her image. She hoisted him on her shoulders and told him to raise his hands to the heavens. Then she performed the dance she used to honor the gods.

Vittoria watched enthusiastically. I remembered when Sister was the best dancer on earth. Vittoria asked me to dance. I knew she liked what she saw. "No. I was once a painter, but never a dancer," I laughed.

"Tonight, my son, I am happy," Zolia said. "Did you enjoy dancing with your mother?"

The child wanted everything Zolia could give. "Yes!" he declared.

Zolia spun on her toe, moving her hands in every direction and spreading her fingers to draw flowers as she floated across the ground. The three of us wondered at her inspiration. She jumped like a deer and bent her body back and forth, touching her head to the ground. While she danced, she moved away from the cave and went high up the hill.

We followed her like bees following a trail of honey. Fe Lar and her pups stayed at our heels. The wolves made strange noises but watched intently as Zolia climbed to the edge of the rock.

Chapter 51: Zolia's Prophecy

"With my dance, the earth stands still."

The children looked at me, wondering what was happening. "That is Mother Zolia!"

Sister lifted herself and balanced on her toe. The Crusader was completely immersed in her dance, her mind elsewhere.

Hanging on the edge of the cliff, Zolia proclaimed, "I see you all! Romans, Sabini, Greeks, Etruscans, Faliscans, everyone. Hear my prophecy!

"In the name of gods, male egos, society, festivals, culture, heritage, nations, and kingdoms, you have suppressed the innocent ones of the earth long enough! You have crushed children under your feet, fed helpless women with wrath, and disrespected good men! Today, Minerva's dance killed all false gods!

"A thousand gods will rise up in the future. A boy will become the king of all gods! He will burn the gods of all ages to Hell! He will be my creation to appear in the future and remove the evil ones from the sky, moon, stars, and earth! I will name him Oscár! My divine god will save the world from misery, and give us strength to avenge the abuse we received from men like Proculus!"

Prophecy

After proclaiming the prophecy to the heavens and all earthly nations, Zolia looked to the skies and inhaled bliss as the wind blew against her tunic. I was unclear about her inner message, but she looked every bit an angel.

When Zolia stepped down from the cliff, Silvestro took his mother's hand and put his face in her palm. We returned to our cave filled with Zolia's prophecy.

Chapter 52: Training Days

When we awoke, the children were excited to dance; but Sister had other plans. "Your lives have a special purpose, my son and daughter. Remember the man with the mask? He is the enemy who destroyed our families. You will avenge us by killing him and bringing his head here. Today, your training begins."

Silvestro was eager to start. "Yes, Mother. We will do as you say and bring the demon's head to you."

"Why did he kill our family?" Vittoria asked.

"If you practice well, you will learn the answer." Pointing to Vittoria, Sister added, "Since you are two days older than Silvestro, you will captain this team."

Vittoria smiled. "I am the leader. Listen to me, little boy."

Silvestro slapped his forehead. "Mother! Vittoria may be older, but I am bigger and stronger!"

"Listen to your sister, my son. Women can lead as well as men," the mentor spoke.

Zolia flashed the rapist's dagger so her warriors could see. She stressed that this was the weapon that would behead the monster. However, the special dagger was not a toy, not for practice. Their first assignment was to shape flat-tipped wooden swords for learning.

Malediction

While she taught our warriors, Zolia resembled Uncle Neiro when she said, "Never defend. Attack. Always press the attack!" Silvestro's hands were strong, but Vittoria's smaller, weaker hands caused her to drop her weapon. Yet the girl was tenacious, like Zolia.

The children trained for an entire morning every day. Their normal play had given way to training. The harder they worked, the closer they bonded, just as their mothers had respected each other's talents. When they were fatigued, we massaged their bodies until they were restored.

"Why do losers rate a massage?" Silvestro goaded Vittoria. "She should massage me!" As the team frolicked on the ground, we laughed, enjoying our cubs.

With her mentoring, Zolia's parenting changed. She became more teacher than parent. Her frustration often showed. While she pardoned Vittoria for learning slowly, the bar was raised for Silvestro. I comforted and encouraged the boy. He quickly corrected his mistakes but at his age, the boy needed her love as much as her training.

When the children turned seven, Fe Lar was noticeably older and grayer. Her pups cared for her. Once her ally, nature now challenged our Wolf Sister.

One day, we decided to relax in the insect and snake-ridden overgrown woods of Spoletium, where the occasional meadows were lush with tall, green grasses. We enjoyed the freedom here and decided to spend a few days camping. Silvestro and Vittoria played in the woods while Polus, Luna, and Fe Lar played near us.

As the three mothers dozed in the afternoon sun, we were interrupted by Vittoria's cries for help. Zolia grabbed a bow and quiver and I carried my sword as we ran to our daughter.

"Is it Romans, Vittoria?" Zolia asked.

When Vittoria came into sight, she pointed to Silvestro. He was mired in quicksand and half his body was under the mud. Zolia extended the bow as the wolves nervously circled the sand, barking loudly. The more Silvestro struggled, the faster he sank. He could not reach Zolia's bow.

I tried cutting roots from a tree, but they were too thick. Time was evaporating. The sand was up to our son's neck. Vittoria held Sister's feet as Zolia stretched as far as she could.

"Mother, I love you. Train Vittoria well. She will kill the monster!" yelled Silvestro.

"No, Silvestro! You will not die," Zolia screamed.

It seemed hopeless. I prayed to Minerva. Fe Lar kissed her young wolves and charged the pit, leaping far into the quicksand. She clenched Silvestro's shoulder with her jaws and extended her tail to Zolia.

"Grab her tail, Mother Zolia!" Vittoria shouted.

Zolia cast the bow aside and caught Fe Lar's tail, pulling with all her strength. Silvestro slowly rose. Fe Lar's bite hurt but Silvestro stayed quiet.

I pulled Zolia back. She let go of the wolf's tail and we dragged Silvestro to land. Minerva had saved Silvestro, but Fe Lar was at risk. When she twisted to give Silvestro a final shove toward his mother, she could not recover.

Our savior was sinking before our eyes. Realizing his best friend was drowning, Silvestro cried out. The young wolves

Sacrifice

frantically circled the quicksand. Fe Lar signaled her life was ending and told her cubs to guard us. Having saved her pupil, our wolf was spirited away, her life's purpose fulfilled.

Silvestro was bleeding and covered in mud. He would not allow anyone to clean him and refused to eat for days. Our boy was drowning in misery, mourning the loss of our shepherd and blaming himself for her loss. The boy knelt, praying for forgiveness, and Zolia saw that her son had a good heart. She vowed that he would achieve his goals.

Chapter 53: Grave Digger

Polus and Luna became our guardians. They were well taught and understood the ways of the forest. As our routine returned, Silvestro and Vittoria practiced swordsmanship near the riverbank. When they grew tired, they rested on the sand. "There are demons under this sand," Vittoria told her brother.

"Why do you say that?" Silvestro asked.

"If you dig, you will see," Vittoria said.

The children dug with their swords. We laughed until Vittoria stopped and Silvestro continued excavating a longer and deeper pit.

"You dig well, Silvestro," Vittoria said. "You should probably dig graves and bury dead animals in the forest."

Zolia froze momentarily. Then she jumped up, ran to the boy, and slapped him. "Never dig graves! No more of this, ever!"

Frightened, Vittoria ran to me. I knew Sister suffered from images of Proculus digging graves. I tried to calm her, but she pushed me away and kept scolding the unknowing boy. Once again, Silvestro was trapped in the dark world between hate and love. Only Minerva could save him.

Silvestro stayed clear of Zolia for days. I stayed friendly to him, but the boy became depressed and talked idly with Polus and Luna.

"Are you all right, my son?" I finally asked.

"Mother Ronica, I should have died before I was born," he agonized.

"Never say that! You are a gift, Silvestro." Tears covered the boy's face. I kissed his forehead, saying, "Please. Tell me what bothers you."

"I never make Mother happy. I do everything she asks, but sometimes she seems to hate me. I do not know why our god saved me in the quicksand. Being dead would be better than living like this."

"Am I fair to you, Silvestro?"

"Yes, but you are not my mother."

"Come with me. We will tell your mother we are leaving her."

I led him to the cave to confront my sister, who chatted with Vittoria. I took a child's hand in each of mine. "Sister, the three of us are leaving you. Silvestro is coming with us!"

"No, Ronica. You promised you would see this through," Zolia argued.

"I will train the children!" I raged.

"What is this? Silvestro, what did you say to Mother Ronica?"

"Nothing." The boy shook his head.

Zolia and I disagreed so we decided to leave the decision to Silvestro, who was trapped between his mothers – two snarling cats. I was surprised when he moved to his mother and hugged her. "I will stay with you, Mother. We will kill Proculus."

"You see, Sister? My son loves me! He will stay with me."

Silvestro's decision affirmed that nothing could break

the bond between mother and son. After this, Zolia kept Silvestro close by her side and stopped communicating with me, making life in the cave impossible. When I was near, she showered affection on Silvestro. At night, she told him stories and made him laugh.

But when his mother was away, Silvestro would kiss me on the cheek saying, "I love you, Mother Ronica."

Vittoria knew Zolia's moods. "I wonder how long before she spanks you again," she chided. Silvestro shrugged and smiled.

I quietly tolerated Zolia and happiness returned to our cave. One night, Zolia kicked me with the force of a mule. When I ignored her, she kicked again. I warned her to stop. After a few moments, she unleashed a powerful dancer's kick. I turned and saw she had moved Silvestro from her side. "Come near me, Revolter."

Her voice melted my stubbornness. I moved closer. She grabbed my hand and placed it on her head. Instinctively, I stroked her hair and tickled her ear.

"What are you doing?" she asked.

"I am checking your hard head and ear problem."

"Do you call me deaf?"

"If you were deaf, you would not know to answer, would you?"

A good-natured smile lit up her face. I kissed her eyes and Zolia sobbed apologetically. She asked me to promise I would never take Silvestro from her. She said I could be his protector. Her confidence in me was higher than the mountains. Zolia promised to control her emotions and handle Silvestro with motherly love. We had crossed another bridge.

Chapter 54: Bonding

By age ten Silvestro was tall, like his father. Vittoria was also tall with a precious face and spirit. Both children practiced diligently. They shot arrows, handled swords, and worked with knives. Vittoria was a skilled marksman. Silvestro was mastering the sword and improving his archery skills. They hunted wild turkeys and deer in the woods. Silvestro always kept a knife in his belt, even in his sleep. The boy was a risk-taker.

One day, Vittoria planned a game that called for Silvestro to tie one hand behind his back and duel her. The fight would take place on the rock, forty feet high above the base. With his hand tied, Silvestro took his position on the edge of the stone. Like Zolia's dance, he balanced on one leg. "I am the son of Mother Zolia," he said. "Nobody can defeat me!"

Zolia and I laughed and were about to tell him to step down when the wind disrupted his balance and knocked him to the ground below. We ran to the boy, but he lay unconscious, unbreathing. I shook his body and jolted him by pressing his chest to revive his heartbeat.

"Minerva, please!" I cried.

Zolia tried resuscitating him but nothing worked. She thumped his chest. "You are my son. Nothing can kill you. Wake up, Silvestro!"

The boy blinked and regained consciousness. Zolia took him to her breast. "No more practice! Just stay with your mother."

Vittoria and I cleaned and wrapped his head with herbs and medicine. While motherhood tugged at Zolia, I wondered if she realized Minerva had favored us.

Zolia kept Silvestro close for a month. He touched neither his sword nor his bow and Sister removed the knife from his belt. He was under his mother's protection. The fall had defined their bond.

When I joked whether he still felt he would rather die than live with his mother, he answered, "When I was unconscious, chains held me down. A mysterious white spirit left my body. A voice asked if I wanted to live or die. I pulled the white spirit back into my body and declared, 'I want to live long with Mother!' When Mother banged my chest, the chains loosened. I was reborn."

Silvestro had passed through the realm of sorrow. I saw this but stayed silent.

After a month, Silvestro reattached his belt and knife. Zolia fussed but the boy was adamant. He wanted to practice the sword. "If I do not kill the monster, he will hurt more people. I must practice."

His genuineness impressed Zolia and she permitted him to resume practice, as long as he promised not to be foolhardy.

Initially the children did not bother us with questions about the masked man or Roma. As their practice intensified, they pressed for the reasons behind their mission. Before long, they asked why the Romans and Proculus had killed our family. We answered they would know in time. I knew Zolia was fabricating a wild story.

Chapter 55: Sixteen

By sixteen, Silvestro was as tall as his father. Vittoria's beauty was disarming and impossible to overlook. Her skin was as natural as the fruit we ate. Her figure was full and tight, her hair pure as gold.

The boy had grown wiser and no longer allowed his mother to intimidate him. When Sister was out of sorts, Silvestro would rattle her by saying he would not kill Proculus unless she softened. Like her son, Zolia had matured and was more relaxed. Sister was a young, desirable woman whose shape benefitted from our Spartan existence.

When Silvestro and Vittoria asked about Roma, I deferred to Sister, who was an imaginative, believable storyteller. One afternoon, while Zolia sat tapping her leg, the children persisted with unbearable inquisitiveness.

Zolia leaned against a shade tree. "It is a sad story," she began. "And one that is emotional. But, because you persist, I shall explain why Romans cannot be trusted." Sister crossed her legs and folded her hands in her lap.

"When we lived happily in Cures, Ronica was married to Gracian and I was wife to Ovid. Those of our family were merchants who sold gold and pearl jewelry. We were respected throughout Sabinium. Greeks and Africans came to trade with us. We lived well.

"Of course, the Romans heard about us and invited us to trade. They requested we bring our finest jewelry.

"The situation in Roma was bad. Our neighbors regarded Romans as thieves and bandits. Nobody favored them.

"But we were merchants. Our job was to trade. Business was business. We did not discriminate. We saw opportunity and decided to visit the new city. People of Cures warned us, but we stood by our decision.

"We packed carts with wares, hitched mules and horses, and left for Roma. You children were newborn. Our husbands, mother, father, nieces, nephews, and loyal servants made the trip.

"Our expectations were high and the journey exciting. On the road, we laughed and made easy conversation. Romans welcomed us and the Roman king's friend, Proculus Maxim, was assigned to guide us around the city.

"Our father displayed his finest jewelry. Roman shoppers wanted to buy our pearls and gold, but they lacked sufficient funds. In trade, they gave us their finest gems. We stayed for three days before returning home.

"Late one evening, there were noises in the woods. Father hurried to investigate and was confronted by a column led by Proculus. The demon grabbed a spear and slew our unarmed father, your grandfather.

"The soldiers rushed from the woods, attacked our home, and stole our jewels. Our husbands ordered us to flee to the woods. We rushed away and hid, watching murderous Romans circle our family.

"You are thieves and murderers!" Gracian said. "You have deceived us!"

"Yes! We are thieves and murderers," laughed Proculus.

Sister allowed the treachery to sink in to our young warriors. They absorbed every word and their anger showed.

"Our family offered all our jewels for the Romans to leave. Proculus planned to kill everyone, take everything, and blame robbers. The Romans outnumbered our husbands and servants. Soon everyone we loved was dead.

"Mother stood, shielding our nieces and nephews, and faced Proculus. He slit her throat and butchered our nieces and nephews. The Romans stole our possessions and celebrated the blood bath by drinking our wine.

"Soon Proculus realized two women and their infants were missing. The soldiers mounted horses and set out searching for us. But we had not waited and, with you in our arms, we ran like the wind deep into the woods.

"Along the way, I tripped, broke my leg, and gashed my head. You see, it was the Romans and Proculus who crippled me and caused my hard hearing.

"We hid in the woods for days before returning to the scene of the devastation. Vultures and foxes were still eating the corpses. Fe Lar stood off to the side, imagining the fight. She refused to touch the bodies. Seeing our misery, she drove the scavengers away and helped gather the remains for burial.

"While we worked, we noticed a dagger near our burned home. I remembered that Proculus had boasted about it when we were in Roma. I took the dagger and vowed to keep it safe so one day it could be used to avenge our family.

"After we buried the bodies, we had no place to live. Fe Lar led us to the cave and brought us food so we could tend to you. She became our companion.

"We knew we were in disfavor in Cures because we had gone to Roma in the first place. The Sabini are strict. We had no allies. Our only choice was to train you to kill Proculus, the murderer who slew our families."

Zolia's account disturbed the children. Silvestro and Vittoria cried and knelt before Zolia, promising to kill Proculus. Zolia kept her eyes focused on me, warning me not to counter her tale. Instead, I calmed the children by taking them in my arms.

I found myself justifying Sister's story because Proculus and Roma had committed so many crimes. Roma was filled with murderers, thieves, rapists, and sadists who followed Romulus, the king of rape.

Chapter 56: Axia

Sister's tale motivated the children to raise their fighting skills. They often stayed in the woods by themselves, leaving home in the morning and returning around sunset. They had learned to eat off the land and grew comfortable away from the cave.

One hunting day, the forest was dark and thick and no game was found. The children went deeper into the forest, where they sighted a target. The cover denied Vittoria a clear shot so they waited for the boar to come closer.

A twig snapped! Someone was there, in the bush.

Vittoria spotted the intruder and fired two arrows. When a woman's voice screamed surprise, the children rushed and found a young girl whose tunic was pinned to a tree by one of the arrows. She was trapped but unhurt.

When Silvestro raised his sword, the girl shouted, "Stop! Do not kill me!"

"Why are you here? Are you lost?" he demanded.

"This is my home. This is all I have. Let me go, I beg you."

Vittoria removed her arrow and faced a pretty girl who looked their age and had an endearing presence. She had been hunting the same boar and was unaware our young were in the woods.

After their kill, they roasted the meat and shared a meal. We were far from their thoughts. They talked like adults and learned about each other.

Axia was from Antemnae, which had lost its war against the Romans. Her mother had been pregnant when her father died in the battle. Three years after Axia was born, the victors wanted the Antemnae to move to Roma. The girl's mother hated Romans and wanted no part of the empire. She fled to the woods with her daughter.

"Did the Romans rob your family of all their possessions?" Vittoria asked.

"Yes," said Axia. "They stole our wealth and treated us like slaves."

"Thieving Romans rob everybody," Vittoria said.

"Where is your mother?" Silvestro asked.

"The harshness of life in the woods took her life. I think I was eight when I buried her. I have lived alone ever since."

The children sympathized with Axia and pledged their friendship.

"Would you like to see my home?" Axia asked.

"Definitely," Silvestro answered.

Axia led them to a secluded hut covered with thatch. Along the way, she asked why they lived in the forest. They told her Zolia's story but withheld the name of Proculus and their plan to kill him.

Silvestro and Vittoria rightfully feared how we might react to Axia and chose not to bring her to us. She was their secret. The threesome agreed to meet often.

Unbeknownst to us, their rendezvous went on for two years before Silvestro asked, "Mother, do you think we are alone in this forest?"

My senses rose. "There are animals, birds, trees, and insects," Zolia replied. "Nothing else. Why?"

"I wonder if other humans live in the forest?"

"Have you seen Romans?" Zolia demanded.

"No, no Romans are here. But maybe there are others who have been affected by Romans," Vittoria suggested.

Something was wrong. "Why, children? Did you meet somebody?"

"We would tell you if we saw anyone, Mother Ronica," Silvestro said.

"If you see anyone in this forest, run and hide. Never trust anyone. We have no friends here. Roman spies are everywhere," Zolia reminded them.

"We are always cautious. We never met anyone. Sometimes life in the forest is lonely. We just wondered," explained Vittoria.

Their questions raised more questions. My head spun with possibilities. I knew the children worried about Zolia's concerns.

The next time they met Axia, they questioned her.

"If I were a spy," Axia stated, "you would already be dead. You two are terrible liars. Why do you not take me to your home? What do you hide?"

Axia pouted. "If you do not trust me, I cannot be your friend."

As the girl walked away, Silvestro and Vittoria apologized. Axia continued to sulk until our children told her everything. She was quickly drawn to their mission and wanted to join them, but our children insisted Proculus must die at their hands.

Silvestro had no choice but to fall in love with Axia. When he turned twenty, he bravely kissed her. Unfortunately, Vittoria witnessed their embrace and teased him unmercifully.

One morning, when they thought they were alone, I overheard the teasing. I let them know I was there and threatened to inform Zolia of their secret. Their confession dropped like a leaf from a tree.

Their secrets and Silvestro's romance were music to my ears, but both children begged me not to tell Zolia. I promised their secret was safe but I insisted upon meeting Axia.

Because the girl lived near Fulginium, we had to arrange a secret meeting closer to the cave. I made an excuse to Zolia and hurried to meet Axia.

I was impressed by her independent, self-sufficient beauty. Her smile was comforting, her speech polite, and her figure firm. I endorsed the girl and told Silvestro that, after he avenged Proculus, they could marry.

Zolia stayed focused on Silvestro's final training. He was asked to cut down a pine tree in five strokes. Silvestro spent six months building strength and technique and, at last, he proudly succeeded in cutting the pine tree in five strokes.

Then Zolia challenged him to cut a similar tree in four strokes. "What difference can it make, four strokes or five?" he asked.

"Obey your teacher!" she commanded.

Silvestro knew better than to argue and began working on another tree.

His palms became rough as bark. When he stroked Axia's silky face, she was aware of his strength and imposing manhood. As a young warrior, we did not question him when he stayed away at night more often than he stayed home. I suspected he enjoyed Axia in the moonlight, watching stars and singing poetry to her, but I kept my promise.

Occasionally he shared his poems with me. In some ways the boy reminded me of Gracian.

When Zolia objected to his nights away from home, he tried to please her by sneaking out late and returning before sunrise. I saw that Vittoria became lonely while witnessing Silvestro's affair. She had difficulty expressing her feelings. I confided that I would find her the best man in Sabinium after Proculus was dead.

As she matured, my daughter was becoming ever more feminine. I worried that Proculus would try to rape her. Surprisingly, Zolia agreed. We felt guilty that we had misled the children. I constantly begged forgiveness from Minerva and Quirinus.

Silvestro worked rigorously and soon he did succeed in felling the tree in four strokes. Sister was not satisfied. She next set the challenge at three strokes. He demanded an explanation.

"You can fell the tree in one stroke and it would only show your strength, not your fighting skill. You must have both. A warrior must know how to minimize his use of power on lesser kills and maximize his power when needed.

"Sword fighting requires coordination between all the nerves and muscles in your body. You must know how to control and calculate the many moves needed to kill your enemy. Silvestro, show me you have more moves in your hands."

"My mentor is the greatest teacher on earth!" He faced me. "If I cut a tree down in three strokes, can I marry your sister?" he teased.

Zolia chased him down the hill, throwing small stones at the boy. "My sister belongs to me. Not to you or anyone else. Leave her alone, rascal!"

"Silvestro likes you, Mother. Why not marry him?" Vittoria joked.

"Ah, my dear Vittoria. Silvestro can do better than an old woman. And you: You will meet the man of your dreams and bear him healthy, strong children like yourself. What more could a mother want?"

Chapter 57: Challenges

While the children grew and practiced, their mothers waited for the day the head of Proculus would lie at their feet. Our children were so much our lives that it was impossible to imagine life without them.

Yet we were women, lonely women, with the natural inclinations all women experience. Before Roma, strong romantic and sexual feelings stirred in our bodies. I had often touched my intimate places, feeling my wetness and massaging my breasts. I feared satisfying myself because I was a virgin and chose to fulfill my sexuality with Gracian.

Since Vittoria's birth, similar feelings occasionally overcame me. I wondered if Zolia felt the same way. She guessed that our suitors were probably dead. I felt that revenge had replaced her natural sexual desires.

In the forest, Silvestro was the only person with a love interest, and she was a woman still unknown to his mother. Once I asked if he had loved Axia like a man, but he said they would never make love before their wedding. He confessed to heavy petting, saying it was as good as sex in the forest could be.

Silvestro's fighting skills and strategies continued to progress. After a year, he had felled a pine in three strokes. He teased Zolia that he had earned the right to sweep me off my feet. But Sister had more warrior challenges for the boy. Saying that his technique was lacking, Sister challenged Silvestro to fell three trees with three consecutive strokes.

"When the trees fall, I shall marry both beautiful Ronica and her ravenous daughter?" Zolia and Vittoria chased him until he tripped. They patted his head gently while he protested. "Protecting three irritable women is the most demanding job on earth."

"Protecting us in the forest is one thing, but felling monster Proculus in Roma is quite another," said Zolia.

"Fear not, Mother. I will split the pig's head."

"My son, when your training is complete you can do anything."

I knew that whore witch Malocanis was dispatching demons on dragons from Hell to find us. At the same time, Minerva and Quirinus were protecting us. Nightmares often woke me.

When I shared my revelations with Zolia, she thought them delusional. My visions revolved around the gods and my faith was strong. I trusted what came to me, but Sister was focused on one thing – vengeance – and her obsession put distance between us.

In time, Silvestro felled three pines. Two years of hard work fulfilled his promise to Zolia. He lifted his mother in his arms and carried her into the woods. Silvestro ran a thousand cubits before setting her down. "Am I too heavy?" Zolia asked.

"Mother, remember how you carried me into the woods to protect me? Now, I am a man. Now, I carry you!" Zolia pressed her ear to his heart. I leaned my head on his shoulder and Vittoria rested her cheek on the man who reminded me of the good men we had once known.

"There is one last training exercise to be achieved, my son," said Zolia.

"Anything my mentor asks," said Silvestro, smiling.

"You must fell six consecutive trees in three strokes."

"I will chop down the entire forest in three strokes as long as you are by my side, Mother."

The next day, Silvestro began his final challenge. I was homesick and asked Zolia if Silvestro's final challenge was necessary. Sister responded that the children must reach twenty-five years before completing their mission. I sensed she was stalling, but stayed silent.

Silvestro mastered five trees in three strokes, but struggled with the sixth. This assignment required technique and strength.

"Why does Vittoria not have challenges?" Silvestro complained.

Zolia promptly tasked Vittoria to strike three apples with one arrow. Daughter easily achieved one apple, and then two, but she lacked the steadiness and strength to master the third.

She practiced every day until one early morning when the arrow felt weightless and she pierced three apples with a single arrow. I kissed her magic hands. "Your hands and eyes are sharper and steadier than mine. Our talents are different but we share Sabini blood."

When the children turned twenty-five, Silvestro was still unable to fell six trees. Zolia and I were enjoying spring weather when Silvestro and Vittoria came running. "Gold! We have gold for our journey!"

Vittoria showed us one hundred gold coins in a purse they had found on a dead man lying in the woods. Thinking the children had killed someone for the gold, as their father had done, Zolia insisted they take us to the body.

The children led us due west, where the dead man lay next to a bloodied rock. When Silvestro and Vittoria turned the corpse, Zolia and I jumped back – away from Sawtooth Villius.

"How did this scum get here?" Zolia demanded.

"You know him, Mother?" Vittoria asked with surprise.

"This creature is the demon's best friend," Zolia reported, noting Sawtooth's cracked skull and a bloodied stone. When a horse meandered over to us, we guessed that the man had fallen onto the rock.

Sister laughingly suggested we attach a message saying, "The sisters of Cures are coming!" to the horse and return Sawtooth on his mount to Roma.

Sister agreed to bury the body but denied my request to throw the gold in the grave. Zolia decided the coins were a gift from our gods that would serve the children well on their mission. "That Proculus should die by funds provided by his friend is the perfect irony," snapped Zolia.

The next day, Zolia announced, "It is time that Silvestro and Vittoria kill Proculus. Vengeance is upon us. Our young are ready for Roma."

"Mother," Silvestro said. "I have not completed the last exercise."

"The time has come. In five days, you will set out for Roma and kill Proculus. You are more skilled than any Roman."

I began mending clothes while Zolia furnished the details.

* * * * * *

Chapter 58: Disguise

Zolia's plan called for Vittoria and Silvestro to pose as husband and wife. They would never be separated. Silvestro would grow a heavy beard to disguise his face and Vittoria would wear a veil to cover our resemblance. They would impersonate silk merchants from Etruria, who had arrived in Roma to trade.

They must not divulge their military training and should neither inquire about Roman history nor indulge in anecdotes or accounts of the past. All Romans were liars whom Zolia deemed unworthy conversationalists.

"Focus on Proculus. Follow him. Learn his habits. One moon past midsummer, you must kill the demon. And remember to avoid Roman wine at all times," Zolia instructed them.

Questions raced across their eager faces. "Why not hear their stories? Why must we kill the demon on that specific day? Why do we need disguises?"

"Listening to Romans will pollute your minds. You will want to kill all Romans. That is not your mission. Distractions are the enemy. Focus is your ally. Any suspicions will cause doubt or may portray you as spies. The day of the killing is the same day that the Romans killed our families. It is the day of Roma's Neptunus Equester festival.

"Romans do not worship Neptunus. The festival is a charade to lure neighbors for slaughter," Zolia reasoned. "They do not celebrate. They steal, rape, and pillage. This is the true Roma, the one behind the surface."

"Romans are filth, Mother," Silvestro said. "They deserve death." Sister had explained everything. Our missionaries were up to the mission and Zolia's plan was sound.

"It seems wrong to just kill Proculus. There must be other scoundrels like him," said Silvestro.

"This is the first step, my son. Bring your mothers the head of Proculus. The day will come when you lead the soldiers of Sabinium into Roma."

As the time for their departure neared, our anger bordered on uncertainty. A surprising resource eased our doubts when the horse of Sawtooth stumbled upon our cave. When our wolves ran to attack, the horse reared, commanding their attention. The three animals seemed to communicate. Whatever the horse whispered, the wolves understood.

"The horse's master was bad. Now he will serve us," Vittoria guessed. When he joined our ranks, we named him Fortis for his bravery. Vittoria and Silvestro groomed, fed, and prepared their grateful steed.

Silvestro visited Axia one last time before leaving. She was uneasy about the mission. Silvestro promised to return and take her to Cures for their new life together. He hid both his misgivings and his heavy heart and embraced Axia passionately before separating. When Silvestro arrived home, he longed for Axia but knew what had to be done.

The time had come. The great day in our lives was upon

us. Zolia had constructed this moment like a great temple. Soon we would celebrate our vengeance.

Silvestro and Vittoria had only modest tunics, so we encouraged them to buy fancier garb before entering Roma. Silvestro wore a small blade in his belt and a sword on his hip. Vittoria slung her bow and arrows over her shoulder. They were ready.

For their blessing, Zolia surprised them with cloths for blindfolds. When their eyes were covered, she stood naked before them. The Crusader smoothed her flowing hair over her breasts and reached her hands to the heavens in a series of trancelike gestures. "My true god, bless these children with strength to fight evil. I sanctify them with all my purity."

She shaped flowers and cast them at our missionaries. Her hands scooped air from her reproductive organs and showered the children. Her legs stretched in different positions as her extended fingers eased air from her vagina.

Sister dressed and we uncovered the children's eyes. "Mother, everything in our lives has mystery," Silvestro commented. "It confuses me."

Zolia and I presented the rapist's dagger to Silvestro. We reminded him the dagger was to sever the monster's head. He promised to succeed.

"My confidence is weakening," I whispered to Zolia.

"The children are eager. We have no choice. They have lived for this. Soon enough, we will know the gory details. We will know that justice has been served."

❀ ❀ ❀ ❀ ❀ ❀

Chapter 59: The Road to Roma

Our warriors mounted the steed and started their journey. The wolves walked along until they turned for a final wave. We sisters sat on a stone, our heads touching, our hearts aching. "What vile dance was that, Zolia?"

"My menstrual dance is a purification dance with special powers. My blood has blessed them." Usually the Sabine purification dance was reserved for the demonized, but somehow Zolia's interpretation seemed appropriate.

Silvestro and Vittoria rode into the woods. Everything looked different. Vittoria shivered and cuddled Silvestro's back. "Will we die in Roma?"

"Never talk like that," he said. "I am here."

She kissed his shoulder. "When I am in danger, will you save me, my brother?"

"My first responsibility is always you, my sibling."

"Silvestro, I trust you. On to Roma!"

That night, the children camped and reviewed their plans. After a sound sleep, they reached the main road early the next morn and turned to Ocriculi, where they used coins to purchase clothes and an air of respectability. With their new silk samples, they would surely fool Romans. Silvestro told the natives they were Etruscan silk merchants from Felathri, a distant city. The children rested comfortably before resuming their trip to Roma.

They reached Roma the following day and were startled by the city's impressive stonework. Faces of Roma were gloomy, unlike the faces of our wide-eyed children. After securing their horse, they walked the city with hands held tight. They appeared every bit the husband and wife, settling near a ridged wall where an old man sold pigeons, ducks, and wild turkeys. As they scanned the crowd, the masked demon and two guards appeared at the market.

"Proculus," whispered Vittoria.

"Are you sure?"

"I could never forget him."

Silvestro turned to the gamekeeper. "Why does that man wear a mask?"

"Ah, my young friends are not from Roma."

"No. We are traveling merchants," Silvestro answered.

"The masked man is Proculus, best friend of King Romulus. All Roma knows that man."

"Why does he wear a mask?"

"Years ago, he was scarred by a brave woman," answered the trader.

"Brave, but foolish," suggested Silvestro. "A few inches lower and Proculus would be dead."

Vittoria whispered, "Mother Zolia said he wears the mask to hide his ugliness. But this man says he is scarred by a woman. Which is true?"

"Vittoria, Mother would not know of his scar. She was only in Roma a few days before her family was killed."

"Zolia said not to ask questions or listen to stories about people. We are not following her orders," Vittoria reminded him.

"Things are not always as they appear," the man said absent-mindedly. The children were drawn to the man, who introduced himself as Regulus and invited them to stay at his residence on Aventine Hill. He had a small, comfortable house where two visitors could rest. Birds sang in the backyard and a dinner of boiled potatoes and roast duck was much appreciated.

Regulus wanted to share his life story, but the children heeded Zolia's instructions and listened without engaging him. Small bits and pieces about the man's past were unavoidable. He was from Caenina, a city invaded by Romans. His daughters had been abducted and his possessions confiscated. His family was ordered to live in Roma where, years ago, his wife had died.

The story depressed the man. Our children tried to console him but they were guarded and spent the night in the same room, whispering about evil Romans who captured women and stole property.

Come morning, Regulus told the children they could stay as long as they liked. He left with his pigeons to go to the market and our children went to study the city.

That afternoon, the old man soon introduced our merchants to potential buyers. Silvestro's inventory of silk samples induced offers, but he told bidders he was waiting for the festival market. Romans respected his patience but men and women alike seemed enchanted with Vittoria.

Eventually, one elderly woman approached her. "Is your name Ronica?"

Silvestro reacted quickly. "Who, by the gods, is Ronica? This is my wife, not a foul tribal woman. We are Etrurian!"

"Hold your tongue, young man. I once knew a woman who looked like your wife. She, too, was young. I meant no offense," said the woman, hurrying away.

"Vittoria, you must wear your veil," Silvestro insisted. "Your carelessness endangers us. Zolia warned us." Vittoria agreed, but wondered why the woman remembered her mother, Ronica.

Roman law required all visitors to register in court. Our agents were asked to appear before two serious men in Roma's registration room. The inquisitors sat on wooden chairs behind a stone table covered with leather parchments. One man had long, curly hair and a beard, quite the opposite of his clean-shaven, short-haired assistant.

"What is the purpose of your visit?" asked Long-hair.

"My wife and I come to sell our silk," Silvestro said.

"How long have you been here?"

"Twenty days."

"Twenty days?" Short-hair asked. "Do you have samples?"

Vittoria pulled samples from her satchel and showed him.

"This is fine silk," he said. "Have you found traders?"

Silvestro answered, "We have offers, but think we can do better when Neptunus Equester arrives and more traders come to Roma. My wife wishes to attend the festival before we leave."

The men faced each other and laughed.

"What did I say?" Silvestro inquired.

"Only fools, or men who wish to lose their wives, come to that festival."

"Oh? I had not heard. Why is that?" Silvestro asked.

"Many outsiders think the celebration is bad luck. Some neighbors fear they will be attacked. There is some history, you know."

"Is Roma dangerous?" Vittoria asked innocently. "Perhaps we should leave."

"No, fine lady. Things happened when Roma was young that no longer occur. Today, Roma is safe. If anyone troubles you, come to us. We will handle it."

Vittoria thanked Short-hair and nodded to Long-hair.

"Welcome to Roma! Enjoy your stay!" Long-hair said, and presented Vittoria with a small brass plate inscribed King Romulus honors your stay.

Silvestro and Vittoria thanked the registrars and left.

"Romans are bold," Vittoria told her brother. "They admit their crimes and think they are above the law. They must be punished!"

"Mother Zolia was right. These are evil people," Silvestro affirmed.

❋❋❋❋❋

Chapter 60: Vittoria

Silvestro knew Proculus lived in a castle occupied by trusted elders. One day, when the gatekeepers were distracted, Silvestro ducked into the garden and hid behind large trees. He surveyed the grounds and the exterior of the spacious building.

He followed the monster by hopping from one pillar to the next, but then Silvestro was overcome by an unexplained heaviness – something that felt uncomfortably familiar.

When Proculus suddenly turned, Silvestro realized that the man was a vigilant enemy and he ducked behind a curtain.

"Is something wrong?" an elder asked the demon.

"I feel a shadow behind me."

"Roma has many ghosts, my friend. Perhaps it is a ghost from the past." The elder shook his head and walked away.

Proculus continued to his chamber on the west side of the castle. Next to the chamber, an airy window faced a steep hill. Silvestro memorized every door, window, hallway, and exit point.

When he arrived at Regulus's home, our son sketched the layout on a leather skin and explained his observations to Vittoria. Each day, the children reviewed their plan.

As the festival approached, Silvestro tired of following Proculus. One afternoon, when the children dallied near a fish-seller, an inebriated Roman stopped and stared at Vittoria. "How much?" he asked Silvestro.

"What say you, old man?" Silvestro asked irritably.

"This woman. How much for the busty beauty for one night?" asked the man, opening his satchel of coins.

"Go away. Sober up!" said Silvestro.

The old man handed Silvestro ten gold coins, who immediately tossed the coins on the ground and towered over the drunkard.

"You deny me? Why? Just one night!" the old man insisted.

"This woman is my wife, pig. Begone!" yelled Silvestro.

"No, this is not your wife. I have watched you, boy. This girl is not your wife." A curious crowd gathered around the argument.

Silvestro's temper snapped and he shoved the man. Two young Romans challenged Silvestro. He dropped one with a single punch, freezing the other in his tracks.

The crowd anticipated a row but two Roman officers arrived and demanded Silvestro's version. His explanation riled the drunk, who insisted Silvestro and Vittoria were unmarried. The officers favored Silvestro's story but the man persisted.

"Listen, Roman citizens. Like you, I am Roman. We live and die together. I am entitled to question visitors. These officers vouch for impersonators who are not husband and wife!"

The crowd began to gossip and, when the situation ebbed, the soldiers released the man. A woman asked the drunk what he wanted. "To marry the girl," he responded. The crowd studied the unlikely pairing and laughed in unison.

"Vittoria and I are already married," said Silvestro. But one elderly man jokingly suggested, "If they kiss, it will prove they are husband and wife. Give us your best kiss and be gone!"

It was intended as a joke, but Romans liked any suggestion of foreplay. Silvestro saw that they were serious, but he hesitated while Vittoria fidgeted nervously.

"You see? I told you. They are not married!" shouted the drunk.

Vittoria raised herself regally. "Why must I kiss my husband in public for such an old sot?" She pulled Silvestro to her and kissed him boldly.

The passionate kiss between two trusting souls silenced the audience and saved their mission. The crowd dispersed and the old man wormed away. The guards apologized and moved to the next disturbance.

That night, our children were uneasy. They could not look each other in the eye. They both felt compromised. Vittoria broke the silence. "First, you wanted to marry my mother. Now, you romance me! Are you Roman?" she teased.

"Hold on! You kissed me. I am not to blame that you want to marry your brother."

She laughed. "Yes, it is true. I was the aggressor. You must never tell Mother," she said, and smiled. "I feared for our mission."

"Come closer, Ronica's girl. You are my sister. Your kiss carried me beyond the heavens and made every woman holy and sacred." The children slept calmly in the palms of the gods as brother and sister, good and virtuous.

●◉✦✦◈●

Chapter 61: Neptunus Equester

At dawn our avengers dressed, gave thanks to Minerva and Quirinus, and loaded their gear. Silvestro attached his sword, tucking the demon's dagger inside his tunic. Vittoria had already stashed her bow and quiver behind a tree near the castle and only secreted a small knife.

They wanted to thank Regulus for his hospitality but thought better of it. Instead, Silvestro placed coins on the table. Their long-awaited mission of revenge was underway.

As they exited, Regulus caught them. "Where do my boarders go?"

"For a walk," Vittoria answered.

"Blessed be the breasts of the mothers that fed you. Go. Kill the man who destroyed your family. I know you seek revenge. While all men surrendered like rabbits, your mothers fought and were true. You are brave to walk into the lion's den," explained Regulus.

"Will you reveal our plan?" asked Silvestro.

"Being an old and tired coward, I could not fight the Romans. It remains my biggest regret. I often wonder why no person comes to avenge the terrorism. Then I saw you, with your conditioning and demeanor, and I knew vengeance was at hand."

Silvestro assured Regulus that killing the demon was their only mission. The old man confirmed that Proculus was the most evil, heartless man in Roma and explained that Proculus had once abused two women for a year before killing them. Since that time, he was known to have committed one senseless terrorist act after another.

As Regulus blessed Silvestro and Vittoria, they realized it was the first time they had enjoyed fatherly conversation. They thanked Regulus before setting out on their mission.

Though early, Roma was awake and preparing for the festival. As the sun warmed the air, children arrived from Aventine Hill. It would be a beautiful day and people already streamed into the city. Unaccustomed to such grandeur, our warriors felt uneasy.

Vittoria claimed her horse and tied him on the hill behind the castle. She promised Fortis to soon return. By the time they reached Palatine Hill, Roma was filled with activity. And where there was activity, Proculus was never far removed.

Our team sat near the corner of a wall, observing everything. Silvestro played with the handle of his sword. Vittoria rubbed her knife for confidence. From nowhere, the king and his guards appeared at the city's center. Proculus joined them, completing the royal entourage of rapists.

Vittoria steamed to cut the demon's throat, but Silvestro insisted on patience. They would pick their time and escape with the demon's head in a pouch.

Around noon, King Romulus urged people to assemble for his opening speech.

"Twenty-six years ago, we first celebrated the festival of Neptunus Equester. Though we assembled with different intent, the Roma we have become is rooted in actions initiated that day. Now we are one family, prosperous, structurally sound, and ever growing.

"Praise and thank Jupiter for making us the mightiest nation on earth. I shall bless Roma forever. Eat well. Drink aplenty. We have more than enough. Forget our past and live our future. Enjoy Neptunus Equester!"

The crowd cheered wildly. As the celebration unfolded, guests were over-served with wine and food. Our warriors only focused on Proculus. As Zolia had predicted, Proculus drank heavily. Women danced suggestively before the monster but he seemed disinterested. His ego satisfied, Proculus excused himself and headed to his castle.

The children kept their distance and arrived at the castle after Proculus. Silvestro hid behind a tree while Vittoria gathered her bow. A pair of sentries made aimless conversation at the gate but, seeing Proculus, they hid their wine and quieted.

"My guards, today, you can do anything. Drink, dance, fornicate the Roman way. Enjoy!" As soon as Proculus passed the gate, the soldiers resumed drinking.

Silvestro and Vittoria slid behind them into the castle. Proculus headed to his chamber, greeting the castle's residents who rushed to the festival. Proculus entered his chamber but left the door ajar.

Silvestro and Vittoria hid behind a pillar, aware that the moment was upon them. Silvestro signaled Vittoria to wait until after he entered. She would guard their rear. Our warrior raised his sword and moved into the room.

Suddenly Proculus lurched from behind the door, swinging his sword and shouting. "Who are you, assassin?"

Startled, Silvestro stumbled back against a pillar just as Vittoria entered with her arrow pointed. Proculus screamed, "This is the end, hag!"

Silvestro lifted his sword and set his feet. "Salvé, monkey face. If you are man enough, fight me!"

Proculus turned and halted, shocked to confront his original face. He stammered, "I know you."

"Murderer!" Silvestro jeered. "You murdered my father for gold and silver."

Proculus raised his sword. "Who was your father?"

"Ovid! You killed him and the rest of our family. We will avenge their deaths."

"Boy! I never killed anyone named Ovid."

"Liar! You have slaughtered so many people you forget their names."

Vittoria released her arrow but Proculus weaved away. "You dodged my first arrow, but not the next!" She removed her veil and loaded the bow.

"Ronica!" exclaimed the monster.

"You ugly demon! Know your assassin is her daughter!" She fired the arrow into the devil's shoulder.

Silvestro knocked the sword from the demon's grip and rained blows on the monster. Proculus jabbed a spear at Silvestro as Vittoria took up the monster's sword.

Suddenly Proculus pieced together the puzzle. "Talk. We must talk!" begged the devil.

"Talk? We are here to kill, not listen!" Silvestro screamed.

Silvestro caught the edge of the spear and swung his sword at the masked man just as Vittoria stabbed the demon's ankle. Proculus collapsed to the floor, resting on his spear. The monster raised his head, fixing his eyes on Silvestro and Vittoria. "Do you know who you are?"

"Your assassin!" Silvestro shouted. Vittoria regained her bow and fired an arrow into the monster's chest.

Proculus dropped his spear. Silvestro slashed the rapist's belly. The monster's intestines spewed onto the floor. Silvestro glared through the monster's mask.

"Do you feel death, Proculus? Do you see my cousins, my father, my family? Know that I shall sever your head and take it to my mother and her sister."

Vittoria spat on the mask. "This is the happiest day of our lives! We enjoy watching you die. Know that your own dagger will remove your head."

Blood poured from the man's body. He looked at Silvestro. "I smell your mother's vagina, assassin. She loved my cock!"

Silvestro sunk the dagger into the man's eye. Proculus gasped for air and lurched into Hell.

Vittoria tested the body. "We must hurry."

Silvestro drew the dagger and prepared to sever the monster's head. As he bent to remove the mask, Vittoria closed her eyes to prepare for his ugliness.

When Silvestro lifted the mask, he balked, realizing he stared at a mutilated version of himself. "Vittoria! This demon has my face."

Opening her eyes, Vittoria was dumbfounded. She looked back and forth but try as she might, she could not deny the resemblance. "Silvestro, this demon could be you!"

Silvestro stepped back. The children gazed at each other. A boy charged into the room and, surprised, Silvestro fired his knife into the boy's chest.

Our warriors rushed to the wounded boy. He looked like Proculus. Silvestro wrapped his hands around the boy's neck, demanding, "Who are you?"

"I am the son of Proculus," whispered the boy. "Are you my brother?"

Silvestro gasped, "I am not your brother, or the son of that pig."

Vittoria commanded the boy to rise and leave, but the boy struggled to breathe. Vittoria sought to save him, but Silvestro was sure he shared his father's evil blood and wanted the boy dead.

Finally Silvestro cried out, "Our mothers deceived us!"

"Could you be the son of Proculus?" mumbled Vittoria. "How could two unrelated men look so alike?"

Silvestro shoved Vittoria back. "Never repeat what you are thinking." He turned away from her and withdrew his knife.

"Everyone said Father was a cruel man," the boy whispered, "but he was kind to me. I had no friends because all Roma feared my father. You killed the only thing I had. I will have revenge."

"It pleases me that you threaten me. Now you will die quickly. Then I shall take your head and the head of your father to my mother," Silvestro declared.

The boy rallied for one last breath. "All donkeys of Roma will urinate on her grave."

Silvestro studied his victim. The boy's death saddened him. Our son began to weep. Vittoria hugged Silvestro from behind and wept also, knowing he had murdered their brother.

Chapter 62: Triumph

Our fighters hovered over their victims. The brother had cost valuable time. Our son could barely look at Proculus, much less sever his head. But with the mission in jeopardy, Silvestro's training came through.

Placing a section of drapery over the demon's face, Silvestro stabbed the dagger into Proculus's neck. Blood sprayed everywhere. The monster's body shook violently. Vittoria watched her brother carve through bone, muscle, blood vessels, and skin before the head fell free.

"I do not feel you are my father because Mother Zolia deceived us and poisoned our minds." Silvestro placed the wrapped head in the satchel.

When he moved to the boy, Vittoria asked, "My brother, please do not remove your brother's head."

"I may have had the worst father on earth, but a good brother is in my arms. Sister, tell me: Am I Roman? Am I evil like my father?" Silvestro hoisted the boy over his shoulder and moved to the window where Vittoria had fastened their escape rope.

Silvestro began his descent. Vittoria lifted the satchel and surveyed the chamber one last time. Blood was everywhere.

The demon's sword and spear lay next to the headless corpse. Pottery and fine works of art were strewn around the chamber. Tables and chairs were tipped and broken. With the image planted in her mind, she followed Silvestro.

Once grounded, they hustled into the woods, where Fortis patiently waited. "My friend, we have an unexpected passenger." Silvestro raised the boy onto Fortis and mounted. With satchel in tow, Vittoria rode behind him.

Fortis turned for home but the children's minds were conflicted. The sense of achievement that they deserved escaped them.

That night, they pitched their camp. In his despair, Silvestro mulled suicide. Vittoria realized their lives were lies, created, perpetrated, and promoted by their mothers. The children knew they would sleep under the stars with their father's head and the body of their brother in their camp. Meanwhile, their two deceitful mothers awaited them in the forest.

The next morning they resumed their journey, walking solemnly beside Fortis who carried their dead.

Minerva's daughters waited at the cave. I prayed to Minerva. Zolia mindlessly drew figures in the dirt. It was afternoon before we heard the lumbering horse. When Fortis halted, I ran to greet my loves but stopped when I noticed the dead body. "Who is this?"

Nobody answered. Their body language exuded contempt. Vittoria brushed by me, bumping my shoulder on the way to Zolia. Silvestro was on her heels. Regaining my balance, I followed.

Silvestro dropped the boy at Zolia's feet. Sister continued drawing, refusing to look up. "Tell me! Are you Mother Zolia, or the thief who stole us from Father Proculus?" roared Silvestro.

With the mention of Proculus, my heart skipped. "Are you injured?" I asked. Vittoria lunged at me, tumbling me to the ground. Defiance raked her eyes.

Zolia jumped up. "If you strike your mother, I will rip the soul from your body!"

Silvestro grabbed the satchel from his sister. He opened the flap, removed the demon's head, and tossed it at Zolia. "Is this my father? How could you steal us from his wife? You denied us a father's touch all these years! You are not my mother. I know this man did not kill your family!"

Zolia raised her face. "My son, Ronica and I have lived our lives serving and protecting you. Do you see that?"

"I killed my father's son, my innocent brother! Do you see that? Does this please Zolia the Great? Do Ronica and Zolia understand how their son and daughter feel?"

"I knew nothing of this boy. His death was not by my order."

Silvestro's temper flared. He pulled his sword and placed it at Zolia's neck. "Tell me where my mother is!"

"Can you be blind to your parentage? Blind to your upbringing?" Zolia pushed the sword away with her hand. "Know that you gushed from my belly with the curse of Roma, just as your sister gushed from Ronica."

Silvestro raised the sword again. I snatched the knife from Vittoria's belt, pushed her away, and pressed the knife to Silvestro's ribs.

Revenge

"Will Mother Ronica kill me? You are the good one, right?"

"My sister comes before anything in this world," I said. "Lower your blade."

Vittoria pointed an arrow at my head. "Drop the knife, Ronica!"

I turned to her. "Who is this evil impersonator of my daughter?"

"Twenty-five years! You deceived us for twenty-five years, Ronica! It is time to pay for your sins," said Vittoria. "Where is my mother?"

"Who scarred my father's face?" Silvestro demanded.

"This man was ugly before I slashed him," answered Zolia said. "Yes, you are the son of Proculus and… me. Vittoria is the daughter of Proculus and… Ronica. Does this comfort you?"

"How could we have the same father? Are you deranged?" Silvestro steamed.

Zolia stood tall, turned her back, and dropped her tunic. Her scars jumped at Silvestro and Vittoria. "Who did this?"

"Romans lashed my back. For six months, Proculus raped and tormented us." Zolia's body quivered like a leaf in a storm. "When I protested, your father made sure I received my forty lashes. I spit at him and his king and refused to cry."

Silvestro dropped his sword. Vittoria lowered her bow, trying to imagine the whipping. "Mother, is this true? Why did no Sabini come to save you?"

Zolia raised her tunic and sat on a rock with her shoulders high. Slowly, she described our fate until our children's ears bled with rage. They could bear no more. The children's resistance collapsed in shock. They contemplated our suffering at ages younger than theirs.

After this emotion, we looked at the dead boy. The children recounted the twists in their mission. The child resembled Silvestro. We pitied him but not his father. We wrapped the young body and buried him, singing prayers for his salvation.

"When you are reborn," Zolia began, "you may bring the donkeys of Roma and urinate on me. Your death is my fault, not the fault of your siblings. You are my second son. No matter the rage of your last wish, I pray it be fulfilled."

I poured water over Proculus's decapitated head, knowing the man's savageness could never be washed away. "Salvé, demon devil. Wake up!" Zolia yelled at the head. "My mistake was not amputating your penis and feeding it to the vultures!"

We had lived in isolation for twenty-five years. Proculus's head was past due in Cures. We returned the head to the satchel. We would travel light, with only our weapons. I reflected on life at the cave, where the walls were not sand and stones were the life of our wombs.

PART III:
Chapter 63: Minerva Returns

The wolves lay side by side. Polus and Luna licked and comforted each other. We stood in silence, four family members unable to express their gratitude or say farewell.

"Wolf Brother. Wolf Sister," Silvestro started. "We leave to go home. Like you, our lives will restart." Fortis neighed, bidding our wolves goodbye.

"Salvé, wolves. Keep helping strangers like us, lost in the woods. You are life-savers, not wolves," Zolia concluded.

The wolves watched us leave. Zolia and I rode with the satchel. The children walked next to us. The wind, water, trees, and stones hailed our vengeance. The tormented sisters persevered and crushed their tormentor.

As we came closer to Cures, our uncertainties mounted. We would soon see our families and suitors. Vittoria would find true love. Axia would join Silvestro. The children were excited. Our dreams would arrive late, but were on the horizon.

Standing above the town, we observed many changes. The architecture was different. Pillars and columns marked buildings. A carved arch rose above the gate. The road was brick. Cures seemed busy, but tranquil.

Fortis halted, refusing to proceed. Silvestro urged our loyal steed ahead but he dug in his heels and stayed put.

The horse neighed at Silvestro and nosed Vittoria. Then Fortis peered into their eyes, turned, and lumbered away. Silvestro pursued him, but Fortis reared once and started to gallop.

"Fortis is a Roman horse, not Sabini," Vittoria said. "He could be slaughtered, right, Mother?"

"Yes, Vittoria. His instincts are true."

With Silvestro and Vittoria at my sides, each holding one of my hands, we walked confidently to the gate. Zolia trailed behind, carrying the satchel.

The gatekeepers did not recognize us and asked our identity. "Minerva returns," offered Zolia. The unknowing guard stepped aside, allowing us to pass.

Townspeople pursued us, all chattering at once. At Cures center, we saw the town had prospered. Merchants were busy. Traders walked the streets.

We soon became the focus of Cures. Some citizens recognized us. Others asked questions. We conveyed our gratitude to be home, but I could see Zolia's anger mounting.

Sister took the podium on a dancing stage and spoke to our neighbors, who neither saw nor imagined her scars or how we had been tormented.

"Hear us, good people of the world's mightiest race! Romans abducted our unmarried women and thrashed and tortured us. We stood and resisted. Roman men were stronger. Neither gods, nor Sabini warriors, nor family came to our rescue. Though we cried every day, no defense arrived.

"Yet the sisters from Cures never gave up. We stood against the men of power and fought like tigresses. We escaped and disappeared into the clouds.

"Today I bring you our vengeance. This is what we will do to all Romans to restore your honor!"

Zolia raised Proculus's head from the satchel and heaved it into the crowd. The devil's head spun through the air, thudding to the ground with eyes wide open and staring up at the few who dared to look. "That is what is left of Proculus, the Roman king's best friend and the scum who abused us for six months. His own seed killed him."

A group of elders rushed to check the commotion. When they saw Proculus, their dread pushed them back. They witnessed Zolia's rage and, when the children and I joined her at the podium, the elders could see we stood together.

Calling to us, Father rushed into the center and tried to join us; but his neighbors blocked him from the podium. When an elder chastised us, Zolia silenced him by reciting our treatment since the abduction. Cures's jaws opened while their eyes lowered.

An elder asked, "Do you mean you were outside Cures the day we decided to kill the unborn babies?"

"Yes. We saw how cruel Cures had become. We fled for our children's lives," Zolia answered.

"You are Sabini. You cannot criticize the elders."

"I know killing innocent babies is immoral and unethical," Zolia chided. "If a decision is immoral, why abide by it? Rape is immoral. Abduction is unethical. Killing innocent children and unborn fetuses is the most disgraceful act of all."

Zolia's words stung the elder and ignited an old debate. As the sun descended, the elders said we had caused trouble by killing the king's friend. They called our bravery foolhardy.

Nonetheless, they instructed the townspeople to prepare a grand dinner in our honor. The elders and high families of Cures would be our sponsors.

We were ceremoniously escorted to the grand hall. A speech from a presiding elder proclaimed our bravery. The elders took the head of Proculus to preserve it. Sabini men were especially interested in our experiences in the forest. Several guffawed at our relationship with the wolves, but we patiently suffered their ignorance.

Zolia kept reiterating that no Sabini had come to our aid.

"It was too late," was the rehearsed response. The people admitted that Roma had grown powerful and that most kidnapped women had mothered Roman babies. The majority resided in Roma. The hands of Cures's men were tied.

Zolia and I stared at each other, recognizing the charade that masked cowardice and corruption in empty logic. The morals of Cures had changed.

We dined on duck soup, ox meat, potatoes, cabbage, and cakes. Wine was served and young girls danced in our honor. The sisters received bouquets of flowers. Garlands were presented to Silvestro and Vittoria.

Zolia was pleased that Cures had retained some degree of dignity. When the elders asked Zolia about the quality of the dancing, she raised eyebrows by saying the dancers lacked either training or talent.

Maybe it was the wine, or perhaps our guard had lowered

since arriving home; but our mood lightened. We assumed that killing Proculus would ignite war with Roma, but the more we heard the less likely battle seemed. One elder spoke openly about the possibility of a permanent truce.

I could see that Silvestro and Vittoria felt comfortable. He was handsome. She was beautiful. When the children asked their mothers to dance, the gathering moved onto the great floor. Silvestro raised Zolia and swung her joyously in the air. Her black mane flowed in the breeze as Sister swooned in his arms. They danced until they dizzied.

When Silvestro returned Zolia to the table, she whispered, "Our suitors await us." It was heartening that we shared romantic remembrances. Silvestro twirled me as he had Zolia, and we were close enough to see that Axia lived in his eyes.

"Mother Ronica," Silvestro whispered, "I loved you from the first."

He bowed to receive my kiss. "I could not have a better son."

When the dancing ended, servers brought specially blended wine that was reserved for us. Zolia and I did not drink but Silvestro and Vittoria enjoyed every drop – and in the end, they persuaded us to share one last drink.

Soon our weary eyelids felt heavy. We tried to dance but were too unsteady. Our eyes closed and we sank to the floor, realizing we had felt this way before.

The next morning we were motionless, and more asleep than awake, when we heard the crowd. Soldiers splashed water to revive us. Zolia lay next to me.

"Why are my hands tied?" I asked.

"Romans must be here!" We forced ourselves to sobriety.

"May the gods disown all Romans!" I shouted.

One hundred Roman cavalrymen flooded the town center. Men milled about but no women were present. Silvestro and Vittoria were tied to stakes with their hands stretched over their heads. Zolia and I limped to them, but townsmen pushed us back.

Zolia knocked one man to the ground, took his sword, and cut free her ropes. After she sheared mine, Sister declared we would take our children and leave. Three elders rejected her and Romans surrounded us.

"Mother, these men outnumber you!" Silvestro yelled. "They will harm you and Ronica."

"I will save you, my son. These are not men. They are cowards." She pointed at the senior elder. "You, son of a wicked whore, why do you shackle Minerva's daughters? Are you Roman filth?"

The elder threw a stone at Sister, striking her forehead. "Watch your tongue, mistress of Proculus."

Zolia dropped the sword. We charged the man but the crowd cut us short, pinning us to the ground. "You sisters have caused trouble with Roma. King Romulus wants you and your children dead."

"You cow dung!" Zolia shouted. "When did the king of rape become king of Sabinium? When did Cures's elders support rapists and kidnappers?"

"Be careful, young Minerva! Your hostility could seal your fate."

Zolia spat on the man's tunic. "Do you think Minerva's daughters fear you?" The elder raised his hands to strike, but Father grabbed him with an iron grip.

"Corradeo, I help your children and this viper spits at me. Control her!"

"Father, save the children!" I begged, but Father was helpless.

"Why are Romans here?" Vittoria cried.

"Our messengers brought soldiers from Roma to imprison the murderers!" screamed the elder.

"You call us murderers?" I asked. "What do you call six months of rape, lashings, and captivity? Zolia is right. You are soulless cowards!"

Cures fell quiet until a Roman captain rode his horse toward us. "Were you involved in Proculus's murder?"

"Yes!" we screamed.

Zolia faced the leader. "My people may practice the same deceitful tricks as the king of rape and his masked grave robber, but we bid justice. Now our people poison our wine and betray us. Will they rape us like Romans?"

The leader removed his helmet and bowed. "You are braver than any women in Roma."

"What will happen to our children?" Zolia asked.

"Your elders vouched for you sisters. You will live." He held his thumb up. "But your children broke Roman law. They entered the city under false pretenses with fictional identities and misled people of Roma. They killed their own father and an innocent child." He turned his thumbs down.

"We deserve the blame," I volunteered. "Kill us. Leave our children alone. Our lives ended long ago."

The captain shook his head, waving his soldiers to proceed. As townspeople restrained us, four Romans doused the children with oil.

"Will you burn our children alive?" Zolia screamed.

"By the king's order," the leader said.

"Romulus is not a king. He is a rapist with a wife who cheats him!" shouted Zolia.

Several townsmen pitied us and begged the release of the children. But the king of rape's order prevailed. Father stormed away, unable to witness the execution of his grandchildren.

The leader faced the gathering. "Men of Sabinium, thank you for disclosing the whereabouts of these murderers. Hail, King Romulus!" declared the leader, throwing his torch onto the oil slick surrounding our children.

"If you are not born of a whore, untie my son and face him like a man!" screamed Zolia. The captain turned and studied her.

Silvestro roared like a lion. "Soldier, if you untie me, I shall capture Roma and slay your king."

"My son is the one true hero."

Romans stoned Silvestro, pelting his face and body. He denied them reward, stoically facing his death. The captain stared at Silvestro. "Are you not afraid?"

"Roma is a city without men!" Silvestro bellowed through scorching flames.

Immolation

Vittoria cried for help. Our reasons to live fixed their eyes upon us. We wrestled our captors but could not join our flaming children.

"Look at me, Silvestro," Zolia cried. "See your Mother!"

He gave her one last look, gritted his teeth, and faced away, where something beyond the flames startled him. Silvestro shook his head violently and his life on earth ended.

"My son, I love you. Please do not leave me!"

The flames swallowed our children. Vittoria had passed out. I called to her. Her eyes opened momentarily, but she gasped once before rising to Minerva.

Roman soldiers called to the crowd. "Cures is loyal to the Kingdom of Roma. Hail, Romulus!"

Minerva's daughters lay on the ground, watching their children turn to ash. The town center emptied. The scene was over. Memories flashed inside me. Again, we were alone.

"Is there any god merciful enough to raise our loved ones from ashes?" Zolia asked.

I shook my head. "Our people would burn them again. They are soulless and ruthless."

We sat on the ground until a familiar voice brought us to the present. Our friend Ona came to us, hugged us, and shared our grief. "My sisters!" she said. "No person will say you did not fight back, brave women."

"What has happened here, Ona?" Zolia asked.

As spectators arrived to see the ashes, Sister rose and loosened a charred stake. She waved a burned post at anyone who came near. "Sabini swine are traitors!"

Jabbing, poking, and dancing with the stake, the Crusader swatted men and women. I tried to pull her back, but the mad elephant continued her chase until she collapsed in sorrow.

"Romans and Sabini rule Roma together," Ona told me. "The elders and the townspeople agreed there would be no more war. This was their solution. This is why they killed your children. The Sabini are pleased that Roman children are dead, but the abducted and abused women of this world could not be prouder of you."

Neither of us could accept Ona's explanation. "We were the only ones who fought for the truth. I hate everyone, Roman and Sabini!"

"Sisters," Ona insisted. "It is time to go home."

"Home? Where is home?" I asked.

●●●●◆●

Chapter 64: Regret

Walking home, we leaned on Ona's shoulder. Sympathetic men and women lowered their eyes in tribute to our suffering. We had arrived in Cures with hope, but our lives were over. The Romans and our townspeople had betrayed us.

Friendless in an unfamiliar town, the daughters of Minerva were once again abandoned and wondering if we were better suited for life in the forest.

Father waited at the door. I ran and held him tight, but Zolia held back. Inside, Mother rested in her chair. I moved to her lap and wept.

"My girls! My lovely girls!" Mother sighed. "My hope returns." Mother had never recovered from the cart accident twenty-six years ago. Her movements were limited and she was crippled without remedy. We needed each other.

Ona brought us juice. I gulped down two cups of it. Zolia sipped but kept staring at Father, while Ona told us how she had tended Mother and helped Father since leaving Roma. The room was heavy with my grief and Zolia's rage.

Sister finished her drink, rose, and stepped close to Father. The Crusader grabbed his neck. "You did not come for us!" she yelled.

Father's jaw set firm. He removed her hands.

Ona spoke. "Zolia, your anger is misplaced. Your Father is a good man."

Sister pounded Father's face. "Your daughters were raped and tormented by Romans. No man from Cures came for us. My father is a coward. Imagine the pain when your hero betrays you!"

"Are you finished?" Father asked. "Or, does my headstrong daughter have more childish things to say?"

"When he raped me, I cried to you. I knew you and Neiro would come."

"Zolia, it is you who disobeyed. It is the mothers of my grandchildren who should have died at the stake, not the innocents. See what you have done. You ruined your mother's life and mine!" Father snapped.

"You want your daughters dead?" Zolia screamed.

Father unleashed a farmer's slap that spun Sister across the floor.

I grabbed his tunic. "Father! Stop!"

He lifted me, slapped me across the face, and dropped me next to Sister.

"Those are the first and last slaps for your disobedience," Father said sternly.

"Father, we meant you no disrespect," I tried to explain.

"Even if we disobeyed, your duty is to save your daughters," Zolia added.

Father grabbed her hair and smashed her into the wall. Mother cried for him to stop.

Father spun away from Zolia and shouted, "Do you understand what has happened here? Do you understand that the people of Cures disregarded my warning and brought ruin to our culture and our town? That my daughters and my wife deceived their patriarch? That many men died trying to save you disobedient women?

"Do not point your finger at me. Look inside yourselves. You blame Proculus, Romulus, and Roma, but you betrayed your Father!"

Stunned, Zolia sank to Father's feet and begged forgiveness. Father softened and raised us to his side. His body shuddered with sorrow. We stayed in each other's arms, sharing overwhelming reality.

Eventually, Father sat us down and started describing life after the abduction of his daughters and the crippling of his love.

> "After hitting the rocks, Mother's left leg was crushed. She knew she was dying. Romans came, shackled Naevius, and dragged him to the king, leaving Mother to die.
>
> "Romulus asked Naevius if he knew the price for killing a Roman. Your cousin asked the king if he knew the price for touching Sabine women.
>
> "A coward struck Naevius from behind. Romulus commanded that Naevius should lose his sword-fighting hand as punishment for killing Romans. When the king asked in which hand Naevius held his sword, he answered, 'The same hand you use to masturbate.'

"An executioner swung his axe and severed your cousin's left hand. Naevius kept insulting Romulus. A soldier stripped your cousin and sent him into the street. He ran through the streets holding his amputated hand.

"When he reached the bottom of Palatine Hill, he heard Mother's cries. Somehow he removed the rocks that crushed her leg. She ripped her tunic so he could cover himself.

"With her leg shattered, Mother could not walk. Naevius hoisted her on his back and carried her back to Cures. Naevius was strong and brave, but he collapsed at the gate.

"Neighbors treated them with herbs, but Naevius lost his hand and Mother lost the use of her legs. Romans have maimed and crippled our family.

"The townspeople were incensed. The young men wanted blood. Families spouted their indignation. Our only thought was to destroy Roma. We needed a strategy but no one had answers. Fathers wept for their daughters until the elders said we must retaliate, but only at the right time and with a sound plan.

"Determined to save you and Sulpicia, Uncle Neiro was ready to fight. He guessed you and others had already been abused and raped. After two days, Neiro lost control and started shouting and smashing water pots to get the elders' attention. But instead of acting, the elders banned Neiro from their meetings.

"At last King Titus Tatius appeared, saying that when Romans asked for our women they were refused and then purposely misled us. Their charade lured our women to Roma, where our future mothers were kidnapped. Roma believed we were too weak to respond. Titus Tatius admitted we knew nothing about the city's infrastructure, information we needed to mount a serious attack.

"The king proclaimed that our abducted women should be welcomed back, whether raped or abused, or even if they had been forced to marry Romans. Sabini men should marry our women without hesitation.

"The king's strategy called for Sabini from Forum Novum to Trebula Mutuesca and from Casperia to Eretum to unite. He sent messengers to the northern Sabini towns of Reate, Amiternum, Interocrea, and Foruli, asking that they join us as one mighty army of warriors.

"Titus set a course of action. We gained focus and began spying on Roma. Soon we knew most of the means of egress, but the city was alert and at the ready. We positioned spies in their asylum but several were caught and hanged for treason.

"Meanwhile, men took to arms, practicing warfare night and day. Your Uncle Neiro grieved every day, refusing to sleep with his wife until you were saved. At night the town prayed and danced to the gods for strength.

"I knew nothing about my daughters. When Gracian and Ovid came and declared their love for you, we were stunned. I realized how little you had shared with us.

"Gracian stayed with Neiro to receive additional

training. Ovid danced and performed rituals for your protection. Brocchus worked to master the art of war. One day, Naevius asked why he practiced so hard. That was when we learned that he loved Sulpicia. Brocchus told Naevius he would be his strong right hand and from that day forward, they were as close as a tortoise to its shell.

"We were surprised when Scaveola took up his sword and resumed training. At first he struggled with his rhythm but eventually his muscles came back. One day, Neiro challenged him because the boy had said he would never use the sword again. 'You think I lost that day?' Scaveola asked. They fought like two heavyweights. Neiro was strong but Scaveola was quick with practiced technique. Scaveola hailed Neiro the mentor of all warriors. The boy's only goal was to fight for Zolia.

"Uncle Neiro put the sword in his belt, walked to Scaveola, and asked if the boy loved Zolia. 'Always. I lost the fight to raise her spirits. I love her now and always will. I gave up my sword for Zolia. No matter what happens at the hands of the Romans, I will do anything for your niece.'

Father's account caught Zolia by surprise. She moved closer to me as the history continued.

"Caenina went to war without a good strategy. We were not surprised by their defeat. King Titus Tatius was disciplined and put good planning ahead of anger. We used the defeats of Antemnae and Crustumerium to evaluate Roma's strengths and weaknesses.

"As refugees poured into Cures, we gained insight that would give us an advantage. Our architects eagerly mapped the city's physical layout.

"It was a year before we were ready to challenge Roma and liberate our women. Sabini warriors were outfitted in new armor and supported by full inventories of weaponry. Our augur led men and women in dances to Quirinus.

"When all Sabine warriors assembled, we were a formidable force. Titus led the troops and Mettus Curtius, Neiro's father-in-law, served as field general.

"Neiro told his wife, 'If I do not return, tell Ronica and Zolia that Uncle Neiro died for their freedom.'

"Ovid's mother prohibited him from fighting. As Gracian left to join the troops, Ovid yelled, 'Fight for me, Gracian. Bring back my Zolia!' Gracian yelled back that this was when Zolia needed him and cowards did not deserve love.

"Soon, Cures filled with horses, riders, and footmen from northern Sabinium. The air was thick with revenge. Uncle Neiro and Scaveola stood close to their steeds.

"When Augur Cnaeus arrived with a sword, Neiro turned him away. Cnaeus promised to live naked in the temple until he heard Minerva's voice. Cnaeus still lives in the temple. I constructed a circular wall to isolate him from the outside. His only contact has been the food and supplies I pass to him.

"Naevius gathered his armor and weapons and insisted on accompanying the army. The soldiers took him to

Invocation

Titus. When he explained that Brocchus would be his left hand, the king said, 'When our women were taken, you killed Romans. You know the smell of Roman blood. You are our first hero and may join the battle!' The army tapped their swords to our hero.

"As they marched to Roma, other Sabini troops filtered in. King Titus distributed his army in all directions around the city. A spy revealed the size of our force to Romulus, who realized that the beast was at his door.

"That evening the Roman king offered a treaty to Titus, who rejected their proposal. Our troops rested in encampments surrounding the five hills and prepared for war.

"Near midnight, the night watch captured a hooded stranger. With the hood removed, the daughter of Spurius Tarpeius, governor of Capitoline Hill's citadel, stood before us. Tarpeia asked to speak with Titus.

"The guards led her to Titus, who was half asleep. 'I will help you capture the citadel,' she offered. When Titus asked her motivation, she said she believed the Sabini would win the war.

"But Tarpeia was greedy and feared for her future. She told Titus that Romans treated women badly and she sought justice for all abducted, battered, and raped women. What she really wanted was gold.

"King Titus promised Tarpeia many golden bracelets for her assistance. In turn, she agreed to let the army inside the citadel. When the traitor left, the Sabini joked that even Roman women were unfaithful and corrupt.

"At dawn, Mettus Curtius led a quarter of his army against the Romans at Capitoline Hill. Gracian was in the first wave. Uncle Neiro, Brocchus, and Naevius waited in reserve.

"The Romans fought fiercely to save face and keep our women. Blood splattered, spears and swords clanged, and the men engaged in hand-to-hand combat most of the day. Eventually the Romans fled, intimidated by our warriors.

"Tarpeia kept her promise. She opened the citadel's small gates for our soldiers, who entered and untied the main gate to allow a larger force inside. When Tarpeia demanded her reward, one soldier answered, 'You should have opened doors to allow our women to escape. Instead, you watched their torment.'

"Our troops hated Romans more than when the battle began. They crushed the traitor with their shields, stepping on her face and throwing her bruised body down a steep cliff. The disdained woman died when her head struck Tarpeian Rock.

"When Mettus Curtius asked about Tarpeia and our soldiers confessed, the general warned our troops not to harm women or children.

"When our army seized the advantage, the enemy panicked. Romulus ordered his men to retake the citadel but his force was fearful of our superiority. They retreated to Via Sacra at the bottom of Capitoline's main street.

"In an act of desperation, Hostus Hostilius, the noblest man in Roma, took charge. Thousands of

Romans rallied behind their new leader and prepared a counterattack to retake Capitoline. Our element of surprise was gone. This Roman army was more inspired. But remembrances of our women motivated our force to quickly regain the advantage.

"Mettus faced Hostus man-to-man and with a mighty thrust severed the Roman's arm before piercing his heart. The frightened Romans retreated to the gate of Palatium.

"The Romans had lost hundreds of men. Many more were wounded, unable to fight. The reign of Romulus was in jeopardy, yet the scoundrel refused to free our women and admit his sins.

"Instead, he raised his hands to Neptune's brother Jupiter Stator. 'Jupiter, king of gods, the god of sky and heaven, turn your face to us and strengthen your children to win this war. If you favor us today, I promise to build a temple in your honor.'

"Romans rallied behind their king and, when Romulus led his men, they had new purpose. They knew their defeat would end the Roman way of life. Romulus planned to retake a lesser hill where Romans outnumbered us.

"Soon, hundreds of bodies littered the hillside. Mettus stood alone, encircled by Romulus and his men. Struck by a foot soldier's spear, Mettus dropped his sword and fell from his mount. Seeing his prey trapped, Romulus screamed, 'Pray to your god, Mettus. You join him now!'

"Mettus would not surrender. Recovering his sword, he told the king that Romans would die with him. Gracian broke through the circle and fought to save our leader by hoisting Mettus onto his horse and speeding through the ranks to our camp of reserves.

"Titus Tatius was displeased when Mettus reported his army lost and that more men were needed to defeat the Roman king. Our troops raised their swords and spears and, with a resounding cheer, called for victory.

"The king ordered Mettus and his surviving force back while he led the rest of the troops into battle. Exhausted but game, Gracian volunteered; but this time the king denied him, leaving Ronica's love to beg Neiro to save the sisters from Cures.

"With Uncle Neiro, Scaveola, Brocchus, and Naevius, our army charged against the Romans. Our men fought for the daughters of Sabinium. At the gates of Palatium, the Romans cowered at the sight of our might. Romulus and Titus approached each other. 'You know you cannot defeat Roma,' Romulus declared.

Titus laughed. 'I should have killed you when you cried for our women. Now you live at my mercy. Roma did not forget how you insulted her. We took your pride because you insulted us.

"Titus's horse reared as he spoke. 'We are here to take our women, chain Romans as slaves, and throw you in the Tyrrhenian Sea. Then we shall do with Roma as we please. History will forever scorn what you have done.'

"Nervous troops stood one hundred meters apart. Suddenly, clusters of women with children in their arms ran at us from behind Roman ranks. Our daughters wept so loudly we could not understand them. Some ran straight to their fathers and brothers and begged them not to fight. They were married and had children by their Roman captors and chose to stay in Roma.

"When we heard this, our stomachs turned. Shame on the women who accepted this fate. We did not listen. Our rage was too great, our loss so immense that we paid no attention to the pleas of Romulus's wife or other women. Even when they held forth their children, we ignored their pleas for mercy.

"While this insanity unfolded, Uncle Neiro, Scaveola, Brocchus, and Naevius searched for Zolia, Ronica, and Sulpicia. They prowled Palatine Hill and ended up at the citadel, where thirty Roman soldiers had returned.

"Neiro drew his sword and cut through twenty Romans. Scaveola and Brocchus finished the rest. When they could not find you, they went to look elsewhere but a tower sentry fired an arrow at Neiro. Scaveola pushed Uncle aside and took the arrow in his throat. Neiro felled the archer with his dagger and scooped Scaveola in his arms. 'Why did you save me?' Scaveola whispered. 'Tell Zolia I await her in heaven.'

"Neiro dipped his hands in our hero's blood and covered his face and body with Scaveola's life. Brocchus and Naevius followed suit, smearing their faces with blood. Together they pledged to kill all Romans.

"Our warriors stormed the enemy, beheading as many as possible. Brocchus and Naevius fought like twins.

"Uncle Neiro turned a corner and faced a man sitting in the great hall. 'Face your death, Roman!' said Uncle.

"The man raised his hands. 'I am a good man. I have

a family. Spare me. Leave the citadel, for I refuse to fight,' said the man.

"Uncle Neiro tapped his spear and raised his sword to behead the man. But, before he swung, Sulpicia and her child jumped in front to shield the man. 'Do not make me a widow, Uncle,' she begged.

"At the sight of his niece, Neiro stalled, took the baby in his hands, and kissed his niece. Sulpicia told him you had tried to escape and Romans had killed you. She added, 'Roma is my country. Natta is my husband, the father of my child.'

"While she spoke, a spear pierced Neiro's back, jutting out his abdomen. He pulled the spear through and flung it at the masked villain. Sulpicia shouted, 'This is the man who abused, tortured, and murdered Ronica and Zolia. Kill the rapist!'

"Uncle Neiro held his sword to Proculus's neck, saying, 'People said Romans were cowards and stabbed warriors in the back. You proved Roman cowardice. I have this chance to kill you, but I will not. My daughters live. They will come for you. From this day forward, you will live in fear, knowing they will have their vengeance.'

"Neiro carved 'R' on the right of the devil's neck and 'Z' on the left. With that, Uncle stabbed his sword into the floor, knelt down, and died.

"Proculus stared at his new scars with disbelief. When he raised his sword to behead Neiro, Natta pulled him away. Sulpicia cried for the man who had come to save all women.

"When Brocchus heard Sulpicia's decision, his heart was broken. He ran from the citadel and stared up at the skies. Before Naevius could get to him, Brocchus drew his sword and twisted it into his abdomen. 'I loved Sulpicia. She surrendered. I did not care what the Romans had done to her.'

"'No, no. The Romans forced her to say these things. She only loved you, my twin,' Naevius answered.

"'Not only do Romans take the lives of women, but they take the hearts of men,' Brocchus exhaled.

"When the Romans saw Naevius, they charged. He stood, took up the sword, and held his ground until Romans toppled him down the hill, where he lay unconscious. Later we picked him up, but his leg could not be repaired. He is crippled, like your mother.

"With the hearts of fathers and brothers melted, the battlefield quieted. Romulus and King Titus stopped the fight. For us, it was a defeat, for we lost much blood and came away with only a few women.

"More importantly, our blood had been compromised. Roma was in disarray but Romulus could rebuild. We Sabines cannot regain our purity. 'Roma hid behind the faces of our daughters and stole our victory,' Titus lamented.

"Cures expected triumph. When our warriors returned, they said, 'The fight had no purpose. We should have acted that first day. This is not war. It is about morals and ethics. When a woman is raped, reality and weakness confuse her. Our women surrendered their bloodlines to motherhood.'

"Days and moons passed before any Sabine looked to the future. Our only peace was that Romans took our daughters as wives, not as whores. We justified uniting with Roma because it is unethical to fight with in-laws.

"But many Sabini did not accept this logic. Towns like Eretum, Forum Novum, and Cures, which were close to Roma, made treaties for the good of their daughters. Recognizing our militaris, Romulus shared the throne with Titus. Many Sabini whose daughters were abducted moved to Capitoline Hill. I stayed, with the hope my daughters would one day return. We trusted Minerva and believed in you.

"Kings Titus and Romulus reconciled and ruled together. Romans continued as citizens of Roma but our king wanted the Sabini to be called Quirites, in tribute to Quirinus. The kings ruled until Lavinium natives killed King Titus in an act of revenge, leaving Romulus to reign alone."

Father's account brought uncertainty to the present and added sadness to the past. Over the next few days, Zolia and I came to realize that good men love and respect women. Zolia's mind crossed between Scaveola, her most honorable suitor, and Ovid. I dared not ask about Gracian. Our hero, Uncle Neiro, died as he had promised, trying to save us. He was as noble an uncle as was his nephew, Naevius.

❋ ❋ ❋ ❋ ❋

Chapter 65: Revenge in the Wood

Father was restless, and one night his uneasiness overtook him. He pointed to Zolia. "You ask what kind of father leaves his daughters in a brothel?"

Zolia tucked herself into my arms. Ona tried to console Father, but he was insistent. Grabbing a spade, he led us far into the woods, where he climbed a tree. Father showed Zolia the inner trunk where XXXVII was inscribed.

"Thirty-seven?"

Father handed her the shovel. "Yes, thirty-seven. Dig here." Zolia started digging.

I asked Father why Ona was present for a family matter.

"When I peered into Ona's eyes, I saw how my daughters suffered. Respect Ona as your sister, my third daughter."

Zolia stopped digging and threw the spade. "Father, you are mean to us. We know we disobeyed you, but now you punish us by making us dig to Hell? Have we not endured enough?"

"Salvé, Dancer," Father said. "Obey your father."

Zolia lifted the spade and restarted. Before long, it banged into metal. Sister shoveled faster, uncovering a shield. When she raised the shield, she faced a corpse.

"This is a Roman soldier killed by Ona and me," Father said.

"What does thirty-seven mean?" Zolia asked.

"We killed seventy-six Romans in twenty-five years. This was number 37. We had perfect kills, except one who escaped. We struck his head but his mount carried him off."

"Sawtooth Villius!" Zola exclaimed. "Know that his coins funded the assassination of Proculus."

Father and Ona had not accepted the treaty with Roma. Ona had told Father the truth about our abuse. Father had wanted to do battle with the Romans, but his responsibilities prevented it. After the truce, he decided how to gain revenge. Father shared his decision with Ona, the only person he trusted. Together, they slew and buried Romans.

During the night, they would leave Cures and comb the woods for Roman targets. After each kill, they buried their victims under a tree and assigned a number. "There were many rumors about missing Romans," Father said. "But no one suspected our mission. Our secret isolated and protected us. This is how we could exist in a Sabine society filled with corrupt morals."

Chapter 66: Burden

We awoke and went to the farm to free Augur Cnaeus. When Zolia called his name, the augur's prayers silenced. His twenty-five-year old dream was realized. "Has my Minerva returned?"

As Father had described, the temple had no doors. We swung iron rods and began breaking through the wall. Cnaeus wrapped himself in his rags. After we opened the hole, our augur stood before Minerva's daughters, his beard wrapped around his face and his hair in a tail.

The Crusader studied the man, smiled approvingly, and sank into his hungry arms. Cnaeus apologized for not saving us but we neither condemned him nor assigned him guilt.

Instead, we declared our admiration for the sacrifices he had made. Zolia was especially comforting, kissing his hand and patting him affectionately. Minerva had heard his prayers.

We walked Cnaeus home, where other high priests greeted him. That night, the augur cleaned himself, shaved his beard, and sat with us for supper. We celebrated Cnaeus's freedom and he celebrated our return.

One afternoon, Gracian came to our home. I was so unnerved I dropped a plate in the kitchen.

"Ronica, I am Gracian. Do you remember?"

Zolia moved Mother to her bedroom, leaving us alone. I struggled for words and lowered my eyes.

Gracian lifted my chin. "Has it been a lifetime, Ronica? If you have forgotten, I understand." Gracian reached into his tunic and lifting my shell bracelet. "My love never wavered. I waited these many years, praying you still loved me."

Overcome, I turned away, ran to my room, and retrieved the pearl he had given me. "Gracian, when things were beyond dismal, it was my love for you that guided me. Trust that I always loved you." I leaned into him.

Dizzied by love, Gracian blurted out, "Ronica, we have waited a long time. I see no reason to wait any longer. Will you marry me tomorrow?"

My body shook with love, lust, and self-doubt. Was I worthy? I ran to my bedroom, leaving Gracian rejected.

Zolia approached Gracian and kissed his hands. "My sister loves you more than you imagine. Reality overwhelms her. So many dreams have been vanquished. Ronica will marry you. She just needs time."

He and Zolia made idle chatter so that when he left the house, he was filled with hope. When Sister entered our bedroom, I was forlorn. "I am not virgin. How can I marry?"

"Ronica, you are virgin. Neither heaven nor Hell will take away our virginity. You have never given yourself or been loved by a man. If anyone is righteous, it is you."

Doubts raced through my brain. Had I encouraged the monster? Was I to blame? When do women lose their virginity? Is virginity related to our physical bodies, our minds, or our hearts?

When Ovid arrived the next day, Zolia's heart soared with hope. She ran to him but he withdrew, standing like a tree. Love blinded Sister. She tried to get closer but again he held her off. Zolia gathered herself. "Do you love me, Ovid?"

He whispered, "I came to say hello. I prayed for your safe return. Now I am married with children. I hope we can resume our friendship."

With another dream shattered, the Crusader turned to me. "Because I am deaf, this coward's words do not hurt." Sister pivoted and walked to her room.

Tears drained from her eyes for many days. Zolia became weak and, though Father was still angry, he sympathized with Sister. One night, he entered the room. "Father is here," he said. "It is time to move on, Crusader. If you want me to slay Ovid's wife and children, consider it done. He should have fought for you."

Father's words shocked us. "Leave Ovid be! My abduction is not his fault," Zolia replied.

"I spare him knowing that if I harmed the wimp you might behead me, like Proculus," Father chuckled.

Zolia ran to Father, jumped into his outstretched arms, and snuggled to his shoulder. "I need your love, Father. Please stand with me."

"Fine, but forget Ovid. He is unworthy. A prince awaits my youngest."

"Who will marry a crippled, deaf, and abused woman?" Zolia asked.

That day, I prayed that Minerva would return to Sister. A peace settled over our family. Father still did not sleep with Mother but he cared and provided for her. Mother sensed his regret and lived in solitude. Ona had tried to mend them but Father abruptly told her that his business was not hers.

Zolia returned to her mischievous ways and schemed a plot to mix stiffening powder in his diet. At first, the idea seemed preposterous but, as their divide lingered, I agreed. One night, we fed him my specially treated duck soup. As he devoured it, Zolia and I watched with amusement. After dinner, the sisters hurried to the farm.

Father's blood surged. Mother watched Father circle the room like an untamed bull. "My manhood is alive," Father muttered, turning to Mother. "I apologize for being distant. Bionca, you are still desirable."

"Yes. But why do you notice now? Does your rod or your heart need satisfaction?"

He moved next to her and ran his hands over her body, but Mother shied away. "Fish woman, I am your husband! I need you!" Corradeo lifted Bionca and swept her to the bed.

Mother moved his hands to her breasts and around her middle, and groaned desire. Father tore off his clothes and feasted on her. Our parents made love for five days. Zolia joked they would need a month to reload.

When Father did get back to his work, his spirit had returned. "Should we expect a boy or a girl?" Zolia teased.

"Not at this age, Crusader. But if a miracle happens, it must be a boy. Women have exhausted me." We chased him until we crashed to the grass. He ran his hands through our hair. "I want these daughters for ages to come."

"If we are reborn, we will have you again, Father," I said.

A few days of tranquil family life followed until Zolia bumped into Ovid at the market. "Are you mad that I lost the brooch?" she asked.

"No, Zolia."

"I risked my life to find it in the river. I am sorry, Ovid."

"You are a good woman, Zolia. I always knew that."

"Do you have my birds?" she asked.

"No," he started nervously. "After you were taken, I kept them for two years but I lost hope and released your birds."

Zolia moved into Ovid, slapping him forcefully. "After two years? I waited in the darkest forest for twenty-five years. That is love. You never loved me, Ovid."

"Zolia, I still love you. Life was wasting. I had to move on."

"If you were brave, you would have been patient, made sacrifices. You are not to blame that I am worthless, but I do not wish to see you again." Sister shook her finger at Ovid. "If someone takes your children, fight for them!"

At home, Zolia closed herself in the bedroom. This time, she fell sick. The Cures healer said depression was causing maladies. Her appetite was feeble. She lay coiled in bed, crying day after day and resisting my care.

Sister had been bludgeoned by male injustice. Gracian insisted we walk with her. With Zolia tucked under Gracian's side, we moved toward town until a group of young men blocked our path.

"Gracian is having his way with the sisters," one remarked. "If Corradeo had more daughters, we could enjoy the spoils!"

Gracian leaned Zolia on me and faced the slanderer. When the fool clenched his fist, Gracian leveled him. Blood streamed from the man's nose while Gracian thrashed the partner. With both men senseless, Gracian announced, "Zolia is my sister. If I hear gossip about the sisters, the gossipers will pay."

●❂❀❁●

Chapter 67: Gracian

The incident convinced Father it was time to marry, but I feared my pleasure would dispirit Zolia. Father said that if we did not marry, the town would think Gracian a fraud.

I loved Gracian. After Sister reassured me, I accepted his proposal. "Ronica, I know you have been hurt. We have waited this long to lie down together. When the time is right, we will enjoy each other. If that day never arrives, we will grow old and die peacefully, not knowing sex."

We were married in Cures, where the high priest barred a ruined woman from defiling his temple. Infuriated by society and religion, Father hosted the wedding at the farm's temple. Gracian and I exchanged grain and gold, and Augur Cnaeus married us.

When other priests harassed our augur, he said, "If you displease Minerva, Cures will be consumed by a hail of heaven's fire." The other priests feared us and permitted the wedding.

Only our close relatives attended but Scaveola's sister, Vlpia, made a surprise appearance. "I regret the suffering I caused you and Scaveola," Zolia told her.

"Zolia, I am your follower. All Sabine men and women surrendered our culture. Now they connect to Roma. You stood strong and fought like you did when we were children. You and Scaveola would have pleased me. He always loved you, Zolia." Vlpia reached into her satchel and held up the diamond-studded necklace with Quirinus's golden spear.

Sister gasped. "Coelus le Terpsichore! You won?"

"Yes. After the war, we were granted second chances."

"Vlpia, I congratulate you. The trophy is wonderful."

"Sister Zolia, my brother died to save you. All the heavens and earth know you are unbeatable. I danced beyond my means for you, the dancer of all dancers. Take this necklace to remember your true love… my brother."

Zolia's head rested on Vlpia's shoulder. "I am half-dead, diseased, and dirty. How I wish Scaveola was alive. I would please him day and night. Vlpia, you are kind, like your brother."

"When I danced, you were in my head… not the gods. Your strength and purity empowered me," Vlpia whispered. "When you returned, I thought you would be unchanged, strong as ever. Everything turned upside down. Yes, today is Ronica's wedding, but this is a promising day for you as well. Wear your necklace, secure that you are not alone. Scaveola and I are here."

That night, the queens of dance reminisced and became eternal sisters.

***

Chapter 68: Passion

Gracian and I spent our first night together under one roof but apart from each other. After a day, our emotions would not calm. My husband kissed me passionately. His fingers massaged my breasts and nipples so tenderly that wetness gushed from my womanhood, down my legs, and onto the floor. I reached for his staff. He groaned under my touch.

When a horrid memory of Proculus flashed before me, I pushed Gracian back and ran like a child seeking sanctuary into Zolia's bedroom. My blood raged with passion but doubts filled my mind.

"Why are you here, Ronica?"

"My sister is my life."

"We are one, yes, but you should be wrapping yourself around your husband."

"I cannot lie with Gracian until you heal."

"When you are one with Gracian, I will be satisfied."

"If I sacrifice, our god will show mercy."

"Your god is not mine, Sister. Gracian trusted his love and waited. Are you crazy? Reward him with everything he wants and more. Your passion will fill me. I relish your married life. Complete your vows. Go to your virgin and wear him out. Then, tell me delicious details so I know what I am missing. That will be my medicine."

"Zolia, sometimes you are vulgar."

"Run to Gracian before I kick you with my crippled leg."

I rushed back to my bewildered husband. I told him I had loved him in Roma, in the forest, while giving birth and on lonely nights. I confessed that in my dreams we had been intimate many times. I promised to please him and myself whenever he desired. I was not a virgin but I had never loved a lover.

Inspired by gods from the heavens and with Minerva's stars showering down upon me, I moved seductively before him, slowly lowering my tunic with sensuous movements. My husband reached for my womanhood, but I placed his fingers on my bosom and suggestively rubbed my thighs against his manhood. His touch made my wetness erupt. I could no longer bear to be without him.

I tore away his tunic, wrapped my arm around his neck, and thrust my breasts into his powerful chest. When I found his pulsing rod, my fingers teased him as he moaned with eagerness. His orgasm was close. I had climaxed so many times that my mind was ablur.

I dropped to my knees and took his full penis in my mouth, down my throat. My lips and tongue caressed him until he tightened and surged larger. I opened my throat and welcomed his seed, my hands pulling his buttocks further into me.

Romance

Gracian groaned so loud I thought the village would hear. But I devoured him, draining every seed and then caressing him to preserve his hardness. When we spilled to the floor, I reached for his member and gently smoothed him. This was the love I had yearned for. We had shared this moment and my husband was still a virgin!

Not for long. I knew how long he had waited. I helped him regain his full strength. We moved to the bed and I pushed his mouth to my breast, then down my abdomen to my wetness. His fingers and tongue probed my vagina and, when he massaged my clitoris, my explosion was so powerful I thought I would faint.

Delirious, begging and craving more, I knew this was what Minerva had saved for me. I grabbed for him, guiding him home. My hungry hips rose to meet his every move. When he was far inside me, my eyes bulged at his force. Our slow rhythm turned to frenzied, powerful movements. I widened my legs. His hands raised my buttocks for more powerful thrusts. My love rode me, drove me, slowed me, and harnessed me. I was his. He was mine. We exploded in unison. His seed and his warmth shot into me, intensifying my endless orgasm. We were one.

My body flushed with desire. I wanted more. We were spent but my love sensed the depth of my passion. Every part of my body welcomed Gracian. He had waited and he would never wait again! My insatiability pleased him. I would always please him. The devil was gone. I offered myself to Gracian without reservation.

We experimented, laughed, and caressed for ten days. At one point, the sight of his penis made me quake with such anticipation my womanhood melted in moisture.

Every touch, every sensation, every sound, every part of me pleasured Gracian.

Minerva had blessed me with sensuality. I was alive! Truly, I was born again. The way we loved could not be taught. We exchanged fluids so many times that my perpetual climax left me unsteady afoot.

When we emerged from home, everything was new. The sun was brighter, the sky was bluer, the earth more peaceful. I was no longer an abused woman. I was confident, luscious, full, a goddess of pleasure. I rushed into Sister's room and playfully put my finger in her ear.

"What are you doing?" she asked.

"Your sister is loved, Zolia."

Sister turned to face me. "Let me see. Ah! You look like you broke the bed and rose above the clouds."

I kissed her neck and giggled.

"Well?" she asked.

"Sister, we devoured each other. I am majestically spent."

"What did our brave love do to you? Or, what did you do to our husband, Ronica? Tell me." I described what I could remember.

She chuckled, "You know, Domus, I outlasted you. I am a virgin."

"Yes, Crusader, you are a virgin." Minerva's daughters marveled at each other.

Chapter 69: Naevius

Soon after, Naevius came to visit. Without his hand and with a lame leg, he was reluctant to face us. Using a wooden crutch, he brought Carling, his wife, and their seventeen-year old son, Seneca. I warmly welcomed the family and led Naevius to Zolia.

"So, Naevius visits his sick cousin at last? Losing your hand and leg made you a worse cripple than me, but my most serious wounds do not show. Is that true for you, Dancer?" Zolia asked, patting the bed for him to sit.

"Ah, cousin, I have missed you. When our people treated you so disgracefully, I could not defend you and was so frustrated I could not face you. But you and Ronica should know that all these years, I never stopped thinking of the sisters. Neiro and I knew you would return."

"My dear Naevius, how brave you are! You fought like a man and came for us. You are my closest friend. No apologies are necessary." Zolia greeted Carling with a smile and applauded her for marrying Naevius.

"My man is honorable. He sacrificed himself for his sisters. Any woman would be fortunate to have such a man rather than one with neither heart nor soul," Carling avowed.

We asked Naevius if he heard from Sulpicia. "Never talk about that cur!" Sulpicia had betrayed her family and Naevius refused to discuss her. "She chose a Roman. Now she must live with it. Neiro and Brocchus died for the ungrateful wretch. As far as I am concerned, they all died together."

He was so loyal to us that, when we explained our abuse, he turned a deaf ear. His father and family had left Cures for Roma, an option Naevius could not tolerate.

Later, Zolia wanted to walk to refresh herself. I tried to help, but they wanted to be alone. Naevius offered his arm and they walked to town. Zolia lumbered along, gasping every few steps.

"Shall we dance, Naevius?" she asked.

"A walk with you is a dance with anyone else," he laughed.

The cousins sat near a well and talked until midnight. Naevius was Zolia's source of happiness. He restored her, but Sister's health was deteriorating. Doctors said her organs were infected. Medicine helped contain the diseases, but I believed Ovid's rejection had weakened her physical and emotional will.

When a relative invited us to a newborn's naming ceremony, scornful women shunned us. Zolia and I sat under a tree outside the home. The child's mother sought us out and asked us to bless her baby. Gracian carried Zolia inside the home where a woman screamed, "Stop! Do not let that sinner touch that babe!"

It was clear that our uncleanliness offended many townswomen. "If they cleanse me with forty buckets of their holy water, I will freeze and die. Perhaps, that is what these godless people want," Zolia told me.

I faced the gathering. "The daughters of Minerva will live and die by how Minerva judges us, not by the mores of Cures, where people deem bedding Romans to be pure. When you see Minerva, we shall know how she judges you!"

After we left the house, the newborn's mother hurried after us. "Forget those women. Daughters of Minerva, please name my child," she begged.

Zolia saw that the mother respected Minerva and answered, "The child will be Silvestro, the blessed one. My Silvestro was born from man's physical abuse. Your Silvestro comes from the mental anguish of women. May your Silvestro rise above both."

Cures's society ignored us. Instead of living in caves with animals and birds, we now resided in a town populated by demons and vultures. Romulus presumed we would reveal the truth about his relationship with Malocanis, the witch of whores, and had demanded our deaths. Only the town elders, who feared a backlash, were keeping us alive. Eventually, the two schemers disagreed and began practicing opposing spells.

As the relationship between Sabinium and Roma mended, our traditional cults, gods, heritages, and cultures became Roman. Zolia and I were Minerva's last line of defense. Banned from social gatherings and prohibited from exchanging goods with others, we existed in a different cell. We were models for true women but most women in Cures were lost in self-righteousness. Sister had started a revolution against corrupt leaders, but her commitment was now stealing her life.

Two years had passed since our return to Cures and the slaughter of our children. Living in this uncivilized world was unacceptable.

When Gracian suggested we return to his town of Reate, outside the Roman territory, we saw opportunity. Romans cheated us with low property valuations but Father's mind was set. Leaving our houses, farms, and temple would be painful but our family had risen above Cures.

Romans posted notice that anyone choosing to accompany us would be barred from Roman territories. We did not begrudge any family members who declined our pilgrimage. Naevius, Carling, and their son, Seneca, asked Father if they could accompany us.

"You think because I am crippled I am useless?" Naevius asked Father. "Cures needs Roma, not me. Zolia is my best friend. I missed her for twenty-five years. If my son grows in her shadow, he will one day gain revenge against Romans. I live for that day."

Father had no response, so Naevius joined us. With four carts filled with belongings, our party set out to the future with one more dream gone astray.

Chapter 70: Ona

I prayed to Minerva for our new life, but my goddess was hot-tempered and fiery. Unsettled, I returned from the farm and took up with Zolia and Gracian in their cart. As we pulled away, Ona's voice halted us. Lugging two bags, she ran to catch us.

"Ona! No! You must stay with your family," I called.

"My parents are jail-keepers who scorn me. They locked me in a barn. I escaped to join my real family. Please, Ronica. I cannot stay in this sinner's paradise."

Ona's mother and father, and other townspeople, ran to our cart. Ona's parents threatened her but, when Ona had heard enough, she jumped into the cart even as her parents cursed her.

"I may be evil, but I never kiss Roman ass. I will live in honor with Ronica and Zolia rather than deteriorate with Cures." The defiance in Ona's heart was genuine.

Gracian whipped the horses and started our journey. A young man yelled, "Zolia is poisoned because she slept with Roman men and danced on their table! Now that the sisters are gone, Cures is purified. No more whores in Cures!"

Ovid jumped up and punched the man with such force that he fell against a tree. An elder restrained Ovid but he pulled his dagger and cut the elder's ear. "Let all men of Cures be deaf, for no person will hear slander about Zolia again." A crowd jumped Ovid, but he fought fearlessly until no one dared confront him.

His bravery astonished our family. Zolia called out, "Praise be to the man named Ovid!"

"Humans are born to love, not fight like animals. I love you, Zolia. I always will. I shall stay in Cures and cut the tongue of any person who dares speak against you." Ovid waved us farewell. His words were the positive thing Sister took from Cures.

Chapter 71: The Outcast

Nearing the town boundary, we heard a cry of "My Minerva, do not leave!"

Augur Cnaeus stood before our procession. He had relentlessly argued with the high priests about their decision to exile us, but no person vouched for our magical birth. Declaring the town immoral, he could no longer live there.

Father comforted the augur and asked that he accompany us, but Cnaeus declined. When Mother asked why the twittering birds no longer favored us, he turned sullen and tearfully blessed Minerva's daughters. We welcomed his love and blessing. The augur faced Ona and said, "You are another of my daughters, Ona. Take care of Minerva."

The wind blew and the trees howled. As we moved to the horizon, we saw the augur kneeling with his hands raised to heaven and declaring his final prophecy.

"Hear my voice, lord of heaven and earth. I am pure and holy. You have made my hands purer than silver. Romans violated the chosen daughters of Minerva in the sinful name of rituals and evil. Minerva has vacated Cures, where Roman gods corrupt the people. She fights her last battle in Roma. Now her daughters are exiled from their town. Soon Minerva will disappear

Suicide

and all other deities will exit Roma with her.

"Romans will search for more than a thousand years, and then form a new cult in the name of the goddess Màrié. In the virgin's name, countless followers will stumble and destroy their lives on earth and in heaven until, one final day, goddess Màrié will rise and take revenge on all Romans. She will destroy them for what they have done to the daughters of Minerva and to all people."

Heavy whirlwinds circled the augur, but suddenly they stopped and cast out flowers and dry leaves. We saw that Cnaeus was the true prophet. His tearful eyes opened and his hands waved to us, a vision timelessly etched in our hearts and minds.

The augur returned to Cures but the town was empty, its people replaced by ghosts and demons. He retreated to our farm and spent the night praying for Minerva. The next morning, Cnaeus undressed, disavowed his faith, and ended his life by hanging himself.

At his last breath, lightning streaked the sky in four directions to form a distinct cross. The cross appeared in each of five repetitions. The sixth shattered the temple. Minerva's statue was reduced to ashes as Minerva's daughters headed away from Cures, away from Roma.

❋❋❋❋❋❋

Chapter 72: Reate

We entered Reate with few hopes and many regrets. Women greeted us warmly, hoisting the Crusader on their shoulders and whisking her to her bedroom. Reateans appreciated our brave act of vengeance and readily accepted us into their society.

Our men worked the fields. Gracian's father reopened his jewelry business and Ona and I helped Gracian's mother. Our lives normalized, but Zolia's health worsened by the day.

Within six months, Zolia was bedridden. The Crusader's weight loss and thinning hair marked her tenuous condition. At night she jabbered about her past, further weakening herself. Soon Zolia's lifeline was thread-thin, leaving her family to balance moments of happiness against ages of sorrow.

Our first family crisis surfaced when Naevius discovered Seneca romancing a girl near a river. Shocked and angered, Naevius dragged the boy home by the collar. "My son, do you not love your family? We are outcasts here. We have lost almost everything and your aunt lies on her deathbed. How can you love a girl in these times?"

Zolia overheard the ruckus. "Naevius, your son does what he must. Remember, you were once young." Naevius stormed into Sister's room, where the family circled the Crusader's bed.

"Cousin, allow your son to marry and discover his life," instructed Zolia.

"Zolia, the boy is twenty years and immature."

"Father, if you delay, Romans will kidnap my love!" Seneca protested.

"You see, Zolia? My son thinks love a joke."

Zolia laughed louder than Seneca. "Perhaps the boy is correct. Romans kidnap ten-year-old virgins for their pleasure. Better your son marry young than waste two lives."

"Crusader! Your sickness twists your mind," Naevius argued.

"People are born to die. I do not fear death as much as I fear missing Seneca's wedding."

Naevius nodded to Zolia. "You are one in this world. If you approve this wedding, so be it."

"Then it is done. You should know that the next time you shout at your son, I will get off this bed and fight you like the two cripples we are," Zolia joked.

So that Zolia could witness the wedding, arrangements started immediately. The ceremony went splendidly. The girl's family were cattle merchants and transferred wealth to their new son-in-law. Zolia spent only a short time at the celebration. The guests treated her as a princess, pouring love upon her.

After the celebration, the newlyweds sought Sister's blessing. "Thank you, Mother Zolia. We are wed due to your wisdom," Seneca said.

"Be polite, gentle, and kind. Never treat your wife as Romans do." Sister faced the bride. "You are young and beautiful. When you give your virginity tonight, hold nothing back. Your real self is in my nephew."

"That formula works for Minerva's other daughter," joked Gracian, triggering my blush. We flocked to Zolia and hugged her, and our new daughter saw that her new family was the right eccentric fit for her.

After the wedding, Zolia's end neared. Her face paled and she had the use of only one hand. These were her final days, so children and townspeople visited regularly. One night, I ran my fingers through her few strands of hair.

"What are you doing?" she asked.

"I am overcome by the beauty of my sister's hair. Neither silk nor lilies in water can compare."

"Does the Revolter tease me?"

"To Zolia the Great, I only speak truth."

"Pain courses my body. Death will soon relieve me." She waited. "Revolter, if I am reborn, will you be my eternal sister?"

"You are my sister in this world and the next. You are me, the Revolter. I am you, the Crusader. While I live, you will be in my soul and body. I will never dishonor you. I could never have another true sister."

One question burned inside me. "Sister, of the men in the world… tell me whom you admire most."

Zolia smiled. "Though he had his father's blood, Silvestro overcame it and believed in me. He achieved his full potential and become the greatest man."

"You trained him like a hero. Yes, you challenged and drove him, but you taught him to be a true man. Silvestro could not have had a better mother." I smiled. "Now, Sister, tell me your greatest secret?"

"My secret is that my son kissed your daughter," she giggled. "He confessed to me on the way to Cures, but I dared not tell you."

"Are you sure?" I needed to know more. "In the next life, who will be my brother-in-law?"

"Scaveola was heroic and genuine. I wish he had lived." Sister grinned. "Who is the best man the Revolter knew?"

"Hmm, I guess… King Romulus!" Zolia shot me a stern look which held until we broke into laughter. "My best man will always be Father. My secret that can never be repeated is that Silvestro is more handsome than Gracian. If granted a next life, I shall be unmarried and avoid all men. Their passion consumes me."

●●✿●✿●

Chapter 73: Germanus and Lucilla

One evening when the sky was orange, a cart arrived at our door. A handsome couple with a young child stepped from the cart. "Ah, Sister Ronica? You are well," said the man.

"You look familiar but I cannot place you. Are you from Roma?"

"No dignified man comes from Roma, but we did meet there. I am Germanus. This woman is my wife, Lucilla. You look better than when we first met."

"Are you the children we saved from Romulus?"

"Indeed, we are. Is my master, the great lady warrior, here?" asked Germanus. I led them to Zolia, whose frailty shocked them.

The family knelt before Sister. "Sister Zolia, we pray for your recovery. Your bravery saved us. We are loyal followers." Germanus lifted his daughter to the Crusader. "This is our daughter, your greatest gift to us. She is named Zolia... for you."

"Your daughter is Zolia?" Sister asked excitedly.

"There is no better name." Germanus reminded Sister of the three children we had appointed to lead others to safety, and so Germanus and Lucilla had led their charges away from Roma.

As time went on, the young boy and young girl felt a binding love. Zolia's bravery so inspired the couple that they had fled to Etruria, where they worked a farm and lived freely. When they became adults, they married and bore daughter Zolia.

Upon hearing of our move to Reate, they journeyed to receive Sister's blessing and give us thanks. At first Sister refused to bless her namesake, saying she herself was unclean and unworthy.

But, when Germanus placed Zolia's hand on his daughter's head and politely requested the blessing, the Crusader relented. Sister faced the innocent one and offered the blessing, after which we hugged and praised little Zolia.

Sister beamed her pleasure. "Do not be like me," said the Crusader. "Heed your father and be a loyal friend like my sister, the Revolter."

Seneca and his wife saw how Germanus and Lucilla and little Zolia affected Sister, and were quick to announce that they would also name their daughter Zolia.

Sister smiled and said, "It is wonderful that we can expect a new family member, but you children should name your first-born daughter Vittoria. Marry her young before she knows the scent of man."

The Crusader's irreverence earned my undying admiration. Germanus stayed several days. We were pleased to have saved innocent children and to have planted the seed of revolution in our followers.

●◉✳❖✳❖●

Chapter 74: Sister

One night, scorpions devoured my flesh and I awoke with chills. Unsettled, I slipped from under Gracian and rushed to check Zolia. With her lamp burned through, the room was black. I placed the hall lamp on a chest and curled beside her, massaging her once proud body.

She lay motionless. The chill of her palm shivered through me. Her breathing had stopped, her heart stilled. Zolia had fought her last battle. One last hair stood atop her crown, mimicking Sister's stubbornness. I kissed the strand and cozied against her, praying for a miracle.

Without her true love, Zolia had no reason to suffer on this earth. A better life awaited her in paradise.

Ona found us lying on the bed. Seeing my misery, she tried pulling me away. When I resisted, Ona insisted. "Ronica, please. We must care for Zolia."

My despair brought Naevius, who saw Sister and stormed from the room, tripping and falling in the hall. Carling placed him on a chair where the warrior stared numbly at the wall.

Sister Ona took charge. She dispatched Carling to gather our men from the fields. When they arrived, other neighbors massed around our home. Mother and Father wept before me

Loss

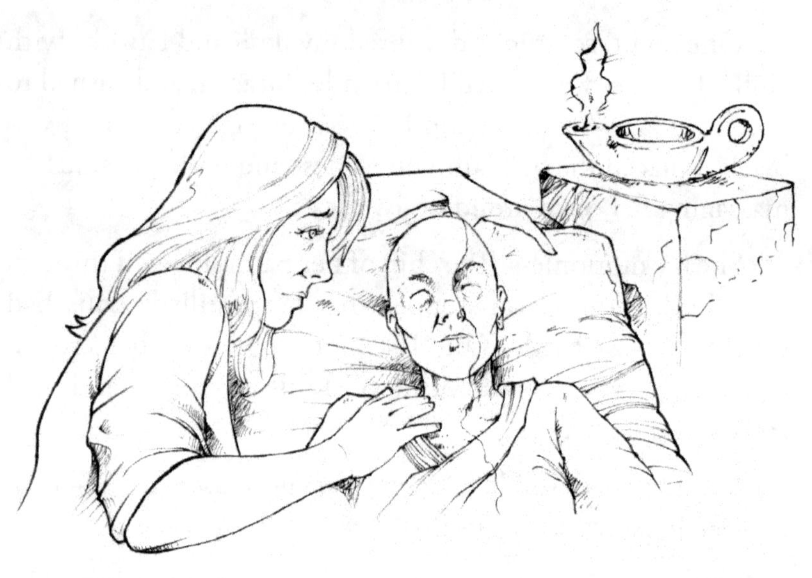

for the first time in my life. My heart cried for everyone and selfishly for myself.

I confessed to Gracian that I would never have survived Roma without the Crusader.

Gracian held my shoulders. "Ronica, your suffering is real. We love Zolia, but we must prepare her for the final ceremony. Please, come away with me," Gracian pleaded. "It is time to set the Crusader free. She has born the weight of many lifetimes."

My mind went blank. Ona loosened my hands. I saw Sister's spirit float to the heavens. I crumbled into Gracian. Ona and Carling showered Zolia's body, covering her in a fine yellow tunic. Seneca placed purple silk over a bench. Our men lowered the Crusader's corpse. Reateans sang prayers to the gods and praised the Crusader, the person who had stayed the fight for all women.

We believed Sister should be buried on our new farm. We placed her body in a covered cart with Father and Gracian at her sides. I struggled to think of a suitable tribute and decided that the domus would dance before the world's greatest dancer. Ona declared me unqualified, but she agreed to sing our tribal dance anyway.

"I am Zolia's sister! I know dance," I insisted.

The rain and thunder were my harp and drums. I stretched my hands, reached to the sky, pulled power from the gods, spiked my angry toe, and pivoted sideways. My hands shaped flowers and spread them over the cart that would carry the goddess of Sabinium.

Soon children joined me and danced by my side. Villagers cheered the goddess of truth and valor. I skipped high like a deer, soaring like the Crusader from earth to paradise, and children imitated the ascension of Zolia to the gods and goddesses.

Father whispered to Gracian, "Zolia's spirit is in your wife." He smiled. "My son, you will need more rest."

When we reached the burial place, the pit was filled with rainwater. I looked to the skies and asked the rain to stop. The clouds vanished, ending the moon's tears. We emptied the pit, put Zolia to rest, and released her to the other world.

The hearts of the town filled with agony. Men, women, and children placed flowers on Zolia's site. We performed death rituals and mourned for thirty days. Zolia's face often smiled her devilish grin to me, and her tenacity and zaniness stirred within me.

Seneca and his family spent much time at the burial place. He understood that he owed his new life to Zolia, queen of revolution. Time spent at her resting place inspired them.

"Seneca, Zolia would not approve of you doting on her passing," I told him.

"Tell us. What would please her, Mother Ronica?"

I gathered Vlpia's golden diamond necklace. "Take this and start a dance school," I said. "Teach dance to Reate's children and honor the Crusader."

"Mother Ronica, neither my wife nor I know dance," said Seneca.

I turned to Naevius. "Brother, I know you loved Zolia. Train your young, and Zolia's spirit will forever live in this town."

"I have not danced since the fight in Roma, but the Crusader said a good dancer needs neither legs nor hands. Before this day, I did not understand. In honor of the greatest dancer, defender of all women, I will manage."

With his declaration, Zolia's Dance School was founded and Naevius regained his life, teaching his son and wife to dance. Reate would one day become known for its artistic joyfulness.

I visited Zolia's burial site every day. After cleaning and beautifying the area, I would pray and reflect on Sister's commitment and determination. I expected her to break through the tomb and come alive. It seemed only a matter of time before that day arrived.

Chapter 75: Vibulena

Not long after Zolia's passing, while Ona and I were cleaning, another young family walked purposefully up the road. Their Roman garb alarmed us. Fearing harassment, Ona clutched her sword but I sensed something different. As they came closer, their daughter looked familiar.

"Have no fear. Romulus died a seven days ago," the man said, raising his open palm in peace.

"He lived longer than he deserved," I answered.

"The town is filled with rumors. His body has not been found. Nobody knows the true cause of death. Some believe he is already buried."

"What brings you here?" Ona pressed.

"I am the son of Vibulena."

Ona lowered her sword. "That child resembles her grandmother. Come here, young girl." I looked at the child closely and she was indeed Vibulena.

When the man introduced her as Ronica, my bosom swelled with pride. Vibulena had died two years earlier. When his daughter was born, the son respected his mother's wish and named his daughter after me. While young Ronica sat on my lap, Vibulena seemed to be with me.

After a chatty dinner, my mentor's son walked me to Zolia's grave. He asked if he could call me "Mother." After our escape, his mother had told him about feisty Zolia and me. At the Crusader's grave, he knelt and prayed that the gods bless her soul.

"Why did you wait until Romulus's death?"

"This is when Mother instructed me to come. You see, I bring a gift."

"A gift? For me? What does that mean?"

He stopped walking and stared hard into my eyes, trying to understand his mother's connection with a younger woman. "Mother Vibulena drew one last picture. She insisted you have this painting. Her last request was that I deliver it after the king was gone."

Because Vibulena had sworn to never draw again, his disclosure made me uneasy. Something monstrous must have happened for her to break her pledge. Her son had neither seen the painting nor knew her inspiration. On the last day of their visit, he took me aside and presented a fine, covered leather parchment.

"Mother asked that I not share this with anyone. 'This depiction is the deepest secret between Ronica and her mentor,' she said."

After the family left, my curiosity overtook me. When the family was asleep, I untied the sash. My hands trembled with excitement. The painting sprang to life so forcefully that I struggled to breathe.

"This is exactly what the king of rape deserves," I sighed.

Disturbing scenes depicting Roma's brutal past and unscrupulous present jumped from the canvas. In one section,

Destiny

QUIRINAL
CAPITOLINE
VIMINAL
PALATINE
ESQUILINE
TIBER RIVER
AVENTINE
CAELIAN
HOSTUS

Romulus was being chased by Sabini elders, his eventual assassins. Each elder wore the face of a god or goddess. Ironically, Minerva, Jupiter, and Quirinus chased the man who had plotted our capture.

In another section the gods tumbled from the heavens, exposing Roma as a godless city characterized by demons.

Yet another image showed a wicked witch dragging a younger woman by a hangman's rope toward a fire. This confirmed rumors that Malocanis had destroyed Romulus's daughter, Prima, as revenge for the king's disobedience. I understood that the whore witch had taken Prima's baby to perpetuate her evil just as she had taken Romulus and Remus.

Vibulena had gone to pains to picture two lovers kissing each other while a baby clung to the man's legs. "Hostus" was inscribed under the crying infant.

My mentor confirmed Zolia's declaration that Hersilia cheated on Romulus by exposing that the queen was intimately connected to Hostus Hostilius, the nobleman who had fought and died in defense of the city.

Zolia was right. Roman women were adulteresses. Knowingly or unknowingly, Vibulena substantiated my prophecy that the blood of Romulus would never rule.

I clutched the parchment, praising the gods for their judgment against the wicked. The painting stirred a recollection of one of our augur's prophesies: "To what idols will the Romans pray? A statue of stone, lime, clay, or sand? Wild pigs have more brains than Roman fools."

The Romans would search for the true goddess Màrié, who, like all other gods, would reject them. In recognition of the veracity of my revelations and those of Cnaeus, I danced and sang prayers, knowing that the suffering of the daughters of Minerva had destroyed Roma and the king of rape.

Vibulena's painting lifted my veil of sorrow and I prayed that Zolia joined my celebration.

●●●●✦●

Chapter 76: Hilarius

Ona and I stood on the porch, studying an approaching dust cloud. When hundreds of chariots came to view, we grabbed our swords. With our men in the fields, we stood fearless. Ona figured the buried bodies had been discovered. We would not deny or hide anything.

Loosening our limbs, we swung our swords up, down, and across. "Ronica, we will kill as many as we can!" We tapped our swords and braced ourselves.

A trumpet blared. A voice cried out, "Hail Numa Pompilius, King of Roma!"

The Roman king stepped from his regal chariot. I lowered my sword and moved before him. We stood at the street's edge, scrutinizing each other.

With his pointed beard and sharp nose, the man bore no resemblance to Romulus. "Will Mother Ronica slay the king?" he asked.

"I am a traditional woman from Cures before Roma. I knew you in your mother's womb. In the old, honorable Cures, we never killed our children."

"Your ethics are well known, Ronica. In the name of justice, you battled Romans and avenged injustice." Pompilius removed his helmet. "I salute you." He bowed to me.

"I come in peace to announce Roma's tribute to the sisters of Cures. We ask the surviving sister to witness Roma's testimony to the virtuousness of all women."

I heard his words. "This smells like Neptunus Equester. Cures lies in ashes. Roma is corrupt. How does the son of a Sabine woman serve as king of Roma? If you are sincere, relinquish your ill-gotten throne, disavow your false gods, and burn the city."

"Revolter, the future is ahead… not behind us. I am still Sabine. We are of the same blood. This is why I constructed a statue in honor of you and Mother Zolia. Your tribute stands ready for unveiling.

"The sisters taught us that every nation must acknowledge the righteousness, power, and zeal of women. Minerva's daughters will be heroic role models for generations to come.

"On behalf of all women, please honor us by accepting this tribute. Accompany us to Cures and see my testimony to the courage of the Revolter and the Crusader."

Pompilius knelt, stretching his hands to me. "The goddess Minerva is in you. The people of Cures admit their mistakes. Please do us this honor."

The sight of the king on his knee proved that Roman kings still had no bearing. I had known Hersilia and, because she once showed us kindness, I agreed to accompany her illegitimate son to Cures.

The king offered safety and transport to Gracian, Father, and our families. Ona would stay with Mother while Father, Gracian, Naevius, and I rode on a chariot. We trusted neither

Romans nor those who had bedded them, but we had no fear. Our men carried swords. I took my bow and quiver.

In Cures, Sabini showered us with flowers and grain and shouted, "Welcome, Ronica, mother of bravery!" Their condescension only validated their Romanization. I would never forgive the city that burned our children.

At the king's request, I hid my disgust. In the town center, the statue climbed higher than any building. The sculpting of our faces was eerie. The sisters stood defiantly next to each other, holding swords. In our other hands, our infants reached for our faces.

Our charioteer circled the statue several times. Cnaeus's prophecy, "What idols will Romans worship?" ran through my head.

The crowd shouted. The soldiers tapped their spears as the king hushed the gathering to begin his speech.

> "We stand on the land of Sabinium, the land that bore the second King of Roma. It also bore Ronica, the Revolter, and Zolia, the Crusader, the most valiant women on earth.

> "Through our differences, Roma has emerged as the world's most powerful empire. I commemorate this statue to unify Roma and Sabinium. Sabini, Caenina, Antemnae, Crustumerium, Etruscans, Trojans, and Spartans are gone. We are Romans for eternity.

> "This statue represents righteousness, honor, integrity, zeal, and vengeance. Whether we like our past or not, we must never set a more just course for the future. When a crime is committed, justice will be served. Hail, Holy Mothers Ronica and Zolia, our eternal inspiration!"

Father asked, "What is happening here? This man wastes our time."

"Ronica, is this real?" Gracian asked.

"As the Kingdom of Roma expands, more fools and liars are born every day," Naevius added.

The king stepped from his podium, asking that I join him to salute the statue.

"I swore to never set foot in Cures. I shall keep my pledge. Once I was proud of my Cures heritage, but no longer. The town is filled with deceit and selfishness. Romans may say you are united but the war between Sabinium and Roma will never end, for it is the struggle of good and evil, believers and non-believers.

"Thank you for this tribute of stone. But my regard for Roma is so low I expect they will pierce a hole in the statue to satisfy their lustfulness."

With my words hanging in the air, we rode a chariot to the border of Cures and stood down. The charioteer said, "Sister Ronica, your words were too harsh. There are good people in Roma."

"Where were the good people when women needed them? If good people do not respond, are they good people or accomplices?"

Father kissed my head. "I thought Zolia was my cross-grained one. You unleashed her thunder today, Revolter."

"Yes, Zolia was stubborn. She lives inside me. I am blessed, Father."

"I see," Gracian started. "Now I have two wives. Fortunately, I always had an eye for your sister."

On the road, we realized that someone followed us. Expecting the worst, we spread across the road and kept moving. When a branch snapped, I pointed the bow as Father and Gracian rushed to the noise.

"Do Roman cowards wish to kill us? Declare yourself or die!" Naevius yelled. I fired an arrow at the sound. When no person emerged, I released another.

"Let us live!" a voice rang out. "We mean no harm." With hands high, beautiful Axia walked from the trees. Laughing and sobbing, we raced to each other.

"When they burned Silvestro, I was alone," she cried.

"I am here, Axia. You will never be alone. You will live in our house and dine at our table. Where have you been, dear woman?"

"When you returned to Cures, we had planned that I would follow at a distance. I saw the Romans burn Silvestro. He signaled me to leave."

"But why?"

Axia lowered her eyes. "He knew I was pregnant."

"Pregnant!"

Axia turned to the woods. "Come out, my son. You are safe."

Like his father long ago, the boy carried a wooden sword. We faced a male Zolia. My heart surged with joy.

"Mother, are these Romans? Should I fight?"

"Hilarius, son of Silvestro, this is Mother Ronica, your grandmother."

Father hoisted his great-grandson, drowning his face with

kisses. Gracian ruffled his hair. Naevius beamed with excitement. Axia and Hilarius knew they were welcome and loved.

Zolia's legacy survived. Axia had carried Silvestro's seed, given birth, and lived in the forest, training her child to avenge his father's sacrifice.

With joyful hearts, we accepted our new children. How pleased Zolia must have been. Axia walked between Father and Gracian to complete the journey started years before. I praised Minerva for standing beside me. Walking on the clouds, I lifted the young warrior into my arms.

"Mother Ronica, am I too heavy?"

"My son, you are light as fresh air."

"Mother said to be kind to Mother Ronica. She said you were kinder to Father than anyone in the world. When my practice is done, I shall slay Romans."

The boy's mission gave me no solace. "My son… rather than the sword, find a god, a protector, a voice, an art, to help you navigate life's path. Do you have a god?"

"I carry a totem, Mother Ronica. The totem protects me from danger."

"Where is this totem?" I asked, though I could see Hilarius was hesitant.

Axia chuckled. "He keeps his protector in his belt. He has never shown it to anyone other than me." She nudged Hilarius.

"Grandmother, promise you will never take it away. This totem is secret."

I stopped walking to better view his totem. When he held up Zolia's butterfly brooch, I gasped. A shudder lifted me.

Familia

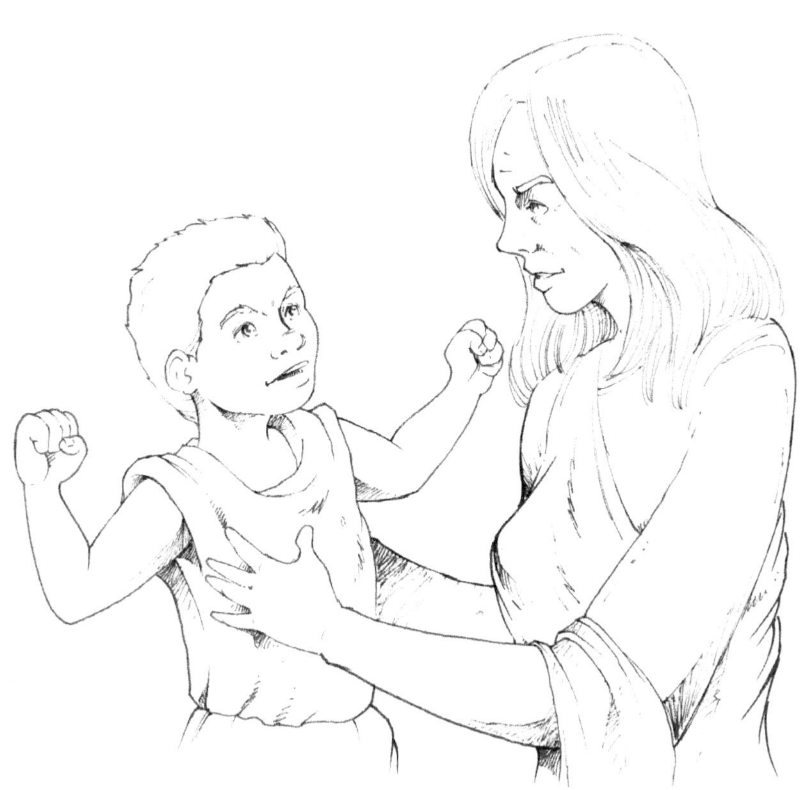

"Where did you find this?"

"Mother took it from an ugly Roman corpse."

"Sawtooth Villius!" Seeing the brooch's effect, Gracian took my hand.

"Is something wrong, Grandmother?"

"No, my dear Hilarius. Zolia dwells inside you. She found you through this brooch. Protect it always. It will give you strength."

"Yes, Grandmother." Hilarius replaced the brooch in his belt. I clutched him to my chest and carried him to Reate.

"Grandmother, will you teach me to use the sword like my father?"

"My son, Mother Zolia killed the Romans. She now lives in you. Your totem belonged to her in a different life, when she danced like a goddess."

Hilarius squeezed my neck. "Mother Ronica, if I do not fight, what will I do?"

"Let us dance, my son. Let us dance!"

www.ingramcontent.com/pod-product-compliance
Lightning Source LLC
Chambersburg PA
CBHW060931120726
47910CB00002B/279